S0-ABO-876

Adjusting one of her gloves that had slipped down her arm slightly, Belle looked up and found herself looking straight into the eyes of a stranger.

There was an expression of utter boredom on his indecently handsome face, an expression that altered dramatically when his eyes met hers, half startled, half amused, and something else—something slightly carnal that stirred unfamiliar feelings inside her and brought heat to her cheeks.

Closer now Lance could see that this was no ordinary girl. He was drawn to the freshness and vitality with which she carried herself, looking at the setting with brilliant eyes and a playful tilt to her mouth. She was exceptionally beautiful, so beautiful that it was impossible not to stand and stare at her.

In her low-cut bodice, revealing the top curve of her firm breasts and the satin smoothness of her bare shoulders, she was a beauty, he decided, simply beautiful—and the light from the chandeliers sparked the diamonds around her neck with a cold fire. His eyes narrowed as they settled on the jewels. Suddenly she had all his attention.

* * *

Diamonds, Deception and the Debutante
Harlequin® Historical #283—May 2010

Author Note

Diamonds, Deception and the Debutante is set in the Regency period. It is one of the most turbulent, glittering and romantic times in our history, when rakes and dandies, outrageous gambling and scandals abounded. It is a period enjoyed by both readers and writers alike. I am no exception.

Every one of my books is special to me, but the one I am working on at the time is always the most important. When I finish a book I always intend having a break from writing to catch up on things I set aside until the story is finished before embarking on another, but invariably my imagination begins to stir and in no time at all I'm off again.

History has always held a fascination for me—it was one of my best subjects at school. I am interested in how people lived, how different everything was from today, and how much one can learn from the past. My inspiration is drawn from many things. I am an avid reader and I enjoy music and walking. My characters are not based in any direct way on anyone in particular and I use my own brush to paint things in a fictional way. I do home in on certain traits and embody them in the characters in my books. I love seeing the people I create come to life and develop personalities of their own.

Writing is something I enjoy tremendously and it gives me a great deal of personal satisfaction. I hope you enjoy reading *Diamonds, Deception and the Debutante* as much as I enjoyed writing it.

Diamonds,
Deception and
the Debutante

HELEN
DICKSON

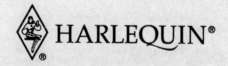

HARLEQUIN®

TORONTO • NEW YORK • LONDON
AMSTERDAM • PARIS • SYDNEY • HAMBURG
STOCKHOLM • ATHENS • TOKYO • MILAN • MADRID
PRAGUE • WARSAW • BUDAPEST • AUCKLAND

If you purchased this book without a cover you should be aware that this book is stolen property. It was reported as "unsold and destroyed" to the publisher, and neither the author nor the publisher has received any payment for this "stripped book."

Recycling programs
for this product may
not exist in your area.

ISBN-13: 978-0-373-30592-6

DIAMONDS, DECEPTION AND THE DEBUTANTE

Copyright © 2010 by Helen Dickson

All rights reserved. Except for use in any review, the reproduction or utilization of this work in whole or in part in any form by any electronic, mechanical or other means, now known or hereafter invented, including xerography, photocopying and recording, or in any information storage or retrieval system, is forbidden without the written permission of the publisher, Harlequin Enterprises Limited, 225 Duncan Mill Road, Don Mills, Ontario, Canada M3B 3K9.

This is a work of fiction. Names, characters, places and incidents are either the product of the author's imagination or are used fictitiously, and any resemblance to actual persons, living or dead, business establishments, events or locales is entirely coincidental.

This edition published by arrangement with Harlequin Books S.A.

For questions and comments about the quality of this book please contact us at Customer_eCare@Harlequin.ca.

® and TM are trademarks of the publisher. Trademarks indicated with ® are registered in the United States Patent and Trademark Office, the Canadian Trade Marks Office and in other countries.

www.eHarlequin.com

Printed in U.S.A.

HELEN DICKSON

was born and lives in South Yorkshire with her retired farm manager husband. Having moved out of the busy farmhouse where she raised their two sons, she has more time to indulge in her favourite pastimes. She enjoys being outdoors, traveling, reading and music. An incurable romantic, she writes for pleasure. It was a love of history that led her to write historical fiction.

Prologue

June 1815

As the rain lashed down to compound the misery of the troops, the scene was set for battle. The British troops had been engaged by the French and forced to retire after a sharp engagement lasting the afternoon and they had to struggle to hold their position. The following morning Wellington drew back, establishing himself at the posting inn at the village of Waterloo.

It was here that one of Colonel Lance Bingham's staff officers brought him a note. It was crumpled and stained, as if it had passed through many hands.

'A lad brought it, sir,' the staff officer said. 'It's urgent, and he said I had to deliver it to you personally.'

Colonel Bingham tore the missive open and read it quickly. He spoke one word, 'Delphine.' Apart from a tightening of his jaw, his expression did not betray even a flicker of reaction. 'There is something I have to do.'

'But, sir, what if General Bonaparte…'

'Don't worry. I'll be back. Take me to the lad.'

Knowing he risked being court-marshalled for leaving his post on the eve of battle, Colonel Bingham rode away from the encampment. With rain beating at his face, following the lad on a small but swift-footed nag, he prayed to God that he was right and that Bonaparte wouldn't attack before dawn, for it was his way to fly at his opponents without waiting to be attacked.

The farmhouse to which he had been summoned was down a dirt track. It was a humble dwelling, the stench of animals and their dung as strong inside the house as it was in the farmyard. The lad, who was the son of the farmer and his wife, hung back, pointing to a room at the top of a rickety staircase. Climbing up, Colonel Bingham paused in the doorway. It was dimly lit, hot and fetid with the stench of childbirth. A man stood next to the bed on which a woman lay, and in a corner of the room a young woman nursed an infant.

The man turned to look at the stranger, who seemed to fill the room with his presence. He saw an officer in military uniform, tall and with broad, muscular shoulders, deep chest and narrow waist, his handsome features ruggedly hewn.

'Colonel Bingham?'

He nodded, removing his hat, his face set and grim.

'I am Reverend Hugh Watson—attached to His Majesty's army,' he said, stepping back from the bed to allow him to approach. 'Thank goodness you have come. Miss Jenkins hasn't much time left. When the midwife who attended the young woman at the birth of her child realised she would not pull through, when Miss Jenkins requested a clergyman to be absolved of her sins, she summoned me.'

Giving the clergyman, who had a prayer book open

in his hands, a cool glance, taking note of his crumpled dark suit and grimy neck linen and that he was in need of a shave, never had Colonel Lance Bingham seen a man who looked less like a clergyman.

Seeming reluctant to approach the bed, his face hardened into an expressionless mask, Lance observed the woman from where he stood. Not having seen her these seven months gone, he did not recognise her as the attractive, vivacious young woman who had kept him happily entertained throughout most of his years as a soldier in Spain. Drenched in sour sweat, she was lying beneath the covers, her lank brown hair trailed over the pillow. Her face was waxen and thinner than it had been, and dark rings circled her deep brown eyes.

As if she sensed he was there they fluttered open and settled on his face. Her heart beat softly inside her with love and wonderment that he had come. A smile lifted her tiredly drooping mouth. 'Lance—you came.' She tried to raise a hand to him, but sapped of strength it remained where it was.

Dropping to his knees beside the bed, Lance took her hand and raised it to his lips. 'Delphine, what in God's name are you doing here? I told you to go back to England.'

'I did, but then I followed you to Belgium—as I followed you to Spain, remember? I—haven't been well. I didn't think I would survive the birth. I did, but I know I haven't much time, Lance—but it gladdens my heart to see you again.'

'Miss Jenkins has just been delivered of your child,' the clergyman informed him.

Colonel Bingham stiffened and for the briefest of

moments, shock registered in his eyes. 'My child? Is this true, Delphine?'

She nodded. 'A girl. You have a daughter, Lance. A beautiful daughter.'

Lance knew he would never again feel the shame, the guilt, the absolute wretchedness that seized him then, as he looked at what he believed to be the dying spirit of the woman who had taken his fancy when he had seen her perform on the London stage, this woman who had followed him to Spain, from one battlefield to the next, without complaint, without demanding anything from him, and was now slipping away.

When they had met, her freshness and vivacity were something his jaded spirits had badly needed. Delphine had proved to be a thoroughly delightful mistress. She had been there to satisfy his craving for carnal appeasement. They had talked and laughed and kissed and shared sweet intimacies. But knowing nothing could come of their affair, he couldn't let her waste one moment of her precious life loving him or waiting for him, and so he had ended it, telling himself that he had done the right thing, the noble thing. But nothing had prepared him for the days and nights of missing her, of the sweet softness of her in his arms.

'Delphine, I have to ask…'

'The child is yours,' she uttered forcefully. 'Never doubt it. There has been no one else. No one was good enough—after you.'

He bent his head over her hand. 'Dear sweet Lord, this is the cruellest thing you have ever done to me. Why did you not write and tell me? I would have come to you, Delphine. I would not have let you endure this alone.'

'I am sorry. I didn't know what else to do. I—I

thought you might hate me—that you would turn me away—but I had nowhere else to go. I couldn't go home and I had to do something, which was why I came to Belgium—to find you.'

'You were afraid of me?' His voice was soft with compassion. 'You were afraid to tell me? Am I such an ogre, Delphine?'

'No…' She trembled and clutched his hand, a great wash of tears brimming in her eyes.

Lance felt his heart jolt for her pain. He would give anything to know how to comfort her, to reassure her that he would not leave her. He was an arrogant bastard, he knew that himself, a man who liked, demanded, his own determined way, but the emotion this woman aroused in him, the sweetness that flowed through him from her, could be matched by nothing he had ever known before.

'Don't cry, my love,' he murmured. 'I'm here now. You're safe with me and always will be.'

'Go and look at your daughter, Lance. You will see she is yours.'

Lance did as she bade and went to look at the flesh-and-blood evidence of the result of their loving. His heart began to beat against his chest wall. The wet nurse pushed away the cover shielding the infant's face. This was his child and he was almost too afraid to look at her because he did not know how he would feel when he did. He forced himself to look at the babe's face, compelled by some force he did not recognise. As he looked she yawned and turned her face towards him, before settling herself to sleep against the woman's breast.

It was his mother's face and his own he saw, the line of her brow with the distinctive widow's peak, the way in which her eyes were set in her skull, the black winging eyebrows, and the tiny cleft in her round chin. On her head her hair swirled against her skull, a clump of curls, coal black like his own, on her crown.

Turning from her, he went back to the bed. 'She is a fine girl, Delphine.'

'Yes, a fine baby girl. I've named her Charlotte—after my mother. As her father you will—look after her, won't you, Lance, be responsible for her—care for her and protect her? She has no one else.'

Lance nodded, a terrible constriction in his throat, for she was so weak, so defenceless against what was to happen to her. He damned all the fates that prevented him from righting the wrong he had done her by casting her from him, the cruel fates that prevented him from having this warm and lovely girl in his life once more.

'You have my guarantee that she will be supported in a manner suitable to her upbringing. But—is there anything I can do to ease your suffering? Anything at all?'

'You could do the honourable, gentlemanly thing and marry Miss Jenkins, sir,' the clergyman suggested stoutly, almost forcefully. 'The child is a bastard and the stigma of being born out of wedlock will follow her all the days of her life. As your legitimate daughter her future will be secure.'

Lance was momentarily lost for words. Before this it would have been impossible, unthinkable to take her for his wife for he had a position to consider and a wife such as Delphine would not have been tolerated, but, by heaven, this changed everything. Lance knew a man's rightful claim to being a gentleman was not something one could inherit. Compassion, honour and integrity were just three of the characteristics. Certainly a man had a responsibility and an obligation to protect those who were close to him, those who depended on him, from the cruelties of the world. Looking from Delphine to the child, never had he felt the weight of that responsibility as he did now. He could not in all conscience and honour cast Delphine aside along with their child like something worthless.

Without any visible emotion, he said, 'Is this what you want, Delphine?'

She nodded, a tear trickling out of the corner of her eye and quickly becoming soaked up in the pillow. 'For our daughter's sake. I am dying, Lance, so I will not be a burden to you and you will be free to go on as before. It won't be long. Will you do this—for me?'

'I shall be proud to make you my wife, Delphine,' Lance said hoarsely. He looked at the clergyman. 'Very well. Get on with it.'

After summoning the farmer and his wife to bear witness to the proceedings, they spoke their vows, the infant beginning to wail lustily when the clergyman pronounced them man and wife.

Delphine smiled and closed her eyes. 'You can go now, Lance. There is nothing more to be done.'

That seemed to be so. With a final sigh her head rolled to one side.

Lance stared at her, unable to believe this dear, sweet girl—his wife for such a short time—was dead. Oh, sweet, sweet Jesus, he prayed as he bent his head, the agony he felt slicing his heart to the core.

The clergyman went to Delphine and placed his head to her chest. Straightening up, he shook his head solemnly. When he was about to pull the sheet over her face, Lance stayed his hand.

'Wait.' He looked at her face one last time, as if to absorb her image for all time. It had taken on a serenity absent before death, so calm and untroubled he felt his throat ache. The eyes were closed, the lashes long and dark in a fan on her cheek. The skin, no longer the almost grey look of the dead, had taken on a soft honey cream.

Not one to show his emotions, after taking a moment to compose himself, Lance signed some papers and then handed the clergyman some money for the burial, telling him to have Delphine interred in the graveyard of the local church. His face stony, his eyes empty, he turned his attention to the woman holding his child.

'You are English?'

'Yes, sir.'

'What are you called?'

'Mary Grey, sir. My own baby died—six days now—and the midwife who attended your wife asked if I would wet nurse your daughter.'

'And your husband?'

'I have no husband, sir. My man died before I gave birth.'

'I see.' He thought for a moment, considering her. At least she was clean and quietly spoken. 'Will you continue to wet nurse the child and take her to an address in England? You will be well paid for your trouble. I will send someone to accompany you—along with a letter for you to give to my mother.'

'Yes, sir.'

The clergyman moved from the bed. 'Don't feel you have to remain, Colonel. I will take care of things.'

'Thank you. I do have to return to my regiment. Battle is imminent. Tomorrow many will die. Your services as a priest will be needed, too.'

The child began to whimper. He looked at it and quickly looked away as if he couldn't bear to look at her, trying to defend himself against the rising and violent tide of anger directed against this tiny being—this infant whose entry into the world had taken the life of its mother. Angry, relentlessly so and unable to understand why he should feel like this, his face absolute and without expression, without a backward glance Colonel Bingham left the farmhouse.

Mary Grey had noted the look on his face and recognised it for what it was. He blamed the child for its mother's death, this she understood, but she was confident it was a problem that would solve itself. But in this she was to be proved wrong.

In silence the clergyman watched him go. What could he say? How could anyone—man or woman—recover from such pain and the agony of such grief?

Lance rode back to his regiment, eager for the battle to begin so that he could lose himself in the fray and forget what had just transpired—and the fact that he had a daughter.

Chapter One

'Miss Belle, I simply do not know what to do with you. Your grandmother is waiting for you in the dining room, and she doesn't like to be kept waiting. Now hurry. You look fine, you really do.'

Isabelle 'Belle' Ainsley spun round from the mirror, the bright green of her eyes flashing brilliantly as her temper rose. 'For heaven's sake, Daisy. I am nineteen years old and will not be hurried. And I will not look fine until *I* am satisfied with how I look.' She twisted back to the mirror, scowling petulantly at her hair, which, as usual, refused to be confined. Daisy had arranged it in twists and curls about her head, but a curl as wayward as the girl herself had sprung free and no matter how she tried to tuck it away, it defiantly sprang back.

Daisy shook her head in amusement, unperturbed by her new mistress's outburst of temper. 'We both know that could take all night and that would never do. You certainly have your grandmother's temper, but she's older and if I were you I wouldn't delay any longer or you'll feel the rough edge of her tongue.'

Belle groaned with exasperation and then in a fit of pique she grabbed a pair of scissors and cut off the offending curl. In a swirl of satin and lace she flounced across the room and out of the door, not deigning to look at Daisy's bemused face.

Belle's descent of the grand staircase was not in the least ladylike and brought a combination of smiles, raised eyebrows and frowns of concern from the footmen who paused in their duties to watch her. She was certainly a wondrous sight to behold, was Lady Isabelle. In the tomb-like silence of the Dowager Countess of Harworth's stately home, the arrival of her granddaughter from America ranked as an uproar and had not only the servants scratching their heads, but the countess as well. And now the countess was in high dudgeon over being kept waiting.

Entering the dining room, Belle steeled herself for the unpleasant scene that was bound to occur. Her grandmother rose stiffly from the chair where she was reclining, her hand gripping the gold knob of her cane. At seventy-two she was still a handsome woman with white hair, elegant, regal bearing, and the aloof, unshakeable confidence and poise that comes from living a thoroughly privileged life. Despite the stiff dignity and rigid self-control that characterised her every gesture, she had known her share of grief, having outlived her husband and two sons.

'Good evening, Isabelle,' she said, looking with disapproval over her granddaughter's choice of dress, which had seen much wear and was not in the least the kind a young lady of breeding would wear in a respectable English drawing room. The sooner her dressmaker arrived to begin fitting her out for a new wardrobe

the better. 'You are inordinately tardy. What do you
have to say for yourself?'

'I'm so sorry, Grandmother. I did not mean to upset
you. I simply could not decide which dress to wear. I
chose this because it is such a pretty colour and looks
well on me. You could have started dinner without me.
You didn't have to wait.'

The Dowager gave her an icy look. 'In this house we
dine together, Isabelle, and I do not like being kept
waiting. How many times must I tell you that I demand
punctuality at all times? Thank goodness we do not
have guests. You have grieved cook, who has been trying
unsuccessfully to keep our dinner warm and palatable.'

'Then I shall make a point of apologising to cook,'
Belle said, unable to understand why her grandmother
was making such a fuss about nothing. 'I have no wish
to put anyone out. I could quite easily fetch my own
food from the kitchen.'

'And that is another thing. You will not do work that
is best left to the servants.' She sighed, shaking her head
wearily. 'You have so much to learn I hardly know
where to begin.'

'But I like to be kept busy,' Belle answered, smiling
across at the agitated lady.

'I shall see that you are—with matters concerning
your future role in life, although I realised from the
start how difficult and unyielding is your nature.'

'Papa would doubtless have agreed with you. He
ever despaired of me.' Thinking of her father, dead these
two months, a lump appeared in Belle's throat and the
lovely eyes were shadowed momentarily. 'I miss him
very much.'

'As I do.' The faded blue eyes never wavered, but

there was a hoarseness in the countess's voice that told Belle of her grandmother's inner grief over the death of her second son. 'It was his wish that you come to England, where you will be taught the finer points of being a lady—and I shall see that you do if I expire in the attempt.'

Belle swallowed down the lump in her throat. How difficult her life had suddenly become and how difficult the transition had been for her to leave her beloved Charleston and come to London. She missed it so much. Would she ever fit in here? she wondered. How she hated having to live by her grandmother's strict rules when her father had allowed her to roam as free as a bird back home. The task of learning to be the lady her grandmother intended her to become was both daunting and seemingly impossible.

She looked at her grandmother, her green eyes wide and vulnerable. 'I'm sure I must be a terrible disappointment to you, Grandmother, but I will try not to let you down. Despite what you think, I am only foolish, not stupid. I am ignorant of your ways, but I will learn.'

'Then you will have to work very hard.'

The countess knew she had her work cut out with her granddaughter. Her manners were unrefined and she knew nothing about genteel behaviour. She was a wild child, as wild as they come. At first sight they had regarded each other, two fiercely indomitable wills clashing in silence. That her granddaughter was proud and strong and followed her own rules was obvious, but the countess would not concede defeat.

Belle crossed to the long table and waited until Gosforth, the butler—who had a habit of appearing and disappearing seemingly from nowhere—had seated her grandmother properly, before pulling out her own chair and seating herself, which earned her another condemning frown from the elderly lady.

The dowager looked at Gosforth. 'We are ready to start, Gosforth, now my granddaughter has deigned to join me. I suppose we might as well see how cold the beef has grown.'

Belle sighed, folding her hands demurely in her lap. The evening was definitely off to a bad start. If only there was some distraction. Anything would be preferable to an evening at home alone with her grandmother, who would endeavour to teach her unsophisticated American granddaughter how young English ladies behaved. All Belle's attempts to try to curb her restlessness and be demure were unsuccessful.

Already—and unbeknown to her grandmother—on her daily rides across Hampstead Heath, Belle had garnered the favours of several curious local young beaux—one with raffish good looks and much sought after, apparently. His name was Carlton Robinson. On occasion he had watched for her when she rode out, and when she had managed to shake off her accompanying groom—who despaired of trying to keep up with her since she could ride like the wind with the devil on her tail—he had joined her.

Carlton Robinson had never met anyone quite like this American girl and he had soon turned to putty under the assault of her big green eyes and stunning looks. Out of boredom it was all a game to Belle, and when she had captured him completely, the game had soured and she had sent the young man packing—blissfully unaware of the consequences of her liaison with this particular gentleman.

She sighed, taking a large, unladylike gulp of her

wine, already wishing the evening would end so she could escape to her room—and to make matters worse the beef was overdone.

The following morning, standing at her bedroom window overlooking the gardens, the countess watched her granddaughter as she cantered up the drive—hatless and astride, her long legs gripping her mount, her hair blowing loose in the wind, and having left the groom somewhere on the Heath.

That very morning one of the countess's acquaintances had hastened to inform her of a scandal that was beginning to unfold concerning Isabelle—a scandal that was entirely of Isabelle's making, if it was to be believed. The countess was incensed by her granddaughter's behaviour. Not in her wildest dreams had she imagined that the lovely, inexperienced young woman would form a liaison with a young man whose exploits were the talk of London as soon as she arrived. And Carlton Robinson! No man but he would dare, would have the temerity, the sheer effrontery to interfere with the granddaughter of the Dowager Countess of Harworth. She summoned Isabelle to the salon immediately.

Daisy had heard the gossip and told Belle she could expect no mercy from her grandmother. Belle's naïvety and inexperience had not prepared her for a young man of Carlton Robinson's reputation. Not to be made a fool of by an ignorant American girl, he had let his tongue loose to do its worst and turned the tables on Belle. He had laughingly told his friends that the American girl was an amusingly peculiar, pathetic little thing from the backwoods of America, and when she was launched, he had no intention of plying his suit.

An inexplicable premonition of dread mounted the closer Belle got to the salon. After listening to what her grandmother had to say, making no attempt to conceal her anger and disappointment, Belle was swamped with remorse and shame.

'Well? What have you to say for yourself?' the countess demanded of the wretched girl.

'I'm so sorry, Grandmother. It was nothing, please believe me. We—met when I was riding on the Heath. We only met three times. He—said he liked my company. I didn't like him, so I ended it. Daisy has told me that the odious man has said some dreadful, wicked things about me that simply are not true.'

'Carlton Robinson says objectionable things about people all the time,' the countess answered drily.

'I never meant for this to happen. I didn't know.'

'There's a great deal you don't know. A girl newly arrived from America—ignorant to our ways—he saw you as easy prey.' She shook her head wearily, blaming herself for allowing Isabelle too much freedom. 'I accept that you are ignorant of how things are done in England, Isabelle. Carlton Robinson is a conceited braggart and the most lascivious reprobate in town. Resentful of your rejection, he has tried to destroy your reputation in the most alarming manner—to make you a hopeless social outcast before you have even made your début.'

'I'm sorry, Grandmother,' Belle whispered brokenly, truly repentant. 'You risked a great deal taking me into your home. Little did you know you would be risking disgrace.' She looked at her grandmother, her eyes wide and vulnerable and shining with tears. 'I've a hideous disposition and I haven't a feminine accomplishment to my name. What is to be done?'

The countess's heart melted for the lovely, spirited, bewildered girl her younger son had borne, and in a moment her old loyal heart had her fighting in defence of her granddaughter, at whose door the blame had been unfairly laid. 'We shall do as the Ainsleys have always done, Isabelle,' she said on a gentler note, 'and weather the scandal. By the time you make your début, hopefully it will have blown over.'

And so the Dowager Countess of Harworth began to shape the artless, unsophisticated girl from America into a respectable English young lady. Isabelle hadn't a grain of sense or propriety in her, but her determination not to be restricted or confined had to be curbed. She knew nothing of fashion and cared even less, but Isabelle had been well tutored in most subjects. She spoke perfect French, read Latin and Greek, and she had a good head for numbers.

Miss Bertram, a woman of unimpeachable character, was to arrive today to begin instructing her on the refinements of etiquette. No one would dare to question the acceptability and character of any young lady in her charge. The Season would begin in just a few short weeks. Hopefully it would be enough time for Isabelle to learn everything she needed to know to make a full-fledged début and to outfit her for the full Season. Until then the countess would begin by taking her to the theatre, where she could be seen but not approached, but apart from that, she must be kept locked away from everyone.

Her grandmother's house, situated close to Hampstead Heath, was unlike anything Belle had imagined. She had been mesmerised by its splendour—imposing without being austere. This was where her grandmother lived when she came to London, preferring the relative peace and quiet of living just outside the city, where the air was cleaner. The ancestral home, Harworth Hall, was in a place called Wiltshire.

On her arrival in England, at first Belle had objected and fought against all her grandmother's efforts to make her conform. Her grandmother was hard to please, over-bearing and possessive, whereas Belle was a free spirit and used to doing as she wished, and she wasn't ready to be buried alive by protocol and the traditional English customs. But now her 'hysterics', as her grandmother called it, had cooled to an acceptance of her situation and a steely determination. Admitting her lack of knowledge about English protocol, Belle was sensitive enough to realise that she was lacking in certain social skills—and she was her own harshest critic. She accepted that her grandmother was the only family she had, and, like it or not, this was now her home, so she had best conform and make the best of it.

Miss Bertram had the formidable task of teaching her social graces, and under her relentless and exacting tutelage, Belle began to settle down and worked diligently to learn anything that might help her win favour in her grandmother's eyes.

Madame Hamelin, her grandmother's personal dressmaker, arrived, accompanied by two seamstresses to fit her for an extensive wardrobe, and Madame Hamelin was full of praise for the beautiful American girl, complimenting her on her natural grace and excellent posture. Belle allowed herself to be pushed, prodded and poked and scolded if she did not stand still for the fittings, and sometimes praised—for she was excited, and what girl would not be?—the centre of attention, admired and exclaimed over.

Next came the dancing instructor, who had her whirling around the room to the imaginary strains of a waltz and to the countess's relief announced that her granddaughter had a natural ability and was far from hopeless.

And so Belle learned how walk properly, how to curtsy, how to open and close a fan, and learned that it had other uses—for flirting and to occupy the hands—other than for cooling oneself. By the time of her début, although she still had much to learn and her wilfulness was far from curbed, her grandmother was confident that she would be ready to be introduced into society. Hopefully the scandal of her brief and completely innocent association with Carlton Robinson would be completely forgotten.

Lance Bingham groaned and pushed himself out of the bed. Reaching for the water pitcher he poured the contents over his hair before raising his dripping head and looking at his face in the mirror. He felt terrible and he looked it. His eyes were bleary, and dark stubble covered his chin. He forced himself to breathe deeply in an attempt to clear the alcoholic fog from his head. Towelling his head dry, he went to the window, shoving it open and breathing deeply the sharp air of a Paris morning.

Today, his life with the army over, he was to return to his home in England, an event he viewed with little joy when he thought what awaited him there. When Delphine had died part of him had died too. Never again would he let his emotions get the better of him. His heart was closed to all women—including his daughter, whose birth had taken away the only woman who had touched his inner being.

Throughout the years with his regiment, he had been motivated by the adventure of being a soldier and driven by the excitement of battle, but the battles' images and the loss of his friends had left their scars. It was going to be no easy matter settling down to life as a civilian. He had everything—breeding, looks and wealth—and however much he would regret its passing, his military career and the manner of Delphine's death and the guilt that would hound him all the days of his life, had made him world weary, restrained and guarded.

The voluptuous French redhead in the bed stirred and lifted herself upon an elbow, her body stiff and aching deliciously from her companion's prolonged and energetic lovemaking. She studied the darkly handsome man, his brooding looks marred by cynicism. He was standing with his shoulder propped against the window frame, looking out. Gazing with admiration and a fresh stirring of desire at the lean, hard lines of his body, her eyes roving down past the rigid muscles of his chest and flat stomach, every inch of him positively radiated raw power and unleashed sensuality.

His latent animal sensuality swept over her. 'Come back to bed,' she murmured huskily, aching for fulfilment, hoping he would, but Lance Bingham seemed not to hear. 'Please,' she persisted, slowly, languidly, running her hands through her hair.

He turned and looked at her dispassionately. 'Get dressed and go.'

'What? Did I not satisfy you, my lord?' She smiled seductively, letting the sheet slip to reveal her swelling orbs, hoping the sight of them would entice him back into her arms. 'You enjoyed yourself, didn't you?'

The voice was lazy and full of promise. A soft smile

played about her mouth, inviting him to her, but he remained unmoved. He hated loose women, but she exuded a rich aura of passion and the full, ripe figure and smouldering eyes promised an obvious knowledge of the art of exciting men. Last night he had invited her to his room and she had come gladly. Now the mere sight of her sickened him and he was coldly telling her to get out.

'That was last night. I was drunk and now I'm sober and not bored enough to want to sleep with you again.'

The woman scowled at him. 'You don't have a very high opinion of women, do you?'

'No. I do not believe in the inherent goodness in anyone—including myself. If you don't mind, I would like you to go.'

The woman's eyes narrowed and anger kindled in their depths. 'Why—you—you bastard,' she hissed.

The look he gave her was one of mild cynicism. 'If calling me names makes you feel better, I'll let it go. For my part I apologise if I've given you grief. I could put it down to your being an attractive woman and me being a long way from home and pretty damn lonely. Whatever it was, it's over. Now get out.'

About to argue, the look on his face made the woman afraid of him for the first time since she had come to his room. Strange and explosive emotions lurked in the hard eyes glittering in the dim light of the room and rendered her speechless. Last night under the effects of drink and full of lust, she had thought him completely malleable, but she now read a hardness of purpose and coldness of manner beyond any previous experience.

Paying no more attention to her, Lance turned away to watch the teeming mass of humanity scurrying along the wide, rain-swept boulevards. The woman threw back the covers and reached for her clothes. Even before she had flounced out of the room he had put her from his mind as if she had never been.

Having sat for what seemed to be hours before her dressing-table mirror, watching as Daisy had painstakingly arranged her heavy hair into an elegant coiffure, deftly twisting it into elaborate curls and teasing soft tendrils over her ears, Belle now fingered the diamonds Daisy had just fastened around her throat—drop diamonds that danced in her lobes and a double row of diamonds with a single, enormous oval-shaped diamond pendant that rested just above her breasts. They were hard and cold and absolutely exquisite in their beauty. They belonged to her grandmother and were famous for their chequered history, and had not been worn for fifty years.

Belle smiled at her reflection in the mirror, a mischievous, calculating smile, a smile those who knew Isabelle Ainsley would know to be wary of.

'Shall I take them off now, miss?' Daisy asked. The countess had agreed to her granddaughter looking at the famed jewels. After handing them over to Miss Belle, the countess had been called away, telling her to put them back in the box and return them to her before they left for the Prince Regent's party at Carlton House.

'No, Daisy.' Belle's eyes were sparkling with defiance, her concentration unbroken as she continued to finger the diamonds. 'I think I shall wear them for the party tonight. After all, what is the point of having beautiful things if they are to be kept hidden away? A necklace of such beauty should be seen and appreciated, and tonight is such a grand occasion, don't you agree?'

'Oh, yes, miss. But your grandmother… Oh, miss,' she said, shaking her mob-capped head, 'she'll have my hide if I don't take them back—and her with one of her heads coming on.'

The anxiety in the maid's voice broke Belle's reverie, and she looked at the terrified girl as she wrung her hands nervously. 'And you will, Daisy. I can promise you that. But not until after the banquet at Carlton House—and if Grandmother is suffering one of her headaches, then she may be so preoccupied that she won't notice.'

'But she will see them when it is time for you to leave. She will never allow—'

'What my grandmother sees and what she will allow is neither here nor there, Daisy,' Belle said sharply, standing up, the transparency of the material of her chemise making no pretence of hiding the softly veiled peaks of her firm breasts. 'The necklace will be concealed beneath my cloak, and not until we reach Carlton House will she see them. By which time it will be too late to do anything about it.' Seeing Daisy's anxiety, she smiled confidently. 'Trust me, Daisy. Everything will be all right.'

She looked at the bed where the gown she was to wear had been carefully spread to await its donning, thinking how the vibrant turquoise silk would enhance the jewels and bring out the lights in her rich, mahogany-coloured hair. 'Now, please help me into my gown.'

With the gown setting off her figure to perfection, Belle turned this way and that in front of the dressing mirror to survey her reflection. 'There, what do you think, Daisy? Will I do?'

Daisy stood back, taking pride in her handiwork—although Miss Belle was already beautiful. She looked positively breathtaking, daring, elegant and special. 'Indeed you will, Miss Belle. Any man, even one in his dotage, who sees you tonight, looking as you do, will surely find his heart going into its final palpitations—as will Prince George himself.'

Belle laughed happily. 'I don't think so, Daisy. The Prince has so many ladies buzzing about him, he will fail to notice an unknown American girl.'

'Don't be too sure about that, miss. Prince George may not be as handsome as he once was—his gargantuan appetite has seen to that—but he cuts a fine figure in his military uniforms and the sumptuous clothes he wears. He is still charming and amusing and has an eye for a pretty face.'

The preparations complete, when the summons came from her grandmother and Daisy had carefully folded her velvet cloak about her shoulders, concealing the necklace, Belle proceeded down the stairs where her grandmother awaited her.

Belle was excited about going to Carlton House and meeting English royalty. Prince George was a splendid host, at his happiest when entertaining on a grand scale. The whole of society aspired to be invited to his fêtes. According to Belle's grandmother, the banquets were always glittering occasions, the point of the proceedings to admire, for the Prince, who spent weeks planning the setting of his next event, liked to show off his aesthetic taste and imagination.

Feeling decidedly gay and definitely light-hearted, Belle had been looking forward to the party for days, and she intended to enjoy every minute of it.

* * *

Having arrived early and trying to work up some enthusiasm to attend Prince George's banquet, which he imagined would be tedious and infinitely dull, Lord Lance Bingham lounged in the shade against the wall to await his good friend, Sir Rowland Gibbon. He idly watched the long line of carriages—a solid block of elegant equipages stretching all the way to St James's Street, depositing the glittering cream of London society at the door.

Raising a lazy brow on seeing a sleek black coach with the Ainsley coat of arms emblazoned on its door come to a halt, his interest sharpened as the coachman lowered the steps to allow the occupants to alight. First of all came the Dowager Countess of Harworth, followed by a young woman. The woman took the coachman's hand and allowed him to assist her.

'Thank you, Denis,' she said.

'My pleasure, Miss Isabelle.'

Miss Isabelle! So, Lord Bingham thought, that was Isabelle Ainsley, recently come from America. Who else could it be? This was the girl whom London society talked about, a young woman who had lost no time in creating a scandal by forming a most unfortunate liaison with young Carlton Robinson—one of London's most notorious rakes and a despair to his father.

Intrigued, Lance stared quite openly, unable to do anything else. A cool vision of poised womanhood, she was undeniably the most magnificent woman he had ever seen, though it was not the way she looked that drew his eye, since the distance between them was too great for him to see her features clearly. It was the way she tossed her imperious head, the challenging set to her shoulders and the defiant stare that did not see the lowlier beings about her.

He stood and watched her as she walked a few steps behind the countess—though walked hardly described the way she moved, for she seemed to glide effortlessly, her body eternally female in its fluid movements, her expensively shod feet barely touching the ground.

As they disappeared through a portico of Corinthian columns that led to the foyer, with a frown Lord Bingham resumed his pose, propping his shoulder against the wall. Where the devil had Rowland got to? he wondered, his patience beginning to wear a trifle thin. He stared into the verdant depths of the ruby on his finger. Gleaming with a regal fire, it seemed to motivate him into action. Slowly drawing himself upright, straightening the folds of his bright red officer's coat, he walked with deliberate strides towards the portico.

Having discarded her cloak, Belle prepared herself for her grandmother's wrath. The countess regarded her granddaughter with an attentive expression in her eyes. For a moment Belle regretted her impulsive action to wear the necklace and quailed at the storm that she knew was coming. She did not have to wait long. Her grandmother advanced on her, her expression turning to stone as she saw for the first time the necklace.

The countess's eyes narrowed dangerously, for it seemed to her that her granddaughter had overstepped the mark. Isabelle's green eyes, so like her own, were fearful and yet at the same time her face wore an expression of defiance.

'Well?' Her voice, which she kept low so as not to be overheard, was as cold as her face. 'I left the necklace with you in good faith, Isabelle—that you would return it to me as I instructed you to do. I did not intend for you to wear it. How dare you disobey me? How dare you?'

'Grandmother—I—I am sorry…'

'It is most unseemly that you should embarrass me before so many.'

'That was not my intention. I saw no harm in wearing it—it is so beautiful and the occasion seemed fitting.' She raised her hands to the back of her neck. 'Of course if it upsets you, I'll remove it—'

'Leave it,' the countess snapped, her tone causing Belle to lower her arms. 'It's too late for that. Its removal—now it has been seen by all and sundry—will only give rise to unwelcome speculation. You may keep it on. This is not one of your finest performances. I am most displeased with you, Isabelle, most displeased.' She turned away to speak to an acquaintance, pinning a smile to her face, but inside she continued to seethe at her granddaughter's disobedience.

Relieved that the moment had passed and the necklace was still in place, Belle was very much aware that the moment she appeared all eyes turned to her. As usual the whispering began and she was surrounded by dozens of people, most of them young men, who obviously thought they might have a chance with the Dowager Countess of Harworth's American granddaughter.

Belle always became the focus of everyone's scrutiny, male or female, when she entered any room. The early scandal of her brief liaison with Carlton Robinson had given her a certain notoriety. Ever since she had made her début, she had become accustomed to the admiring looks of the young bucks, either at some society event or on those occasions when, having taken account of her customary rides with her grandmother through Hyde Park, they often waited for her somewhere along the route with the hope of gaining an introduction from her guardian.

It was quite a distinction to have been named as the most beautiful débutante of the London Season, and the most desirable to join the marriage mart, which was quite an achievement for a girl newly arrived in London from the Carolinas. She wished she weren't so beautiful, because people, especially the young bucks, behaved like complete idiots around her.

But an interesting fact to some was, upon her marriage, the man who married her would become the recipient of a dowry generous enough to elevate his status considerably. Hardly a day passed without some new request for her hand being addressed to her grandmother.

Belle had met rich men, she had met handsome men, but she had not fallen in love. Disheartened and thoroughly disenchanted with the opposite sex, she scorned them all, much to her grandmother's dismay, for she was eager for her to make a good marriage, and with so many eager young males of good families posturing about, she could have the pick of the bunch.

Adjusting one of her gloves that had slipped down her arm slightly, Belle looked up and found herself looking straight into the eyes of a stranger. There was an expression of utter boredom on his indecently handsome face, an expression that altered dramatically when his eyes met hers, half-startled, half-amused, and something else—something slightly carnal that stirred unfamiliar things inside her and brought heat to her cheeks. She was struck by two things: the man's obvious good looks and some kind of arrogance in those eyes, an arrogance that told her he knew who she was, knew everything about her, which unnerved her slightly.

He was dark, dark as the American natives who roamed the plains. The expression on his face was calm and controlled—he was obviously a man much used to being looked at. His close cropped hair was black, like the smooth wing of a raven, but it was his eyes that held her attention. In a face burnt brown by a hot tropical sun, they shone vivid and startling, and as blue as the speedwell that carpeted the summer meadows. They were heavily fringed with thick black lashes above which his eyebrows swooped fiercely. His broad shoulders were adorned with gold epaulettes affixed to the bright red fabric of his military tunic, and narrow-fitting white breeches encased his legs.

Lance gave her the same inspection. Closer now he could see that this was no ordinary girl. He was drawn to the freshness and vitality with which she carried herself, looking at the setting with brilliant eyes and a playful tilt to her mouth. She was exceptionally beautiful, so beautiful that it was impossible not to stand and stare at her.

Her eyes were wide set and accentuated by wing-swept black brows; the patrician nose, the heart-shaped face, the fine texture of her skin, the haughty set of the queenly head crowned with a glorious mahogany mane, upswept and sporting a silk flower matching the vibrant turquoise of her gown, all bespoke aristocratic blood. In her low-cut bodice, revealing the top curve of her firm breasts and the satin smoothness of her bare shoulders, she was a beauty, he decided, simply beautiful—and the light from the chandeliers sparked the diamonds around her neck with a cold fire. His eyes narrowed as they settled on the jewels. Suddenly she had all his attention.

Belle stood in shock beneath his leisurely perusal, and was she mistaken or did his gaze actually linger on her breasts, or was it only her imagination? His close study of her feminine assets left her feeling as if she'd just been stripped stark naked. Indeed, she could almost swear from the way he was looking at her that he had designs on her person and was already deciding on the areas where he would begin his seducing. She was bewildered, embarrassed and insulted, all at the same time. The gall of the man, she thought with rising ire. He conveyed an air of arrogance and uncompromising authority which no doubt stemmed from a haughty attitude or perhaps even his military rank. Whatever it was, it was not to her liking.

Sensing her granddaughter's distraction, the countess turned and looked at her, following the direction of her gaze. Her expression became one of severe displeasure when she saw the object of her attention.

Belle saw an odd, awed expression cross her grandmother's face as she scrutinised the dark-haired man in military uniform and was both puzzled and troubled by the look in her eyes. She had no way of discerning what thoughts were being formed behind that hard mask of concern.

'Isabelle,' she reproached severely, her gaze swinging sharply to her granddaughter, 'you look too long at that particular gentleman. Pull yourself together. We have an audience, if you hadn't noticed.'

Belle had and she couldn't suppress her amusement when the stranger gave her grandmother a mocking smile and affected an exaggerated bow.

The dowager countess was relieved to move on, away from the man who had looked at Isabelle with the hungry admiration of a wolf calmly contemplating its next meal. Lance Bingham was one gentleman she would prefer not to show an interest in her granddaughter. She had planned for too long to see Isabelle become just another conquest of the notorious Lord Lance Bingham, fifteenth Earl of Ryhill in a line that stretched back into the dim and distant days of the early Tudors, and whose reputation left very much to be desired.

For years gossip had linked him with every beautiful female of suitable lineage in Europe, and before he had gone to Spain to fight Napoleon's forces, wherever he went he left a trail of broken hearts, for marriage was not what he offered. She was not at all happy to see him back in England. He was the last man in the entire world she wanted her granddaughter to associate with—but there were other reasons too, reasons that went far back in time, and when she glanced at the necklace adorning Isabelle's neck, glittering in the light of the chandeliers, she shuddered at the painful memories it evoked.

It was all a long time ago now. The young people wouldn't know what a fool she had made of herself over Stuart Bingham, the only man she had ever loved, but the older generation remembered and any kind of association between Stuart's grandson and Isabelle would resurrect the old scandal.

'Who was that gentleman, Grandmother?' Belle ventured to ask as they passed into another room, where great arrangements of flowers filled the air with their fragrance.

The countess turned and gave her a baleful look. 'His name is Colonel Lance Bingham—the Earl of Ryhill, or Lord Bingham as he is now addressed since the death of his uncle over a year ago—and I am amazed that a man could ignore his duties as prime heir for so long a period of time. He is only recently returned to London—not that it concerns you, since I would rather you did not have anything to do with him. I saw the way you looked at him, Isabelle; it is true enough that he is a handsome devil, but he's a cold one.'

Belle remembered the warmth of those vivid blue orbs and doubted the truth of her grandmother's observation. There was a vibrant life and intensity in Lance Bingham's eyes that no one could deny.

The countess went on. 'I remember him for his arrogance. I pity the woman who marries him. He may be a revered soldier, but before he went to Spain he was a rake of the first order, which young ladies such as yourself should be wary of, for I doubt things have changed now he has returned. I don't want you to have anything to do with him, is that understood?'

Belle nodded. 'Yes, Grandmother,' she answered dutifully, shaking her head to banish the vision of the man who continued to occupy her mind, and hinted at what the strong, straight lips had not spoken. The memory of the way he had looked at her sent a dizzying thrill through her. Her face flamed at the meanderings of her mind and angrily she cast him out.

'Sorry I'm late, Lance,' a calm voice said beside him. 'Had the deuce of a job getting away from my club—interesting game of dice kept me.' He took a deep breath. 'Ye Gods, just look at this place. I think the Regent must have invited half of London.'

Recognising the voice of his good friend Rowland Gibbon, grateful for the distraction, Lance tore his gaze from the delectable Isabelle Ainsley and turned to the man next to him. 'I see that you have still not had a shave,' he commented casually, drawing his friend to a quiet spot beside a rather large exotic oriental plant. 'How long is this rebellion against the fashionable world going to last?'

Rowland grinned, proudly rubbing his whiskers. 'As to that, I've not yet decided. My valet chastises me about it daily. I fear that one night when I crawl into bed deep in my cups, he will take a razor to it and shave it off. If he does I shall have to get rid of him, for I am determined to bring back the fashion for beards. Damn it, Lance, the London beaux need someone to keep them in check.'

Rowland, tall and lank and seeming rather disjointed in his gangling limberness, was too untidy to be described as a beau. His mane of light brown hair looked forever in need of a brush and his clothes often looked as though they had been slept in—which they often had on the occasions when he was too drunk to remove them and his valet had gone to bed. Wild, disreputable and outrageous, he was also warm hearted and possessed an enormous amount of charm, which endeared him to everyone and was the reason why he was invited to every fashionable party. The two had been close friends since their days at Oxford.

'It's good to have you back, Lance, and that you've assumed your earldom. Have you been to Ryhill?'

'I've just got back.'

'Your mother will be relieved you're back. Is she well?'

He nodded. 'She visited me at Ryhill prior to leaving for Ireland to visit Sophie. My sister is expecting her first child and naturally Mother insisted on going over to be with her.'

'And your daughter—Charlotte?' Rowland enquired cautiously. 'You have seen the child, I take it?'

Lance's face was devoid of expression as he avoided his friend's probing gaze. 'No, but I have it on good authority that she is thriving and being thoroughly spoilt. She is with Mother in Ireland.'

Rowland knew not to pursue the matter of Lance's daughter. It was a subject he would never discuss. 'And you're finished with the army for good?'

Lance nodded, looking down at his uniform. 'The old uniform will have to go, but it's the best I have until my tailor provides me with new clothes—tomorrow, I hope. After Waterloo I had intended carrying on with my military career, but on learning of the death of my uncle, as his heir I had a change of heart. So I left the army, casting my sights towards home. I swore an oath to do my duty to my newly acquired title. Even to think of the estate being bestowed upon another went against everything I hold dear.'

'Well, you've certainly set tongues a wagging since you got back, with every mama with daughters of marriageable age setting their sights your way. There's one right now,' he said, indicating a young woman standing close by with her mother.

Lance casually glanced their way and acknowledged first the older, then the younger woman with a slight inclination of his head. The mother smiled stiffly and the daughter blushed and giggled behind her fan.

'There you are. You always did have women falling over themselves,' Rowland remarked casually. 'You were always viewed as the biggest fish in a very small pond. Every time you're in town they begin casting nets in hopes of scooping you up.'

'I'm particular as to which bait I nibble at, Rowland, and that particular morsel is not tasty enough for me.' Lance withdrew his gaze from the young woman and fixed his eyes once more on Isabelle Ainsley, who wandered back and forth in admiration of her surroundings.

Rowland followed his gaze to the source of his distraction. 'You look at that particular young lady with a good deal of interest.'

'You are too observant, Rowland,' Lance replied shortly.

Rowland raised one eyebrow. 'Well, out with it, man. Am I to know the identity of the lady?'

'Isabelle Ainsley, the granddaughter of the Dowager Countess of Harworth, recently come from America.' Lance didn't turn to look at Rowland, but he could sense his surprise.

Rowland made a sound of disbelief. 'You have been involved too long in the wars, my friend. See a pretty face and you lose your wits over her. Good Lord! You've only recently returned from France, and already you know who she is.'

Lance grinned. 'You know me, Rowland—always one to keep ahead of the rest.'

'You know how to live dangerously, I'll say that.'

'Who said anything about living dangerously? I have not laid eyes on her until tonight.'

'You wouldn't since you've been out of the country fighting those damn Frenchies. The American girl has certainly hit the London scene by storm and is no nitwit, that's for sure. Wherever she goes men are dazzled by her. She received countless marriage proposals before she came out, and countless since. The dowager countess is aiming high—the greater the title the greater the chance for the suitor.'

'Now why does that not surprise me?' Lance murmured drily. 'Nothing but the best for the great lady.'

'Yes, only the best. The real test for any man is fairly simple. All he has to do is win the lady's heart, for by winning it, he will then gain her grandmother's approval—maybe. Foolish logic indeed, for they will soon learn that many a pompous lord, after striving to gain the young lady's favour, has toppled from their plinth with scarcely an excuse from the young lady herself. As a consequence she has been dubbed the Ice Maiden and I have to wonder if she is as cold and haughty as those rejected suitors have claimed. I'd say her beauty is unparalleled. I wonder if she's as beautiful on the inside.'

'That, my friend, is immaterial to me,' Lance said quietly. 'It's what she has around her neck that counts.'

'I did notice that she had some rather pretty sparklers adorning her equally pretty neck.'

'The famous diamonds.'

Rowland looked at Lance, realisation dawning on him. 'Ah, how interesting—*those* diamonds. I think this needs further examination, old chap. I thought they were under lock and key, never to see the light of day again. Now I understand. It certainly explains the attraction—although after all that has happened in the past between your two families, I doubt the Dowager Countess of Harworth would consider a Bingham suitable for the hand of her granddaughter.'

'Who said anything about wedding her?'

'Then it's time you gave it some thought. Besides, you do realise that not a woman in town will spare the rest of us a glance until you have been claimed. You're not getting any younger, you know. If you intend to sire a dynasty, then you'd better get started.'

'I have already started, Rowland, and after my tragic marriage to Delphine I am not looking for another wife, and won't be doing so for a good many years.' Lance grinned, a hint of the old wickedness in his eyes that Roland had not seen in a long time. 'I have a few more years of grand debauchery to enjoy before I settle for one woman.'

If he had thought to convince his friend he failed, for although society thought otherwise, Lance's days as a debauchee were long and truly behind him. Lance was the stuff ladies' dreams were made of, fatally handsome and with the devil's own charm. Having spent several years as a soldier, his daring and courage in the face of the enemy had won him praise from the highest—from Wellington himself. His skill and knowledge in numerous bloody battles added to his reputation as a clever strategist and an invincible opponent.

The Lance Bingham who had returned to England was very different from the one who had left. The changes were startling. In contrast to the idle young men who lounged about the clubs and ballrooms with bored languor, Lance was full of energy, deeply tanned, muscular and extremely fit, sharp and authoritative, and although he laughed and charmed his way back into society, there was an aura about him of a man who had done and seen all there was to see and do, a man who had confronted danger and enjoyed it. It was an aura that women couldn't resist and which added to his attraction.

'I wonder why the old girl's suddenly decided to show the diamonds off,' Rowland mused.

Lance shrugged. 'I have wondered myself.'

'Have you never tried to get them back? After all they are rightfully yours.'

'No—at least not lately.'

'And now you're back in England, will you attempt to get them back? Although I don't see how you can. Getting the great lady to part with those precious diamonds will be like getting blood out of the proverbial stone. I'd stake my life on it.'

'I wouldn't want your life for a gold pot, but I am always game for a friendly bet. A hundred pounds says you're wrong. I will have the diamonds in my possession by dawn tomorrow.'

Rowland chuckled, happy to pick up the gauntlet. 'Make it two hundred and you're on. I love a sure bet. But the fascinating young lady will be returning to Hampstead after the ball, so how will you be settling this bet?'

Lance shrugged nonchalantly. 'You'll have to wait and see.'

Rowland smiled smugly. 'I doubt you'll succeed. I'll call on you tomorrow to claim my winnings. Now, as much as I would like to stay and chat, right now I see the delectable Amanda, the daughter of Viscount Grenville, has just arrived. If you'll excuse me, I'll go and secure a dance or two before her card is full.'

Left alone, Lance considered the amazing bet he had made, and he knew he would have to act quickly if he were to see it through. Normally he would have kept his money in his pocket, but there were reasons why he'd impulsively made the bet. There were benefits to be obtained from securing the diamonds, for not only were they were worth a fortune, by rights they belonged to him.

Lance continued to watch the two Ainsley women as the dowager countess greeted those she knew. There was insolence and arrogance written into every line of Belle Ainsely's taut young body, but its symmetry was spell-binding. She was exquisite and he had already made up his mind to be formally presented to her. If her dragon of a grandmother objected, then with the inbred arrogance and pride of a man who is not accustomed to being denied, which of course he did not expect to be, he would find a way of introducing himself.

At some point during the evening he was confident that he would succeed in separating her from the laughing, chattering throng and whisk her away to some quiet arbour, where they would drink champagne and engage in the dalliance that was the stuff of life to him.

Chapter Two

Nothing had prepared Belle for the splendour that was Carlton House, which faced the south side of Pall Mall; its gardens abutted St James's Park.

Following her grandmother past the graceful staircase and through the spacious, opulent residence, which was packed with hundreds of people—nobility, politicians, the influential, the wealthy, the elite of London society—admiring the superb collection of works of art hung on the walls of every room, ornate fireplaces, crystal chandeliers—dripping with hundreds of thousands of crystals and ablaze with blinding light, marble busts in niches, mirrors and gold leaf—Belle, finding it all magically impressive, absorbed every detail.

The dowager countess smiled at her mixture of fascination and bemusement. 'Wait until you see the rest of the house—and the table. The food will be delicious—even though it does have so far to travel from the kitchens that it invariably arrives cold. The Prince shows great imagination in planning these parties and one always enjoys his hospitality.'

Belle stopped and closed her eyes, dizzy with the incomprehensible sights of so much dazzling splendour. Quickly recovering, she snapped open her fan and briskly fanned herself. 'It would be impossible not to. I've never seen anything like it,' the dazzled girl said. 'How can all these people not be struck blind by all this beauty?'

'The Prince stresses there is nothing in Europe that can compare with Carlton House. As for being struck blind, why, these people have seen it for so long that it's lost all meaning to them.'

'You mean they don't appreciate it?'

'Not as much as you evidently do. The Prince would be well pleased.'

Belle said not a word, merely drinking in every sight as though she had never before in her life seen such beauty. The supper table was covered with linen cloths and laden with delicacies far more numerous than Belle could ever have imagined. It glittered and sparkled and gleamed gold and silver on both sides, running the length of the dining room and into the conservatory beyond. The oriental theme the Prince had chosen for the table decorations was exquisite in every minute detail. At equal distances elaborate crystal fountains bubbled musically, the liquid in them not water but wine.

The atmosphere became electrified when the Prince arrived, looking larger than life and extremely grand in a military uniform heavily trimmed with gold braid. His eyes twinkled good-humouredly as he welcomed everyone and there was a great deal of bowing and dipping of curtsies.

While waiting to be seated, Belle looked about her, her eyes drawn to Lord Bingham, who stood across the room conversing with a group of young bucks. She studied him surreptitiously. His blue eyes glinted with a sardonic expression. Broad shouldered, narrow of waist, with a muscular leg, he gave the appearance of an athlete, a man who fenced and hunted. Yet, she thought, with that determined, clefted chin there was a certain air of masculinity, something attractive, almost compelling, about him, and certainly dangerous.

As Lance became tired of standing around, his eyes sought out the delectable Belle Ainsley, which, despite the house being almost full to capacity, wasn't too difficult. He saw her surrounded by doting swains enthralled by her uncommon beauty, a premise that, curiously, strangely nettled his mood on finding himself observing her audience of aristocratic suitors. She was enjoying herself, laughing and at ease, a natural temptress, he thought, alluring and provocative and with the body of a goddess. He had to fight the insane impulse to disperse her personal entourage of admirers, carry her to a quiet place, take hold of that lithe, warm, breathing form, crush it beneath him and kiss the irreverent laughter from her soft, inviting lips.

Belle was seated next to her grandmother, Lord Bingham several places away from her on the opposite side of the table. She tried hard not to look at him, but found her eyes turned constantly in his direction. At one point he caught her glance and held her eyes with his warmly glowing blue orbs. His lips widened leisurely into a rakish grin as his gaze ranged over her, and he inclined his head to her in the merest mockery of a bow and raised his glass.

Considering the perusals she had been subjected to so far, Belle deemed his perusal far too bold. At least other men had the decency to size her up with discretion, but

Lord Bingham made no attempt to hide his penchant for studying and caressing and feeding on every aspect of her person so that she felt she was being devoured.

Hot with embarrassment over being caught staring and the smug manner in which he'd acknowledged her, Belle curled her lips in derision and, lifting her chin in an attitude of haughty displeasure, looked away, aware that if she didn't stop it and take more interest in the general conversation that was going on around her, her grandmother would notice.

It proved to be an especially fine banquet and, continuing to find herself the recipient of Lord Bingham's careful perusal and feeling the dire need of its numbing effects, Belle imbibed more wine than she normally would have done. There was no protection from that rogue's hungering eyes, and at times the warm glow she saw in them made her feel quite naked. She was not at all surprised when she realised her nerves were taut enough to be plucked.

Three hours later when the banquet had ended, Belle strolled through the lantern-lit gardens with her grandmother, who had become overcome with the heat and thought some fresh air might help alleviate her headache, which had become quite intense. She also strove to keep Isabelle in her sights.

People collected in groups to gossip while high-spirited young couples sought privacy among the shrubs. After she had excused herself to go to the ladies' retiring room when her grandmother stopped to acknowledge an acquaintance, on returning and finding herself alone for the first time since she had entered Carlton House, Belle followed the sound of music and stood in the ballroom, watching dancers attired in satins and silks swirling around the floor in time to a lilting waltz.

Suddenly she got that unnerving feeling she got when someone was staring at her. The sensation was so strong she could almost feel the eyes on her, and then a deep voice seemed to leap out from behind her, and said, 'Dance with me.'

Belle turned in astonishment as the officer materialised from the shadows. Belle recognised that mocking smile—it was identical to the one he had given her across the table, when he'd caught her inadvertently staring at him. His voice was deep and throaty, like thick honey. It was a seductive voice that made her think of highly improper things. It seemed to caress each word he uttered, and she knew there couldn't be many women who could resist a voice like that, not if the man speaking looked like Lord Bingham. But she told herself she needn't worry, for she was completely immune to that potent masculine allure.

'That would not be appropriate. I don't know you.'

Lance laughed at her. 'Well, my fine lady, you should indeed know me—and if you don't, I will tell you that I am Lance Bingham, at your service. Now does my name sound familiar?'

'My grandmother has already told me who you are,' Belle replied coolly.

'I thought she might.'

She looked at him directly. 'Why does she not like you?'

Instead of reacting with offence, he merely chuckled. 'You should ask your grandmother. You may find what she has to tell you—interesting.' He grinned, his mouth curving up at one corner. Beneath his heavy, drooping lids his eyes were filled with amusement, and idle speculation. 'What's the matter? Cat got your tongue?'

She cocked a dark, finely arched brow above a baleful glare, which, with the chillingly beautiful smile, could have frozen the heart of the fiercest opponent. Woe to the man this woman unleashed her wrath upon.

'I'm minding my own business. I suggest you mind yours.'

He grinned. 'You're outspoken.'

'None of your business. Why don't you just go away?'

'Hostile, too. I don't often encounter hostility from young ladies.'

'I'm surprised.'

'You're not impressed?'

'Not a bit.'

Those seductive blue eyes settled on her. 'Well, Miss Isabelle, I find you quite challenging.'

'You do?'

'Did anyone ever tell you you're quite lovely?'

'All the time.'

'And you've got lovely hair. You're got a provocative mouth, too.'

'Save your breath. I am not interested.'

'No?' He arched a brow.

'Not in the slightest.'

'I find that hard to believe.'

'You are very convincing. You actually make a woman believe you are speaking the truth—but then you have undoubtedly had a great deal of practice.'

He grinned. 'True, but I am sincere.'

Belle could feel her cheeks warming as she met those smiling blue eyes. 'You seem terribly sure of yourself, my lord.'

'And I can see you're not easily taken in, but can you not understand what a man like myself experiences in the presence of such a beautiful woman?'

Belle peered at him frostily. 'And I can see you're all talk.'

Leaning forwards, Lance ensnared her gaze and carefully probed those dark green eyes as a slow smile curved his lips. 'You've got me all wrong. You've awakened emotions within me that I was sure I was incapable of feeling—some of which are appreciative—others I'm simply struggling to restrain.'

'Then you will just have to curb your emotions, my lord, for I am not interested.'

He cocked a sleek black brow. 'No?'

'Conceited, aren't you? Conceited and arrogant.'

He pretended offence. 'You do me a terrible injustice. In fact, you make me feel quite downcast and disconsolate. Here I am, complimenting you on your beauty, and you start casting aspersions on my character. You think I'm insufferable?'

'Quite,' she agreed heatedly.

'That's quite a temper you have,' he said, shaking his head in teasing, chiding reproof. 'And here I was thinking that you wanted me to ask you to dance.'

Her eyes flared. 'Do you actually think I was waiting for you to ask me?'

Her show of outrage bestirred his hearty laughter. Thoroughly incensed, Belle glowered at him until his amusement dwindled to nothing more than a slanted grin. 'You can't fault a soldier recently returned from the wars for hoping that such would be the case. You really are quite the most enticing female I've met. So, what do you say? Will you dance with me?'

'No. Like I said, you are insufferable. I don't think I like you very much.'

'A little would do. Actually, I'm quite delightful once you get to know me. I do have a reputation, I admit it frankly—but I've been dreadfully maligned. You shouldn't believe all you hear about me.'

Belle gazed at him with a cool hauteur. After a moment he smiled a devilishly engaging smile, offended demeanour gone.

'Are you sure you don't want to dance?'

'Quite sure,' she retorted.

'You don't know what you're missing.'

'Sore feet, probably.'

'It's a long time since I trod on a lady's toes, Belle.'

Her heart lurched at his familiar use of her name. 'Maybe so, but I will not risk it. I did not invite you to ask me to dance.'

He grinned unrepentantly. 'I know. I took it upon myself. Always was impetuous.'

'Now why doesn't that surprise me? If you will excuse me, I see my grandmother beckoning to me.'

Lance Bingham gave her a mock-polite nod, eyelids drooping, a half-smile playing on his mouth. Lowering his head, he spoke softly into her ear, his warm breath fanning her neck. Mingled with an underlying essence of soap, the pleasantly aromatic bouquet of his cologne drifted into her nostrils and twined amazingly through her senses, and she found the manly fragrance intoxicating.

'Go if you must, but I will not give up.'

True to his word, Lance Bingham didn't. His mind never wandering far from the diamonds around her neck, Belle Ainsley's delectable form fully visible to his hungry eyes was an inducement he was unable to resist.

The Dowager Countess of Harworth had watched him throughout the evening carefully. She had seen him approach Isabelle and noted her rejection. However she was unsettled by it. Countless young women surrounded him all the time, all vying for his attention. Lord Bingham, she noted, treated them with amused tolerance, for his attention was on the only female at Carlton House who seemed immune to his magnetism—her granddaughter.

Having serious cause to doubt that he had never seen such perfection before and tempted to dally with the lady to his heart's content, half an hour after he had spoken to her, Lance threw caution to the four winds and approached Belle once more.

From where she sat conversing with two elderly ladies who were friends of her grandmother, glancing up, Belle saw his head above the crowd and instinctively knew he was looking for her. When he turned his imperious head his eyes locked on to hers and he smiled, a lazy cocksure smile. When he strode arrogantly towards her, she was not in the least surprised when the crowd parted before him like the Red Sea before Moses.

Belle lifted her eyes to look into his face. He was smiling down at her, the bright blueness of his eyes catching her breath. She was used to male admiration, but this one was the first to rouse her hostility while at the same time stirring her senses and capturing her imagination. Not that she'd let him see it, for that was not her way, but she had never reacted like this before to any man.

'As you do not appear to be taken for this dance, I wonder if I might—'

Belle raised her chin haughtily. 'Thank you, but I am not dancing at the moment.'

'I can see that, which is why I am here. Now, if the ladies will excuse us…'

Bowing in the direction of the open-mouthed ladies, Lance took Belle's hand, pulled her out of the chair and whisked her into the middle of the swirling dancers where he took her into his arms. Belle was so unused to anyone forcing her to do something against her will that she went with him, automatically falling into the right steps of the waltz before she realised what she was doing.

Her astonishment at his outrageous audacity was short lived and anger took over. For two pins she would walk off the floor and leave him standing, but she was acutely aware that almost everyone was watching them and she could not do that. To do so would be a slight to him, and she could not do such a thing to him in front of all these people. Nor could she shame her grandmother by creating a scene, even though she did not hold a high opinion of Lord Bingham and had told her in no uncertain terms that she must have nothing to do with him. So she made up her mind not to speak to him and leave when the dance ended

They danced in silence for a few moments, a silence in which Lance noted the strange lights dancing in her shining hair, and her slender shoulders gleaming with a soft, creamy lustre. 'This is pleasant, is it not?' he said at length, and there was a touch of irony in his mocking tone.

Feeling his arm tighten about her, Belle stiffened and for an incredulous moment she was speechless. Looking into his eyes, she forgot her intention not to engage in conversation with him. 'I would be obliged if you would not hold me so tightly. I am only dancing with you because you dragged me on to the floor,' she said with an effort, in the coldest and most condescending manner. 'Do you usually snatch your partners away from their chaperons so ungallantly?'

He raised one thick, well-defined eyebrow, looking down at her. A faint half-smile played on his lips as if he knew exactly what was going on in her mind. 'Only when I think they might refuse to dance with me—or need rescuing.'

'I did not need rescuing, as you well know, Lord Bingham,' she retorted, resenting his effect on her, the masculine assurance of his bearing. But she was conscious of an unwilling excitement, seeing him arrogantly mocking, and recklessly attractive. Here they were, together in the middle of the dance floor, in an atmosphere bristling with tension. 'I was perfectly happy where I was.'

'I don't believe you. Besides, it's not every day I get to dance with an American girl.'

Belle looked at him condescendingly and gritted out a menacing smile. 'Lord Bingham, I am curious about your name. You see, I knew some Binghams in Charleston. Scurvy lot they were—thieves and cutthroats. Are you perhaps related, sir?'

The sweetness of her tone did not hide the sneer she intended. He met it with a flicker of amusement showing upon his lips. 'It's not impossible. I have distant family scattered all over the place. Who knows? Some of them may quite possibly have settled in the Carolinas. You dance divinely, by the way,' he murmured, spinning her in an exaggerated whirl that made her catch her breath.

'Will you please behave yourself?' She spoke sharply, jerking away from him.

'I do,' he murmured, his warm breath fanning her cheek as he pulled her back to him. 'We are partners. How else should I behave?'

'Do not hold me so tightly. Be a gentleman—if that is not too difficult for you.'

'A gentleman?' he said, flashing his white teeth in a lazy grin, his gaze dipping lingeringly to her soft lips. 'How can I do that? I am but an ignorant soldier, un-schooled in the postures of the court, trained only to fire a gun and fight the enemy.'

'Do not play the simpleton with me. It won't work. Why have you singled me out from all the other ladies to dance?'

'Is it so very strange for a man to want to dance with the most beautiful woman in the room? You are a very beautiful—enough to drive a man to madness.'

'I really had no idea,' she apologised sarcastically. 'Perhaps you would like to prove your words.'

'Prove?'

Calmly Belle met his gaze. How she yearned to erase that smirking grin from his lips. 'Your madness!' She sounded flippant and casual. 'But you need not burden me. A few flecks of foam about your mouth would serve as well to prove the claim.' She ignored the amusement that shone from his eyes and was sure her remark would have had him laughing out loud had they not been in the middle of a crowded dance floor. 'Am I the first female you've ever met who didn't want to dance with you?'

'I confess to being somewhat spoiled by women who seemed to enjoy dancing with me. And you,' he added, knocking back her momentary sense of triumph, 'have been too long surrounded by besotted beaux who would willingly kiss the ground on which you walk, begging your permission to be your lord and master.'

'Heaven forbid! I will never call any man my lord and nor will I allow a man to be my master. When I marry it will be a partnership. I will not be a dutiful little wife expected to behave like an obedient servant.'

Lance glanced down at her with an odd combination of humorous scepticism and certainty. 'No I don't suppose you will. You have quite a following of admirers,' he commented, his eyes skimming over the bachelors who had been among her audience earlier. They were now eyeing him enviously and with keen attention. 'I must say that I'm relieved you didn't walk off the floor and leave me standing.'

'Had I done so, I would have put my own reputation in jeopardy.'

His eyes, sweeping over her face and coming to rest on the sparkling gems around her throat, narrowed. 'Even so. You should know that if I want something I take it, whatever the consequences.' He lowered his head as he spun her round, his lips close to her ear. 'I've never seduced a girl from Charleston before.'

Deeply shocked by his remark, Belle had the urge to kick his shin and leave him standing, regardless of the consequences, but instead she controlled her expression and met his look head on. 'No? Then might I suggest you go there and find one. I am not so easily seduced,' she retorted, too angry to be humiliated.

'No?'

'A very *definite* no. I wouldn't let you touch me to save me from drowning.'

He looked down at her with mock disappointment. 'I am mortified to hear that—but it's early days. I always enjoy the chase. You will think differently when you get to know me.'

Belle looked at him with withering scorn. 'Why, of all the conceited, arrogant—what a thoroughly selfish, insufferable individual you are, Lord Bingham. Do you make lewd remarks to all the women you dance with?'

'And do you treat every gentleman who dances with you with such animosity—or only me?'

'Lord Bingham, in the first place, you are no gentleman—which I have already pointed out. In the second, I don't like you. And in the third, you should not be speaking to me at all.'

'I shouldn't?' Her hostility didn't offend him in the slightest. In fact, it added to his determination to get to know her better.

'We have not been properly introduced.'

'Do you mind?'

'No—not really,' she confessed honestly, hating the protocol that now ruled her every waking moment, tying her in knots lest she do or say the wrong thing.

'Good. Neither do I. I would like it if you would call me Lance,' he said, his gaze settling on her face, 'since I intend for us to become better acquainted.'

'Forgive me, but that would go against the basics my grandmother has tried to teach me since coming to this country. I have been taught to show proper respect for gentleman of any standing.'

Lance considered her at length and had to wonder why she refused to be so informal with him after he had invited her to be. 'I must assume by your answer that you're averse to the familiarity.'

'It is what my grandmother would demand of me.'

'Does that mean you insist on me addressing you in like manner?'

'Whether you adhere to the strict code of gentlemanly conduct is entirely your affair.'

His eyebrow quirked with some amusement. 'Come now, Belle—and in case you're wondering, I know that is what you are called since I have made enquiries—'

'I wasn't,' she cut in crossly.

'—but your grandmother is stuck in the past,' he continued. 'Times are changing—at least I hope they are.'

Belle had never known her name could sound so very different, so warmly evocative when spoken by a man, or that she could feel as if she were dissolving inside when those soft, mellow tones caressed her senses.

'Can you not agree that if we are to get to know each other on more intimate terms,' Lance went on, lowering his head so that his mouth was very close to her ear, 'it should allow us privileges above the usual stilted decorum of strangers?'

His husky voice and the closeness of his mouth so that she could feel his warm breath on her cheek was almost her undoing. She blushed scarlet. There was still so much of the girl in her at war with the young woman, and this man had the knack of bringing it quickly to the surface. Yet for all her annoyance with him, she was aware of everything about him—of the handsome face above the scarlet jacket, tanned and healthy. She was surprised to see, at close quarters, faint lines of weariness about his face as silently, reluctantly, she felt drawn once more towards him. Recollecting herself, she tried to change her thoughts, finding her emotions distasteful.

'But that is precisely what we are, Lord Bingham,

strangers—and I intend for us to remain that way. I am convinced you have plied many light o' loves with similar persuasive reasoning. I can well imagine that you have become quite adept at swaying besotted young girls from the path their parents have urged them to follow.'

His eyes twinkled down at her. She was right. Apart from Delphine, there had been temporary light o' loves—and one or two had lasted longer than others—but he had never considered his involvement with them of any consequence. 'You are very astute, Belle, but if you think you have the measure of me, then you are very much mistaken. I saw you the moment you arrived and I've wanted to speak to you all evening.'

'And now you have,' she said, staring into those eyes that had ensnared her own. 'And don't get any high-minded ideas that you're any better than the other gentleman I have partnered tonight, because if you do you will be wrong.'

Belle thought he was too much aware of her physically, and that the banter was leading to something. He made her uneasy and yet at the same time he stimulated and excited her. He did seem to have a way about him and she could not fault any woman for falling under his spell, for she found to her amazement that her heart was not so distantly detached as she had imagined it to be. To her amazement his voice and the way he looked at her evoked a strangely pleasurable disturbance in areas far too private for an untried virgin even to consider, much less invite, and she didn't quite know what to make of them. They seemed almost wanton. But she didn't intend making it easy for him.

'Clearly I didn't make my aversion to conversing with you plain enough,' she retorted hotly.

He chuckled low. 'I thought you were merely playing hard to get.'

'I don't play those sorts of games,' she retorted hotly. 'My pleasure would be to walk off the floor and leave you standing, so be thankful that I've let you retain some of your pride. My grandmother will reproach me most severely for dancing with you.'

'That is for you to deal with, Belle, but heed my warning. I do not run from fierce old ladies, no matter how hard or how loud they huff and puff. Her dislike of me is quite unfounded.'

'My grandmother has never said that she dislikes you, and she never says anything about anyone without good reason. And, of course, you're the poor innocent and undeserving of any condemnation.'

His eyes glowed in the warm light as he gave her a lazy smile. 'I never claimed to be an innocent—in fact, I am far from it.'

'I would hardly expect you to admit it if you were,' she retorted crisply.

'I could show you if you like.' His eyes seemed to glow, laughing at her, mocking her.

'Not a chance.'

'Are you enjoying the Prince's hospitality?'

She looked at him boldly from beneath her long eyelashes, her lips parted, her tongue visible between the perfect white of her teeth, and a tell-tale flush having turned her cheeks a becoming pink. 'Very much, and Prince George seems very charming—unlike some of his guests.'

'Oh? Anyone in particular?'

'I don't think I need spell it out, do you? The Prince is awfully good at giving wonderful parties.'

He gave her a penetrating look through narrowed eyes. 'So, Belle Ainsley, your grandmother has warned you about me?'

Belle leaned back in his arms and looked up at him. His taunting grin made her realise the folly of baiting him. He had all but stated he was no gentleman and did exactly what he chose to do. She felt a perverse desire to shatter a little of his arrogant self-assurance.

'If she has, it's because you have a certain reputation. She cannot bear me out of her sight, for in her opinion every male in London has designs on me. Not that she would object to it being the right man, you understand, since she's forever reminding me that the Season is for young ladies to find husbands.'

'Which is true. Otherwise what is the point of it all?'

'Indeed, and I'm afraid that at present I have more suitors than I know what to do with. Grandmother sets great store by propriety and everything must be done according to the rules of courtship.'

'And you? Did you want to leave America?'

'No. It was my home, where I wanted to remain, but on my father's demise my grandmother—who had become my guardian—insisted I come to England.'

'Well, I for one am very glad she did.'

'I don't see why you should be, for since my grandmother seems to have an aversion to you she will see to it that we are never in the same company.'

The brief shake of his head dismissed her remark. 'If I have a mind to get to know you better, Belle, your grandmother won't be able to do a thing about it,' he said in a deep, velvety voice.

Belle saw the look in his eyes, and her heart began to hammer uncontrollably while a warning screamed along her nerves, a warning she knew she should take heed of if she was to retain her sanity. He had set her at odds with his insolent perusal of her earlier, but she had to admit that he was the most exciting man she had met—and the most infuriating.

As the dance progressed, couples dipped and swayed, but Lance Bingham and Belle Ainsley were unaware of them. They made a striking couple. There was a glow of energy, a powerful magnetism that emanated from the beautiful, charismatic pair, he so handsome, she so lovely—so everyone thought, everyone, that is, but the Dowager Countess of Harworth. Sitting with a group of elegant men and women who composed her personal retinue, as she watched her wilful, headstrong granddaughter skim the ballroom floor in the arms of and in perfect unison with the notorious Lord Bingham, her expression was ferociously condemning.

Even the other dancers turned their heads to watch, making way for them as they circled the room. Guests, who had been chatting and laughing and drinking champagne, aware of the enmity that existed between the Ainselys and the Binghams—that there had been much strife and that emotions were still raw—grew watchful and quiet, glancing now and then at the dowager countess, so enormous was her consequence among the *ton*, to see what she would do.

The countess observed through narrowed eyes that the famous diamonds had created a lot of interest and drew a good deal of comment and envious glances—not least that of Lance Bingham. Already the air was buzzing with whispered conjectures and she knew the word would spread like wildfire that, by singling Isabelle out to dance, Lord Bingham was sending out the message that the age-old feud was over. This thought the countess found most displeasing and was not to be borne. The last thing in the world she wanted was for her granddaughter to capture the interest of this particular aristocrat, but it would appear she had done just that. By breakfast the affair would be being discussed in every household in London.

Belle was whirled around in time to the sweeping music by a man who danced with the easy grace of someone who has waltzed a million times and more. Lance was a good dancer, light on his feet, keeping in time to the rhythm of the music. Belle could feel the muscles of his broad shoulders beneath the fabric of his coat, and her fingers tingled from the contact.

And then the dance was over and he released her, but he was reluctant to part from her. Belle Ainsley intrigued him. She was the only woman who had dared stand up to him, and flaunting the diamonds that by rights belonged to the Binghams—the sheer injustice of it—was tantamount to a challenge to him.

'Would you defy your grandmother and dance with me again?'

'Why? Are you asking?'

'Would you like me to?'

'Yes, just to give me the satisfaction of saying no.'

He grinned. 'Don't cut off your nose to spite your face, Belle.'

'Don't flatter yourself. One dance with you is quite enough. Please excuse me. I think this brief encounter has gone on long enough.'

She turned from him, about to walk away, but he caught her arm. 'Wait.'

She spun round. 'What?'

'Protocol dictates that I escort you back to your grandmother—or do you forget so easily what you have been taught?'

'Are you sure you want to? Do you have the courage?'

'After confronting Napoleon on the battle field, confronting your grandmother is mere child's play.'

Belle elevated her brows in question. 'You think so? Would you like to tell her—or shall I?'

'I wouldn't bother. Your grandmother might take offence to being compared to the mighty emperor.'

'I don't think so. Both are stoic and determined people, and unafraid of the enemy. I think they would get on remarkably well.' She tossed her head haughtily. 'I suppose you must return me to my grandmother—it will be interesting to observe the outcome.'

Taking her hand, Lance led her off the dance floor. He sensed that, in her belief she could do whatever she fancied, there was an air of danger about her. Nothing will ever beat her, he thought. He would wager she had teeth and claws. Determined too. What she wants she'll go after—a girl after his own heart. But she was still young, still impressionable—trembling on the edge of ripe womanhood. Isabelle Ainsley would not be long without a husband. The Regent's court possessed many handsome beaux, who would be willing to wed the beautiful granddaughter of the Dowager Countess of Harworth. She thought she had his measure. He smiled, confident in his own power over the female sex. She was only an apprentice compared to him.

He liked his women to be experienced, experienced

in the ways of pleasing his own sexually mature body, and there was no doubt Belle Ainsley would make a perfect bed mate. But she must be shown that it was Lance Bingham who called the tune. However, Lance knew full well that though it was not in his nature to care what people thought of him—especially the Dowager Countess of Harworth—he must, for the time being, do the right thing and return this beautiful baggage with her reputation intact.

Lance bowed to the countess, his smile courteous. 'Your granddaughter dances divinely, Countess. I hope you will forgive me for stealing her away. I was somewhat precipitate in rushing her on to the floor as I did.'

The dowager countess regarded him with an expression of acid tolerance for which she was known—and feared—by all the *ton*. A deep shudder passed through her and she felt as if she were being taken back in time, for Lance Bingham, with his lean, noble features, stunning good looks and tall, broad-shouldered frame, was so much like his grandfather. She was shocked by the likeness. He had the same mocking smile that she had always found so confusing. It had promised so much and yet meant so little.

'Yes, you were. So, Colonel Bingham, you are back from France.'

'As you see, Countess. I am especially honoured by this opportunity to renew our acquaintance.'

The countess considered it prudent to ignore his remark. 'You are back for good?'

'Indeed.'

'You have been to Ryhill?'

'I have, but pressing matters of business brought me back to London for the present.'

'Wellington and Prince George have sung your praises often during your campaigns. From all reports, your regiment was a shining example of a well-disciplined force, which proved itself as valiant in battle as any in the British Army—in particular the battle at Waterloo. You are to be congratulated, Lord Bingham.'

'No more than any other. Waterloo was a great victory for Wellington. Any officer would have deemed it a privilege to serve under his leadership. You kept up with what was happening?'

'I read the newspapers,' the countess replied, her tone stilted.

'Of course you do.' Lance's eyes flicked to Belle. 'I should be honoured if you would permit me to partner your granddaughter in another dance, Countess.'

'I imagine you would be. However, I believe her dance card is full. I'm sure you will find some other young lady willing to partner you.'

Her face became alarmingly shuttered and without expression and her eyes darkened until they were almost black. That this impertinent man, whose family had done her so much harm in the past, should have the effrontery to try to ingratiate himself with her granddaughter was insupportable.

Lance nodded, understanding perfectly, but he was quite ready to be summarily dismissed. 'I'm sure I shall, Countess.' He looked at Belle and bowed his torso in a courtly gesture. 'I enjoyed dancing with you, Miss Ainsley. Should one of your partners be unavailable, I am at your service. The night is still young. Who knows? Anything might happen.' Without another word or so much as a glance at Belle, he bowed and walked away.

Determined to dedicate herself to keeping Lance Bingham away from Isabelle, and having planned to leave for the Ainsleys' ancestral home in Wiltshire at the end of the Season, the countess considered it might be as well to leave in the next few days. Although even in Wiltshire it couldn't be guaranteed that Isabelle would be safe from the officer if the wily rascal had a mind to see her.

She was pleased with the way Isabelle had turned out—even if she had enjoyed frustrating all her tutors' efforts to correct any part of her like some precocious child out to tease her elders. However, her demeanour was much improved. She was at ease and content fraternising with affluent aristocrats with lofty titles and well respected. But there were still times—like tonight and her disagreeable and defiant behaviour over the necklace, and her refusal to send Lance Bingham packing when he'd asked her to dance—when the old Isabelle surfaced to remind her that the spirited, wilful hoyden was still present.

'If Lord Bingham approaches you again, you will have nothing to do with him, Isabelle. The man believes he can talk his way into, or out of, any situation and I have no wish to see him do you harm. He has charm in abundance, but you will have nothing more to do with him. Do you understand?'

'Yes, Grandmother,' Belle replied dutifully, knowing that if Lord Bingham had a mind to approach her again, there wasn't a thing she could do about it.

As the evening progressed, from a distance Lance watched Belle Ainsley, making no attempt to approach her for the present, though this had nothing to do with her grandmother's displeasure. No matter how he tried to clear his mind of her, the more difficult it became, for the woman was entangling him in desire and he hadn't even kissed her yet, never mind possessed her. But he would. Yes, he would. Although Lance considered himself an experienced ladies' man, with justification he knew when to take a step back. His senses were giving him that message right now.

However, his attention never wavered from the provocative sensuality of her as she danced with more men than she would be able to remember. There was a natural, unaffected sophistication and exhilarating liveliness that drew men to her, and he took pleasure in looking at her, at the vibrancy of her, her laughing face, his gaze shifting now and then to the glittering diamonds resting against her creamy flesh that brought a quiet, secretive smile to his lips.

The festivities were drawing to a close when he saw her standing by a pillar alone. He lazily regarded her, his eyes following her, snapping sharply. Going to stand behind her, he lightly trailed his skilled fingers down the soft nape of her neck, reassured when she did not move away.

Belle recognised the scent of his cologne. She gasped and quivered, a warmth suffusing her cheeks. Though she commanded herself to move, her legs refused to budge. She felt it so strongly, it was as if her whole body was throbbing suddenly and in her head her thoughts were not orderly—just odd, strong responses. And in her breasts—how could a touch, a caress, reach her breasts? Yet it had; it was making them desperate to be touched and it was all she could do not to reach for one of his hands and place it there.

And the sensation moved on, lower, sweetly soft and liquid; small darts of pleasure travelled as if on silken threads to her stomach and inner thighs as the infuriating man continued his rhythmic stroking, with Belle unaware as he did so that he was giving particular attention to the clasp of her necklace. The heat of his hand seemed to scorch her cool flesh and she licked her dry lips. Recollecting herself, she shrugged away from his caress, but not too forcefully.

'You overstep yourself, sir,' she murmured, a little breathless.

'But you enjoy me touching you, Belle, do you not?' Lance breathed in a tight, strained voice. 'Would you deny either of us the pleasures of being together?'

Oddly feeling no grudge against him, Belle turned and looked at him surreptitiously. His bold gaze stirred something deep within her, and the sensation was not unpleasant. 'You go too fast. I hardly know you at all.'

Lance's eyes gleamed with devilish humour, and his lips drew slowly into a delicate smile. 'You're quite right. You must allow us to get to know each other. You could be the light of my life. Have mercy on me.'

Belle lifted her chin. 'I am hardly the first or the only one. It passes through my thoughts that you are a rake, Lord Bingham, and have probably said those very words to so many women you have lost count.'

'I cannot deny any of what you say—but then I had not met you. You impress me. You attract me. It is a long time since I said that to a woman.'

Confused by the gentle warmth of his gaze and the directness of his words, Belle was moved by what he said. It was impossible to determine whether he mocked her or told the truth. He was not like any man she had ever met. When she had spoken to hurt him, to insult him, he had taken it in his stride or with humour, with patience, and still he complimented her.

'You must forgive me if I appear confused. *You* confuse me.'

The softening in her manner enhanced her beauty, and Lance boldly and appreciatively stared, encouraged by it. He leaned closer so that his mouth was close to her ear. 'At least we have something in common.'

His warm breath stirred shivers along her flesh, and a curious excitement tingled in her breast. She had to fight to keep her world upright. What was the matter with her? Had she consumed too much wine and was now feeling its effect?

'Is it too hard to imagine that we could become lovers?' he asked softly. 'I find you absolutely fascinating, and yet you suddenly seem afraid. Is it me you fear—or something else?'

The endearment spoken in his rich, deep voice had the same stirring effect on her as his finger on the back of her neck. 'I am not afraid,' she said, trying to control herself and the situation, 'and nor do your words sway me. I realise that this is merely a dalliance to you.'

'Liar.' A seductive grin swept across his handsome face. 'Admit it. You are afraid—afraid of the things I make you feel.'

'Lord Bingham,' she gasped breathlessly, 'I am not a woman of easy virtue and certainly do not intend giving myself to you. Now please go away before my grandmother sees us together. You have no idea how angry she can be.'

'Yes, I do.'

'Then you should take heed and leave me alone.'

He moved round her to stand in front of her, his eyes hooded and seductive. 'Come now, you don't mean that.'

With trembling effort Belle collected herself, and, as he stared at her, she drew a deep, ragged breach. 'She says I must have nothing to do with you. I'm beginning to think she's right.'

He chuckled softly. 'Is she afraid I will lead you astray? Is that it, Belle?'

She gave him a level look. 'I believe she does, but that isn't the only reason, is it? My sixth sense tells me there is some other reason why she dislikes you.'

'Your sixth sense does you credit.'

'So I am right.

He looked at her, his eyes amused, a smile curving his full mouth, and when Belle met his gaze she was struck by the sheer male beauty of him. And then she was struck by something else, very strongly indeed—it shocked her with its violence, a great blow of emotion, emotion for him.

She wasn't quite sure what it was even, but she acknowledged it—it was startling and unexpected and absolutely new. The evening—the privilege of being at Carlton House, the build up to it, of being with so many people, the music, the laughter, the champagne, all far removed from what she knew—had heightened her emotions, made them raw, even a little reckless and dangerous. She knew quite clearly—they both did, for she could see in his eyes that he acknowledged it too—that this was a new and important thing, only just beginning. And yet she knew she must not accept it, not let it happen. That she must fight it.

Chapter Three

When their coach finally arrived at the front of Carlton House, Belle was glad to climb in. Her feet ached and she was tired and couldn't wait to get into her bed. She was travelling alone in the protection of the grooms, for her grandmother's headache had become much worse. She was feeling so poorly that Lady Canning, a close friend, had invited her to spend the night at her house in town. She was expected to return home the following afternoon.

With two armed footmen travelling at the back of the coach, the coachman urged the horses forwards. The Dowager Countess of Harworth took no chances when travelling after dark.

Not only did one have to beware of highwaymen, but discontented soldiers—soldiers once loyal to the country, who had been cashiered from their regiments to eke out a miserable existence in the slums. Many of them took out their spite on the gentry as they travelled the quiet roads after dark to their elegant residences, robbing them of valuables before retreating back into the dark city streets.

A light wind blew, sending heavy rain clouds scudding across the sky, veiling the moon so that it shone through in a pale, diffused glow. The Ainsley conveyance lurched through the London streets and headed north. The house was close to the picturesque suburb of Hampstead. It stood high outside London, where the air was fresher. Beyond the orange glow of the carriage lamps, the trees all around them seemed to have taken on strange, moving shapes.

Suddenly a gunshot sounded ahead of them, startling the occupants of the coach. The coachman was heard to shout, 'Robbers up ahead.'

Belle leaned out of the window, but could see no assailant, and in an urgent voice ordered the coachman to set the horses to a faster pace. But it was too late. The footmen had no time to load and cock their pistols. There was a sudden movement to the side of them, as if the trees had come to life, and they found themselves confronted by a menacing, ominously cloaked rider who called upon the driver to bring the coach to a halt.

The driver pulled on the brake lever and hauled at the reins to bring the team to a halt. Belle heard a muffled voice ordering the footmen and the coachman to climb down. Belle was beset with alarm. After what seemed like an eternity, but could not have been longer than a minute, the door was pulled open and the muzzle of a pistol appeared in the doorway held by a man in full cape and a tricorn low over his brow.

'What do you want?' she demanded. 'If you mean to rob me, I have no money on me.'

'Step outside, if you please,' the man said from behind a concealing scarf half-covering his face, his voice low and rough sounding. 'I will see for myself. I will be on my way when you've handed over your valuables. Be kind enough to oblige without causing me any trouble.'

Struggling to gather her wits about her and trying to quell the fear that threatened to overwhelm her, with great indignation, Belle said courageously, 'I most certainly will not! You'll get nothing from me, you thieving rogue.'

The pistol was raised, its single black eye settling on Belle where it stared unblinkingly for a long moment. Beneath the threat, even that brave young woman froze, as the man growled, 'Then I'll just have to take it. Get out of the coach—if you please, my lady,' he added with mock sweetness.

With the pistol levelled on her, she knew there was nothing for it but to comply with the thief's demands. He was ominously calm and there was an air of deadliness about him. Stepping down, she gasped with concern on seeing the footmen and the coachman all bound helplessly together. Unconcerned for her own safety, she turned her wrath on their assailant. The cold fire in her eyes bespoke the fury churning within her. She held herself in tight rein until the rage cooled. What was left was a gnawing wish to see this highway robber at the end of a rope.

'How dare you do this? Please God you haven't harmed them. What is the meaning of this?' she demanded.

The robber scorned the words and would heed no argument. 'Quiet, lady,' the tall, shadowy figure rasped.

Belle's eyes were glued to him. This was not how she had imagined highwaymen to be—fearless cavaliers, carefree, chivalrous, romantic knights, in masks and three-cornered hats, adventurers, 'Gentleman of the Road'. Reluctant to submit to this footpad's searching hands, she stepped back and looked around her, considering the idea that she might be able to disappear into the confines of the trees.

He read her thoughts. 'Don't even think about it,' he rasped. 'It would be foolish to think you could get away. You could not escape me if you tried.' He swaggered closer. 'What have you got, pretty lady, hidden beneath your cloak? A well-heeled lady like yourself must have something. Show me. Come now,' he said when she shrank back, 'it's not worth dying for, no matter how much your valuables are worth. Are they so concealed that my fingers may have to forage?'

She shook her head, taking another step away from him. 'Keep away from me. You are nothing but a thieving, unmitigated rogue out for easy money.'

'True,' he agreed almost pleasantly. 'Come now—a bracelet, a brooch, a pretty necklace—a rich lady like yourself will not miss a bauble or two. I must ask you to hurry. I find myself getting impatient and that causes my finger to twitch on the trigger of my pistol.'

When he reached out to her with his free hand, incensed with his boldness and at the same time terrified of what he might do to her, Belle slapped his hand away. 'Get away from me, you lout.'

He uttered a soft curse. 'For a wench who has no help at hand, you're mighty high minded. Do you think you can stand against me with your impudence? You'll come to heel if I kill you first.'

'I'll shred your hand if you dare to touch me. I swear I will. Leave me alone,' she cried, her body trembling with fear. 'You have no right to touch me.'

'Stop your blustering.' In the blink of an eye he had reached out and flicked open the frogging securing the front of her cloak, which slid from her shoulders to her feet. Catching the light of the carriage lamps, the necklace sparkled. The man emitted a low whistle of admiration.

'So, milady, you say you have nothing of value. Those sparklers look pretty expensive to me. Remove it.' When she made no move to do so, he bowed his head in mock politeness. 'If you please.'

'You can go to hell,' she hissed.

'I shall—and very soon, I don't doubt, for my chosen profession usually includes death at an early age.'

'And well deserved,' she retorted indignantly. 'Hanging's too good for the likes of you.'

He chuckled low in his throat, the sound feeding Belle's anger. 'You think you're not afraid of me, don't you?' he said. 'You sneer at me with your pretty face and big monkey eyes. When I take to the road I feel like a king and I'd like to think tonight is to be my lucky night and come daybreak I shall be as rich as one. Now turn around,' he ordered, 'if you value your life. If you try anything rash, I have no qualms about shooting your coachman.'

Afraid that he might carry out his threat, Belle reluctantly turned her back to the robber, who moved to stand directly behind her and, using one hand, his fingers reached to the back of her neck. A deadly sickness came upon her and she flinched when she felt the cool contact on her flesh. It only took him a second to unclasp and whip the necklace away.

Shoving the precious gems inside a pocket of his cape, the thief backed away, keeping the pistol levelled at her. 'There, that wasn't too painful, was it?'

'You have what you want,' Belle uttered scornfully. 'Now what do you mean to do with us? Shoot us?'

'Nothing so dramatic.'

'Then you can leave us. I have nothing else to give.'

The man laughed. ''Twill be more than your jewels I'll be having my fun with, your ladyship.'

When he moved closer Belle took a step back. Reaching out, he caressed her cheek with the back of his hand, amused when she drew back. Tiny shards of fear pricked Belle's spine while a coldness congealed in the pit of her stomach. She was wary of angering him and bringing him to a level of violence that would destroy her. She had heard tales of how highwaymen sometimes killed those they waylaid—and a lone woman wouldn't stand a chance against the strength of such a powerful man.

'You wouldn't dare,' she whispered, almost choking on the words.

'Wouldn't I?'

'And don't look at me like that.' She could feel his eyes devouring her, and could well imagine the lascivious smile on his lips behind the scarf. A shudder ran through her, and it was not because it was cold. 'You'll hang for sure.'

He placed the pistol beneath her chin so that the barrel touched her throat and tipped her face up to his. 'Madam, if looking is a hanging offence, then I'd rather fulfil every aspect of my desire and be strung up for a lion than a lamb.'

She stared back at him in horror—the colour drained from her face. After a moment, which seemed like an eternity to Belle, he removed the pistol and stepped back.

'Please don't touch me again.'

He cocked a brow. 'Please, is it? So the lady has remembered her manners. But worry not. I have neither the time nor the inclination, lady. I have what I want—you have been most generous. I thank you for your co-operation.'

'Don't think you'll get away with this—you—you devil.' Belle cried, unable to contain her fury. 'I'll find out who you are and see you hang. I swear I will.'

The thief laughed in the face of her ire. 'Dear me, little lady. You have a strange preoccupation with seeing me hang. I'd dearly like to see you try.'

Having got what he wanted, without more ado the man took the reins of his horse and leapt into the saddle with the agility of an athlete. Turning about and giving her a farewell salute and a cheeky, knowing wink—a playful, frivolous gesture that infuriated Belle further—he galloped off into the night.

Seething with rage, her heart pounding in her chest, Belle watched the animal speed along, matching the wind over the narrow road. His hooves flashed like quicksilver in a brief spot of light, and his coat glistened as the muscles beneath it rolled and heaved. She did not move or utter a sound until the thief's muffled laughter and the hoofbeats could be heard no more.

Quickly releasing the footmen and the coachman and assured that they had not been molested in any way—while concealing her anger at their incompetence, for to her mind their pistols should have been loaded and cocked in the likelihood of such an event occurring—her face as hard and expressionless as a mask, she ordered them to take their positions on the coach.

Picking up her cloak, quivering with outrage and deeply shock by what had happened—and slightly bewildered, for something about the robbery and the highwayman did not make sense—Belle climbed inside the coach. The consequences of the theft of the jewels were too dreadful to contemplate.

How was she to tell her grandmother? They meant

so much to her, not to mention their value. Dear Lord, this was a calamity—a disaster. Her grandmother would be livid, and rightly so. She should not have been wearing them in the first place. Even if the robbery was reported first thing in the morning, the thief would be far away by then so it would be difficult to apprehend him. And if he was apprehended, he would already have disposed of them.

They arrived home without further incident. Not until Belle was in bed did she give free rein to her thoughts. She was relieved her grandmother was still in town and had not been party to the ordeal she had suffered. Grandmother didn't intend returning until the following afternoon, so she had a reprieve until then. But she would have to be told eventually. There was no way of escaping that.

Tossing and turning and unable to sleep, she went over and over in her mind what had happened. There had been something about the thief that was familiar. But what? It bothered her and she couldn't shake it off. Then a strangled gasp emitted from her and she shot bolt upright as a multitude of thoughts chased themselves inside her head—a pair of familiar blue eyes glinted down at her as he danced her about the floor. A deep voice tinged with laughter as he lowered his eyes to her neck and said *if I want something, I take it.*

In the space of five seconds, all these memories collided head on with the reality of what had happened on the road. And something else. The scent the thief wore—the faint smell of his cologne when he had stood directly behind her to remove the necklace—was the same scent that had assailed her earlier, when she had been dancing with Lance Bingham.

Flinging herself out of bed in a tempestuous fury, she paced the carpet, unable to believe what she was thinking, unable to contain it. She remembered the moment when he had stood behind her and caressed her neck, when she had thought… What? What had she thought? That he wanted to touch her, that he desired her?

Oh, fool, fool that she was. Why, that arrogant lord had merely been checking the clasp on the necklace, familiarising himself with it, to make it easier for him to remove. He had set out to use her to get the necklace. Why he should want to eluded her for the moment, but she would find out.

The blackguard! The audacity and the gentlemanly courtesy with which he had demanded that she part with her valuables was astounding. There was no doubt in her mind that he was the thief. The man she had met at Carlton House had turned into the Devil when determination to steal the necklace had removed all semblance of civility from him, frightening her half to death. But he wouldn't get away with it. Oh, no. She would see to that.

Every nerve in her body clenched against the onslaught of bitter rage. She continued to pace restlessly. After allowing the tide of emotion to carry her to the limit, nature took command of her again and she was strengthened, something of the old courage and force returning. She stewed. She seethed. Never had she been this angry before in her life. She had to decide on what course of action to take, ways she could make him pay for this outrage, how she could retrieve the stolen necklace before her grandmother returned—and she would, even if she expired in the attempt. Nothing could stop her doing anything once her mind was made up.

But beneath it all was the hurt when she remembered

the tender words Lord Bingham had spoken to her on their parting at Carlton House, words she now knew to be empty, without meaning. How could he have said all those things to her and then do what he did—terrify and threaten her at the point of a gun?

The man was cold and heartless and without a shred of decency. She wanted to hurt him, to hurt him badly, and she would find a way to do it without letting him see how much he had hurt her—without letting him see how much she cared.

But why had he taken the necklace? She was utterly bewildered by his actions. And why did bad feeling exist between the Ainsleys and the Binghams? Whatever it was, she suspected it had something to do with the past.

Belle had always been self-willed, energetic and passionate, with a fierce and undisciplined temper, but her charm, her wit and her beauty had more than made up for the deficiencies in her character. She hadn't a bad bone in her body, was just proud and spirited, so determined to have her own way that she had always been prepared to plough straight through any hurdle that stood in her path—just as she was about to do now.

But what was she to say to her grandmother?

As it turned out she was granted a welcome reprieve. The following morning a note was delivered to the house from Lady Channing, informing her that the countess had taken a turn for the worse and that the doctor advised her it would be unwise for her to leave her bed to make the journey to Hampstead until she was feeling better.

Later that day, with a groom in attendance, Belle rode from Hampstead to visit her grandmother. She did indeed look very ill when Lady Channing showed her to her room—too ill to be told about the theft of the necklace. Before returning to Hampstead, she joined a large gathering of fashionable people riding in Hyde Park, struck forcibly by the noise and colour and movement and wanting to feel a part of it. It was a glorious day, hot and sunny. Roses bloomed profusely and she could hear a band playing a jolly tune.

Serene and elegant atop her horse, she looked striking and stood out in her scarlet riding habit. Daisy had brushed her hair up on her head in an intricate arrangement of glossy curls, upon which a matching hat sat at a jaunty angle. She was greeted and stopped to speak to those who recognised her, who expressed their distress when told the dowager countess was unwell.

Suddenly she felt a small *frisson* of alarm as all her senses became heightened. Ahead of her a man atop a dark brown stallion had stopped to speak to an acquaintance. She did not need to see his face to know his identity. He was dressed in a tan jacket and buff-coloured breeches. He sported a tall hat and a snowy white cravat fitted snug about his throat.

As he turned slightly, and not wanting to be found looking at him, Belle averted her gaze, but not before she had seen a world of feelings flash across his set face—surprise, disbelief, admiration—but only for an instant.

Lance nudged his horse forwards, eager to introduce Rowland to this vision in scarlet.

Watching them ride towards her through the press of people, Belle braced herself for the encounter.

Lance bowed very coolly before her, his gaze calmly searching her face. 'Miss Ainsley. I had hoped to have the pleasure of seeing you, but I did not think to find you here. Allow me to compliment you. You are exquisite.'

Aware that every person in the park seemed to be watching them, Belle straightened her back and lifted her head, unaware that she had been holding herself stiffly, her shoulders slightly hunched, as though to defend something vulnerable. She stared at him uncomprehendingly.

'Why—I—thank you,' she said, having decided to be tact and patience personified. She had also decided to play him at his own game and give him no reason to suspect she had identified him as her highwayman of the night before. 'For myself, your presence took me wholly by surprise. I did not expect to see you again so soon.'

Belle studied his features, looking for something that would give her some hint of what had happened on her way back to Hampstead last night, but there was nothing to suggest he had been the thief. But there was something different in him today. His manner was subdued and his tone of voice made her look more closely at him. She detected some indefinable, underlying emotion in it as his brilliant blue eyes gleamed beneath the well-defined brows. Belle was not shaken from her resolve that he was the one, and before she had finished she would prove it.

'May I introduce you to this gentleman?' Lance gestured to his companion. 'This is Sir Rowland Gibbon, an old and valued friend of mine. Rowland, this is Miss Ainsley—the Dowager Countess of Harworth's granddaughter. Rowland wanted to meet you, Miss Ainsley, having recently returned from America, where he travelled extensively.'

'You exaggerate, Lance.' Rowland bowed to her. 'Although I did find the country interesting and exciting and hope very much to return there one day. I believe you are from America, Miss Ainsley.'

'Indeed,' she answered, liking his easy manner and trying not to look at Lord Bingham. Sir Rowland was not a handsome man by any means, but he had obviously spent a goodly amount of coin on his attire, for, completely devoid of prudence, he was garbed in a flamboyant fashion in dark-green velvet coat with a high stiff collar, frothing neck linen and skintight white trouser that clung to the line of his long legs above his black riding boots. He sat his horse with an easy swagger and the dashing air of a romantic highwayman.

Highwayman? Belle sighed. Highwaymen were very much at the forefront of her mind just now. 'I was born there—in Charleston. And you are right to say it is exciting. I too wish to return there one day, but I can't see that happening in the foreseeable future.'

At that moment someone caught Rowland's eye and he excused himself to go and speak to them.

Lance's unfathomable eyes locked on to Belle's. 'Ride with me a while, will you, Belle? I should like to hear more about America,' he said, reverting to a quiet informality.

Belle hesitated. She was aware of the curious stares and of a hushed expectancy from those around them.

'Is it my imagination, or is everyone watching us?'

'It is not your imagination. In the light of the bad feeling that exists between our two families, it is hardly surprising. Ride with me and I will show you just how inflamed the gossip is.'

'You are extremely impertinent and I do not think I should. The last thing I want to do is to create a scandal that will upset my grandmother.'

Lance's eyes darkened and his gaze was challenging. 'What's the matter, Belle? Afraid of a little gossip? Your grandmother isn't here to see—and by the time she hears of it it will be too late.'

Something of the man she had met at Carlton House resurrected itself when he suddenly grinned wickedly, and despite Belle's resolve to remain unaffected by him, she could not quell the small shiver of delight that ran through her. His teasing eyes were so lovely and blue, so blissfully familiar and admiring.

'Very well,' she murmured, forcing an uninterested politeness into her voice. 'But instead of riding in the park, perhaps you would care to ride with me a little way back to Hampstead.'

'Gladly.'

Together they rode out of the park, her groom following at a discreet distance. Belle could feel the fascinated stares of everyone in the park as they left. As they rode up Park Lane, the steady pace of their mounts eased their tensions and they began to unbend, each filled with the other's presence.

Just like the night before when they had danced together, they drew attention from passers-by. Isabelle's beauty and Lord Bingham's tall, lean handsomeness made them unique. And he was handsome, perhaps the most handsome man Belle had ever seen, so there was little wonder he attracted attention, she thought, smiling to herself as she quietly admired her partner. In his broadcloth jacket, which fit his wide shoulders perfectly, his dark hair beneath his hat shimmering in the sunlight, he was devastating. She had to keep her eyes away from his, or at least she tried to, because it was so easy to get lost in his gaze and forget what he had done.

Lance turned his head and looked at Belle. She was like a magnet to his eyes, and now he felt an odd kind of possessiveness. Not the kind one felt on owning material things, but something else. There were different types of possessiveness, and he didn't even want to think of the more common form, which had no place in his emotions.

'I see you've dispensed with your military attire, my lord,' Belle commented airily at length, the cut and seam of his coat evidence of the tailoring only noblemen could afford. 'Your tailor must delight in the opportunity to clothe such an illustrious hero of the wars with Napoleon. Why, a gentleman with such expensive and stylish apparel will be the envy of every roué in London.'

Lance met her cool stare. From all indications it seemed she was none too pleased with him, which did much to heighten his curiosity. 'I count myself fortunate in my tailor, who has made my wardrobe for a good many years—military uniforms, mainly. Now I have retired from army life he is delighted at the opportunity to finally outfit me with all the clothes of a gentleman.'

'Indeed, I think even that master of style and fashion Mr Brummell will have to sit up and take notice.'

'My tailor is a man of sober tastes and it would go against the grain to kit me out in garish garb—and I have no desire to emulate the overdressed Beau Brummell. Besides, that particular gentleman has fallen out of favour with Prince George and it is rumoured that he is heavily in debt and no longer as stylishly garbed as he once was.' He frowned across at her. 'Was your comment about my attire because you find it flawed in some way?'

'Not in the slightest. In fact, I must commend your tailor's abilities, although I imagine you must feel strange in civilian attire after wearing a uniform for so long.'

'It will be something I shall have to get used to—even to tying my own cravat. Thankfully my valet is a master.' After falling silent while they negotiated a congested part of the thoroughfare, he said, 'Your grandmother is well?'

Belle glanced at him, wondering what had prompted the question. Was he curious as to how she had reacted on being told about the theft of the necklace? She answered carefully. 'No—as a matter of fact my grandmother is not feeling herself.'

He glanced at her sharply. 'She is ill?'

'Indisposed,' Belle provided, not wishing to divulge too much. If he thought her grandmother was so distressed over the loss of the diamonds that she had taken to her bed, so much the better—although if a man as cunning as he could rob people at gunpoint and scare them witless, then she doubted he would be moved over the plight of an old woman grieving her loss.

'I am sorry to hear it,' he sympathised, his gaze searching. 'I hope she will soon recover.'

'I doubt it—that she will recover soon, I mean. She really is quite distraught over the loss of something that was close to her heart.' Apart from a narrowing of his eyes, Lord Bingham's expression did not change.

'She is? And was this item—valuable?'

'You might say that—but then—' she smiled, tossing her head and urging her mount to a faster pace '—it is a family matter and I am sure it will be resolved very soon.'

Although she hadn't objected to riding with him, Lance was a little taken aback by the courteous, but impersonal smiles she was giving him. He decided it prudent to let the matter of her grandmother drop.

'I am giving a supper party tonight. There will be a

large gathering. I would very much like you to come, but I realise you would encounter difficulties with your grandmother.'

'Yes, I would. You know she would never allow it—but I thank you for the invitation all the same.' They had been riding for some time and on reaching the place where she had been accosted last night, she drew her horse to a halt and faced him. If he thought there was any significance in her stopping in the exact spot, he didn't show it. 'I can manage quite well from here. I'm sure you have more important things to do than play escort to me, Lord Bingham. I shall be quite safe with my groom.'

Lance frowned across at her. 'What's wrong, Belle? You weren't like this when you almost melted in my arms before we parted at Carlton House last night. '

Belle's green eyes widened in apparent bewilderment. 'Did I really almost do that? Goodness, I must have imbibed more champagne than I thought. I danced so many dances with so many different beaux, I forget. I recall dancing with you and you were hardly the soul of amiability—unlike my other partners—and some of them were much more desirable than you.'

'Really?' he said frostily. 'In what way?'

'For one thing, they were younger than you,' she replied, trying to seem cool and unemotional. She longed to slap this insufferable, arrogant lord down to size. 'I have decided that you are much too old for me.'

Lance's eyes darkened very nearly to black. 'What the hell are you saying?' he hissed. 'Don't play games with me, Belle, because you'll find you are well out of your league.'

She looked at him in all innocence and said breezily, 'Games, my lord? I don't play games. If I said anything to mislead you, then I apologise most sincerely.'

Lance's eyes hardened and his jaw tightened ominously. When he spoke it was with a cold savage contempt, his voice dangerously low. 'You're nothing but a common little flirt. Take care how you try to bait me,' he murmured softly. 'I'm not one of the besotted fools who dance attendance on you night after night. I might want more from you than you are ready to grant—and when I want something, I do not give up until I have it.'

Drawing her horse away from him slightly, reminding herself not to let him annoy her and that she must carry out the charade to the end, Belle feigned innocence. 'But—surely you have what you wanted?'

She saw something move behind his eyes and for a split second his gaze went to her unadorned neck before rising to her face. She waited, her eyes holding his, challenging him, aware of the sudden tension inside him, the stirring of suspicion behind his gaze.

'I have?' he answered, not without caution. 'What are you talking about?'

'Why, you asked me to ride with you—and here I am.' She tilted her head to one side and smiled, her eyes questioning. 'Why, were you referring to something else?'

He studied her carefully before saying coldly, 'I think this unpleasant encounter has gone on long enough. I bid you good day.' With that he rode away.

Without a backward glance, Belle headed for home, a sense of triumphant jubilation in her heart, for Lord Bingham's invitation to his supper party had given her an excellent idea as to how she might recover the diamonds.

* * *

At nine o'clock Belle, dressed in breeches and a jacket and a low-brimmed hat, with no time to lose and with much chiding from Daisy, who knew all about the missing necklace and what her mistress had in mind, left the house and climbed into the waiting coach.

The driver knew it was not his place to ask questions—although he did look startled at Miss Isabelle's male form of attire. She gave him the address of Lord Bingham's London residence, which had not been too difficult to procure, since he was so well known that the servants had been able to provide her with the address. Settling into the upholstery, in an attempt to still her wildly beating heart she took a deep breath. There was so much depending on this night. She could not expect everything to go well and doubt thwarted her attempt at calm.

By the time she reached her destination—a fine Palladian mansion located close to Hyde Park on Park Lane—she had worked herself up into such a knot of anticipation and foreboding that she was tempted to tell the driver to return to Hampstead. Quickly she recollected herself and, sternly determined, fought to bring her rioting panic under control, thinking of the immense satisfaction and triumph she would feel if her plan succeeded, which would have very little to do with retrieving the necklace, and everything to do with outwitting Lord Bingham.

Belle left the coach some distance from the house, telling the driver to wait, that she hoped not to be long. She avoided the front of the house, where several smart equipages were lined up. Quickly becoming lost in the dark, she found her way to the back of the house and into a yard with buildings that housed Lord Bingham's carriages and horses. Standing in the shadows she carefully surveyed his town residence.

Lights shone from the windows and people could be seen strolling about the rooms and sitting about. Thankfully several of the upstairs rooms were in darkness and it seemed quiet enough. Suddenly she was overcome with a sense of urgency, for there was a need for haste if she was to find what she was looking for without being seen. Letting herself in by a door that led into a passageway, she paused and listened. Sounds of domesticity and cook issuing orders to the kitchenmaids could be heard from a room on her right—the kitchen, she thought. Fortunately the door was only slightly ajar and she managed to creep by. A narrow staircase rose from the passageway and gingerly she made her way upwards. With a stroke of luck she found herself on a landing, on the top floor of the house, off which were several rooms.

With her ears attuned to every sound—conversation and laughter from Lord Bingham's guests and the clink of glasses—she went from door to door, pressing her ear to it before opening it a crack and peering inside. They were bedrooms mostly—though not one of them gave the impression of belonging to the master of the house. Undeterred, she crept along another landing, peering into each room until eventually she found it. Looking through the slightly open door she waited, afraid Lord Bingham's valet might be in an adjacent room. After a few moments when nothing happened she stepped inside and closed the door.

Only one lamp was lit, giving off a dim light. She could have done with more, but decided she would have to manage. She set to work, starting on a tall bureau beside the door. Thankfully the drawers slid open soundlessly. After rummaging inside and being careful to leave things as she found them, she went on to the next piece of furniture, working quietly, admiring the expensive quality of everything her fingers touched.

She glanced at a rather ornate clock on the mantelpiece as it delicately chimed ten o'clock. Wondering where the time had flown and disappointed that her search had produced nothing as yet, she knew she would have to hurry. Looking about her, she saw a door that she assumed must lead into a dressing room. Slipping inside, she searched the chests of drawers and among racks of clothing, but all to no avail.

Feeling crushed and extremely disappointed, she emerged into the bedroom once more. She was about to admit defeat when her eyes lighted on the bedside tables. She paused to listen. Had she heard a noise on the landing, or was it the noise of the wind that had risen? Whatever it might have been, she decided to get on with it. She had no wish to be caught red-handed.

With one last desperate attempt to locate the jewels, she looked inside the first bedside table, almost shouting out in triumph when, on opening a small velvet pouch and seeing its sparkling contents, she realised she had found what she was looking for.

'Got you, you thieving rogue,' she whispered, pocketing the pouch. Quickly she closed the drawer and then halted abruptly. This time she could not mistake the footfall on the landing as someone came towards the bedroom. Her heart thumping wildly in her chest, Belle flew to the lamp and blew out the flame, placing it on the floor so it could not be lit in a hurry—although there were others in the room to light, so she needn't have bothered. The room was now in almost total darkness. Belle stood in the middle, turning about indecisively. She had to find a place to hide. Her eyes lit on the dressing screen and she flew behind it just as the door handle turned.

Lance came in, uttering an oath under his breath when he found his room in darkness, and an even louder oath when his foot made contact with the lamp and it toppled over.

'What the devil has happened to the light?' His voice bore an edge of sharpness that bespoke of vexation. Without more ado he picked up the lamp and, striking a sulphur match, soon had it lit. He stood for a moment in puzzlement. His eyes did a quick sweep of the room. Seeing that everything appeared to be in place, he removed his jacket and threw it on to the bed.

From behind the screen Belle listened to him moving about, wondering why he had come to his room and how she was going to get out without being seen. Her heart racing in confused fright, she took a deep breath, trying to calm her rapid pulse and to peer through a crack in the screen. She saw him loosen his neck linen and remove his waistcoat—and what was that dark stain? It looked like wine. So that was it. He'd clearly spilled some on his clothes and come up to change. Hopefully he would do it quickly and go. Seeing him disappear into his dressing room, she waited in trembling disquiet, horrified when, having changed his clothes, he came back into the bedroom and approached the screen.

Lance was just reaching to fold it back when it was shoved towards him by a decisive force. He was almost toppled over by its weight and was momentarily stunned as a shape leapt past him and ran towards the door, pausing for a split second to blow out the lamp. Angrily Lance tossed the screen aside and with quick long strides reached the intruder before he could escape, snatching a handful of his coat and pulling him back.

A rending tear preceded a startled cry and then a booted foot kicked at his shins.

'Dammit, who the hell are you, and what do you think you're doing in my house?' Lance ignored the hands that flailed the air, hitting out at him, and jerked the figure around roughly.

Belle stumbled against the bed and in great trepidation scrambled across it to the other side.

Angered beyond bearing, Lance lunged after what he thought to be a man, since the figure was wearing breeches and the face was concealed by a low-brimmed hat.

Making a concerted effort to escape, Belle picked up his jacket and threw it at him, but swinging round the bedpost, Lance tossed it aside, his fingers again reaching out to ensnare the shadowy figure. Belle side-stepped and darted about the room, but the vague blur of bodies in the dark room gave away their movements. When he was near her, Belle abruptly changed directions and scurried to the door. Lance was faster and leapt after her in time to catch her full against him, clamping a hand over her mouth when she opened it to scream.

'Be still. If you continue to fight me, I'll knock you senseless. Do you understand me?' His captive nodded, in which case he began loosening his grip slightly.

The moment he did, Belle sank her teeth into the fleshy part of his palm and flung herself away from him. He grabbed her before she had taken two steps and held her prisoner in his arms.

'So, you want to draw my blood, eh?'

The sudden contact of their bodies brought a gasp to Belle's lips.

Lance continued to hold her, finding the form too slender, too light to be that of a man. A youth, perhaps?

Taking her with him to the door, he turned the key before releasing her and lighting the lamp. Giving all his attention to his captive, who continued to squirm against him, he reached out and tore the hat away, his mind rebelling in disbelief at what he saw—the dark brown hair, with highlights of red and gold, framing a creamy-skinned visage. The lips were soft and sensuous, the eyes a clear, sparkling shade of green.

'What the hell… Good Lord!' he cried. 'Belle!'

Belle turned from him, but he caught her wrist. Blindly, insanely, she fought him, wildly twisting and writhing and clawing at him in an attempt to get away from him.

'Will you be still?' he growled, pressing her back against the wall and trying to still her frantic threshing with the weight of his own body. When she wouldn't he increased the pressure of his grip upon the delicately boned wrist. Stubbornly Belle resisted the pain until Lance finally loosed his hold, not wishing to hurt her unduly. Feeling what little fight she had left drain away, slowly she quieted, breathing heavily, very much aware that his thighs were crushing her own quaking limbs.

'Stop fighting me, Belle, and I'll step away. Then I will listen to what you have to say. You owe me that much at least.'

'I owe you nothing,' she hissed through clenched teeth, open mutiny in her tone, her eyes hurling daggers at him. She sidled away from him, rubbing her wrist. 'I swear I'll break your hands if you dare touch me again.'

Lance stepped away from her. A wave of anger that she could be so reckless, that she had put herself in danger like this, washed over him. 'Do you realise I could have killed you, you stupid girl?'

Belle tossed her head in defiance, her expression indignant. 'Desperation leads me to do stupid things.'

'Desperate? You? Don't make me laugh,' he uttered sarcastically. 'How nice of you to drop in to my party. Do you mind telling how you got past my butler— looking like that?'

'I came in through a door at the back of the house. It wasn't difficult.'

'Are you going to tell me what the hell you think you're playing at?'

'Do I really have to tell you—thief?' she hissed accusingly, looking at him with withering scorn.

He looked at her very calmly now, everything beginning to fall into place. 'Thief? Now, that's debatable.'

'Not to me.'

'You know, if you're going to take this defensive attitude, we're not going to get anywhere. I take it that you have found what you were looking for?'

She nodded.

'So, you saw behind my disguise.'

'That wasn't too difficult when I had time to piece things together. It was your cologne that gave you away.'

His lips twitched with the hint of a smile. 'How astute of you. Trust a woman to notice that—and it certainly explains your attitude towards me at the party.'

'What you did, holding up a coach on the King's highway and forcing—at gunpoint, I might add—a woman to part with her valuables, is a criminal offence—one you could be hanged for.'

'As you took great pleasure in informing me last night. Please don't go on,' Lance drawled in exaggerated horror. 'You will give me nightmares.'

His ability to mock his fate and ignore his crime was more than Belle could bear. Her voice shook with angry emotion, and she stared at him as if he were something inhuman and beyond her comprehension.

'And my grandmother? Did you not spare a thought to how your actions might have affected her had she been in the coach? She might have suffered a seizure on being confronted by a violent highwayman.'

'I doubt it. Your grandmother is made of sterner stuff than that. However, I heard it mentioned that she wasn't feeling well and was to remain in town with Lady Channing.'

'And if she had been in the coach?'

'I would not have held you up.'

'How perfectly noble of you,' she scoffed. 'My grandmother could bring charges against you for what you did.'

'And who would believe a high-ranking lord of the realm—as well as being a highly respected and decorated officer in Wellington's army—would stoop so low as to take to the road as a highwayman?'

Belle glowered at him. 'Is there no limit to what you will dare?'

'No,' he said. 'No limit whatsoever. If you suspected it was me who took your necklace, didn't it occur to you to simply ask me about it when we met earlier today, instead of taking matters into your own hands and sneaking into my home to look for them?'

Belle shrugged. 'It's no worse than what you did to me—you—you wretch. Besides, what was the point in asking you? You would have denied it.'

'And you know that, do you?'

'Don't you feel any guilt at all about stealing the diamonds?'

'No. Should I?'

'I don't suppose you would. One has to have a conscience to feel guilt,' she said, shrugging out of her coat to examine the tear in the back.

'If I were guilty of taking something that didn't belong to me, maybe I would deny it. But I didn't.'

'What are you saying?'

'The diamonds belong to me—to my family. I was merely retrieving them.'

Belle stared at him, surprised by his revelation and clearly shocked. 'To you? But—they are Ainsley diamonds—my grandmother—'

'Told you they belonged to your family, I know. Maybe after all these years she has come to believe that. Is the loss of the diamonds the reason why she has taken to her bed?'

'No. You were right. She wasn't feeling too well at Carlton House last night and stayed with Lady Channing. She is still not well, so I thought it wise to wait until she is feeling better before I tell her the diamonds were stolen.'

'One cannot steal something that legitimately belongs to them.'

'But why go to all that trouble of pretending to be a highwayman?' Belle demanded.

At that moment Lance preferred not to think about the bet he had made with Rowland. 'Because I wanted you to think the person who took your valuables was nothing more than an ordinary thief. Would you have given them to me if I'd asked?'

'Of course not.'

'There you are, then. You have your answer, but I cannot believe you planned this—to come here dressed as…you are,' he said, contemplating her attire, thinking that in her white silk blouse, long and shapely legs encased in buff-coloured breeches, she really was a wonderful sight to behold, 'and that you were foolish enough to come to my house to steal them back.'

Suddenly Belle felt suffocated by his nearness. Her whole being throbbed with an awareness of him, but she knew that if she gave any hint of her weakness, it would only lead to disaster. She saw where his gaze was directed and, glancing down, realised the twin peaks of her breasts were standing taut and high beneath her blouse. Her cheeks grew suddenly hot with embarrassment, and she folded her arms across her chest, glowering at him.

'I never would have, if not for the fury I was beset with at the time—and there's a confession for you. I have a temper—I can't help it, and I'm rarely able to control it once it snaps.'

'I'd already figured that out for myself,' Lance said drily. By his actions he had woken a sleeping dragon.

'Then perhaps you'll think twice about provoking it in future.'

His eyes narrowed dangerously. 'I, too, have a temper, Belle. You would do well to remember that.' He stared at her for a moment, his jaw tight and hard, and then he sauntered to the fireplace, resting his arm on the mantelpiece.

'If I were a man, I'd call you out for what you did to me last night.'

'That would not be wise, Belle.'

'No? After threatening my life and the men whose duty it was to protect me, nothing would satisfy me more that to put a bullet between your eyes.'

'What? You can use a gun?'

'Of course I can—I'm a very good shot, as it happens. Where I come from it is not unusual for women to learn how to shoot. I can hit a target with the best of them.' She smiled wryly. 'I suppose you will say my vanity is showing itself.'

'No, I'm impressed. Not one of the ladies of my acquaintance would know which end of a gun to fire.'

'Then you should become more selective in the ladies you associate with.'

'I don't think so,' he replied drily. 'To become intimately acquainted with a woman whose skill with any weapon might exceed my own, could prove to be dangerous.'

'Then that lets me off the hook,' Belle retorted flippantly.

'How so?'

'Last night you let me believe you were as enamoured of me as the rest—just to get your hands on my grandmother's diamonds. You certainly know how to dent a girl's pride.'

Lance would like to have told her that she had jumped to the wrong conclusion, and that he was enamoured with both her and the necklace. The truth was that she was too beautiful, too sensational for a man not to be enamoured of her. But he refused to feed her vanity more than it already was by the doting swains who trailed in her wake.

'I have every confidence that your pride will soon recover.'

Belle was disappointed that he wasn't attracted by her, but didn't show it. Why had she to say that? How absolutely embarrassing. He probably thought she'd been making advances toward him, fishing for compliments. She should have known that her remark would be pointless. But damn it all, why did he have to point it out?

Chapter Four

For the first time since the diamonds had been taken, Belle had a feeling of self-doubt. Carrying her jacket, she moved towards Lord Bingham, confused as to what she should do. If the diamonds really did belong to him, then by rights she should give them back.

'So, Belle. What are we to do? You have the jewels. Will you return them to me?'

'I think I should wait and see what my grandmother has to say about that.'

'Belle, they really do belong to me. If you don't give them to me voluntarily, then I shall have to take them from you. Is that what you want?'

'What?' she uttered, her eyes flashing with scorn. 'Will you threaten to shoot me like you did last night—and I seem to recall there was a moment when you implied that you would. What kind of man are you, Lord Bingham? What was it that drove you to play such a despicable game? Is there some quirk in your nature that you enjoy doing that to people? Why should I believe anything you say?'

'Because I am a fairly honest person. Trust me. Something happened between our families concerning the diamonds when our grandmothers were in their prime. My grandmother kept a journal. Everything explaining proof of ownership and what happened at that time is written there. I will show it to you if you like, but there isn't time now. I have to return to my guests.'

Belle turned to the door. 'I think I should go. I told the coach driver to wait for me at the corner of the street.'

'Belle…' She turned and looked at him. His eyes were steadfast. 'The diamonds.' Slowly he walked towards her, holding out his hand.

Belle knew he wouldn't let her out of that room unless she gave them to him. Reluctantly she fumbled in the pocket of her coat and took out the pouch and handed it to Lord Bingham.

'Thank you,' he said, taking it.

'What do you advise me to tell my grandmother?'

'The truth. She'll understand. Come, I'll take you back to the coach—although I can't think what your driver was thinking of bringing you here, dressed like that, in the first place.'

'I can be quite persuasive when I want to be—even with coach drivers when I use my best smile on them.'

She didn't need to elaborate. The effect of her smile was highly predictable. Lance could well imagine the driver's dilemma, how dumbstruck and willing to do her bidding he had been when she had flashed her pearly white teeth and fluttered her eyelashes.

'What a truly vain creature you are, Belle Ainsley.'

'You may see it as a flaw, but at times it can be useful.'

Lance shook his head. The way the female mind worked sometimes was beyond his comprehension.

'There are some things that would tempt a man beyond good sense. Your smile is one of them. However, the ease with which you have managed to get into my house tells me that I must have a word with my butler about increasing the security. Any miscreant from the street could enter. You encountered no one?'

'No—and I can find my own way to the coach.'

'I'll make sure you leave the house without being seen. I insist. I certainly don't want any of my guests confronting you looking like that.' Taking her jacket from her, he held it while she thrust her arms into the sleeves. 'I apologise for the rip. A good seamstress should be able to repair it.' Placing his hands on her shoulders, he turned her round to face him. 'I would like to apologise for last night,' he said calmly. 'I can't remember the last time I apologised for anything, so you must forgive me if I appear awkward.'

Belle was not to be so easily mollified. 'What an arrogant man you are to think that after what you did to me last night and the violence that you threatened, I can be placated with a few words of apology. You can apologise all you like, but it still does not absolve you or solve the problem I shall have explaining what you have done to my grandmother.'

His face darkened with annoyance, and Belle could almost feel his struggle to hold his temper in check. 'I could say that your own behaviour—by coming here tonight and breaking into my home, is not beyond reproach either. However, I am truly sorry if I frightened you last night. Despite how it looked, it was never my intention to hurt you.'

'You didn't hurt me. I was simply furious that you should have the audacity to do what you did. And now if you don't mind I would like to leave.'

Turning on her heel, she went to the door. Lance followed, halting her by catching hold of her arm and speaking close to her ear from behind. 'Of course you must go, but before you do, Belle, I will give you a warning. Just one,' he enunciated coldly. 'Call it advice, if you prefer.'

'If I wanted advice,' Belle retorted, spinning round, her eyes sparking green fire, 'I would not come to you.'

'I don't normally receive guests in my bedroom—but then, you are not my guest, are you? If you break into my house again and come to my room and search through my personal belongings, I will lock you in and not release you until you are well and truly ruined. Do you understand me?'

Belle felt a sudden stillness envelope them. Vividly aware of the heat of his body and the spicy scent of his cologne, she was overwhelmingly conscious of the man behind her. She was irritated by the way in which he had skilfully cut through her superior attitude. She knew she had asked for it, but the magnetic attraction still remained beneath all the irritation.

'I'm sure you would like nothing more, but I will not give you that satisfaction. Now, can we go?' He was far too close and Belle was beginning to feel distinctly uncomfortable. The tight tension of regret was beginning to form in her chest that she had dared to come here.

Lance continued to hold her arm. Now the issue of the necklace was out of the way he was reluctant to let her go, and to his way of thinking it was time she received her come-uppance and realised the danger of coming uninvited to a man's bedroom.

'Not yet. I have not quite finished with you.'

'Are you saying I am in danger?'

Black brows arched above gleaming blue eyes. 'Of the worst kind, I fear. Tell me, Belle, have you ever been kissed?'

The tension in her chest was tightening. 'No man kisses me except the man I want.'

An almost lecherous smile tempted his lips as his eyes did a slow perusal of her lips before travelling to the slim, erect column of her neck, to the beckoning fullness of her breasts straining beneath her blouse. The all-too-apparent womanliness of her and the heady scent of her perfume evoked a strong stirring of desire, and he felt a familiar stirring in his loins.

'Then I will have to *make* you want me, Belle.'

He moved closer, close enough so that she was trapped and could not move without coming into contact with him. He braced his forearms against the door and gazed down at her face. He ached to caress the womanly softness of her, to hold her close, and ease the lusting ache that gnawed at the pit of his belly.

His nearness threatened to destroy Belle's confidence and composure, but only threatened. This man was far too bold to allow even a small measure of comfort. She lifted her head imperiously, and her eyes glinted as they glared into his.

'I don't want you to show me. I don't want you to touch me, so kindly step back and let me go at once.'

'Not a chance,' he drawled. Gripping both her upper arms, he pulled her to him, holding her tightly against his chest, his fingers digging cruelly into her soft flesh.

Resolutely she squirmed against him. She saw his eyes darken in the dim light, his lean and handsome features starkly etched. A strange feeling, until this moment unknown to her, fluttered within her breast, and she was halted for a brief passing of time by the flood of excitement that surged through her. With renewed determination she forced it down.

'I asked you to release me. I really must go.'

'What's the rush?' he murmured against her ear and brushed warm kisses along her throat. 'I'd like to show you that I in no way resemble those fancy bucks who dance attendance on you night after night, pouring flatteries and endearments into your ears they do not mean.'

'Leave me be. And don't get any high-handed ideas that you are any better than they,' she stated shortly.

'Say what you like, Belle, but I suspect that you'd prefer a real man to warm your bed than any of them.'

His statement brought a bright hue creeping into Belle's cheeks. 'I find that remark extremely insulting and uncalled for. The conduct of the men I meet at the affairs I attend has been exemplary and I have no complaints. You speak as if you are some great gift to womankind, whereas you could learn a lot from them. And now I wish to leave. Anything is preferable to this. At least they are gentlemen and wouldn't take advantage of a woman as you are doing.'

'Don't you bet on it, but relax, Belle. I'm not going to hurt you.'

An iron-thewed arm slipped about her waist and brought her against that broad chest. Belle thought to remain passive in his embrace and did not struggle as his mouth lowered upon hers, but they flamed with a fiery heat that warmed her whole body. That was when she realised the idea was ludicrous and a gross miscalculation of her power to deny him, for the kiss went through her with the impact of a broadside.

Her eyes closed and the strength of his embrace and the hard pressure of his loins made her all too aware of the danger she was in, that he was a strong, determined man, and that he was treating her as he would any woman he had desire for. Her head swam and she was unable to still the violent tremor of delight that seized her, touching every nerve until they were aflame with desire. Her world began to tilt, and she was lost in a dreamy limbo where nothing mattered but the closeness of his body and the circling protection of his arms.

Moments before she had thought herself knowledgeable about men, but now, as Lance slid one hand down to her buttock and pressed her to him, she became acutely conscious of her innocence.

His lips caressed and clung to hers, finding them moist and honey sweet, and for a slow beat in time, hers responded, parting under his mounting fervour. She leaned against him, melting more closely to him, as though the strength had gone from her. Aware of her weakening, he raised his head and lifted her in his arms.

'Put me down,' Belle panted breathlessly, panic rising. 'This is not at all what I want.'

'To hell with what you want, lady,' Lance muttered thickly. 'I can feel your need, Belle. It is the same as my own.'

'Please,' she cried. 'This game has gone on long enough.'

'Games are for children. But this is something more between a man and a woman.' His eyes burned into hers as he strode purposefully to the bed with her. Kneeling on the mattress, he lowered her to its softness and before she could move his arms came down on either side, trapping her between them.

'You beast,' she hissed. 'You filthy beast. How dare you lay your hands on me…?'

He silenced her with his lips, kissing her long and deep and hard. She struggled, but her physical resistance was useless against his strength and his unswerving seduction. Lowering his weight on to her body, he cradled her head between his arms. He was strong, muscular, savage even and very determined, and for a moment Belle felt her insides lurch—she didn't know why—and in the pit of her stomach flared a spark of something, and again she didn't know what or why.

'Don't be afraid,' he breathed against her throat. 'I won't hurt you. Let yourself enjoy it.'

'I can't,' she argued.

'Yes, you can.'

Again he found her lips and parted them. Shuddering excitement passed through her, and the strength ebbed from her limbs. Not for a moment did Lance break the kiss that was inciting her. His mouth was hungering, turning to a heated, crushing demand. Her anger had become raw hunger, cindered beneath the white heat of their mutual desires. It was sudden, the awakened fires, the hungering lust, the bittersweet ache of passion such as Belle could never have imagined.

His position gave him full access to her body. Pulling her shirt out of the waistband of her breeches, his hand slowly snaked its way up to the tantalising fullness of her naked breast, cupping it, teasing her nipple until it was a hard bud. She made a sound deep in her throat. She wasn't sure if it was a protest or merely a sound of pleasure she couldn't contain, so wonderful did it feel. She was kissing him voraciously as the pleasure swiftly escalated, her entire body trembling with desire. She moaned again and wrapped her arms around his neck, shoving her fingers in his hair without even thinking about it, for she couldn't seem to help herself and it seemed the most natural thing to do.

Lance closed his eyes, intense desire for this woman torturing him and making him acutely conscious of the celibate life he had led for some time now. As he caressed the sweet, young body, his flesh betrayed his need, rising up against his will. He was hungry for her and could hardly restrain himself to free her from her garments, possibly even tearing them if they resisted his fingers.

His hands slid from her breast and Belle felt him fumbling with the fastenings of her breeches. Instantly her sanity returned and with a horrified gasp, she broke away from him, her whole manner conveying her fury, which reappeared with shocking speed. With a tremendous effort of will she flung herself away from him and rolled off the bed. She stood glaring at him, breathing hard, her hair tangled in disarray about her shoulders, her green eyes burning, completely unaware of the vision she presented to his hungering eyes.

'How dare you?' she hissed. 'How dare you do that to me? I will not be forced.'

Struggling for control, finding it with effort, getting off the bed, Lance straightened his clothes. 'Come now, Belle,' he managed to say, smiling, though he himself was shaken by the moment. 'It was only a kiss—an innocent kiss, nothing more sordid than that.' But he was not convinced by his words. With her long sleek legs encased in breeches, he was led to think that he had never caressed any that had evoked his imagination as much as those. The lingering impression of those trim thighs entangled with his own had done much to awaken a manly craving that had gone unappeased for some months.

He cursed himself for letting Belle Ainsley affect

him in this way. He went from hot to cold, a sensation not normal for him, a man who had always had a woman at his whim, had enjoyed a woman casually and made love to her for his pleasure. Now this young woman needed to be taught a lesson and he could hardly keep his hands off her.

Belle's anger was boiling. Every single word she uttered seemed to make it worse, as if it were feeding upon itself. And having no other outlet for this anger, it would continue to grow and fester.

'A kiss that would have led to other things—which was what you had in mind you—you lecher—had I not had the presence of mind to end it,' she flared, furious with herself for not only responding to it, but *liking* what he had done to her. 'You forced your will on me, forced me to kiss you. I did not invite you to do that.'

'I forced nothing,' he said, raking his fingers through his hair. 'You brought it on yourself when you decided to invade my bedchamber, don't forget.'

He sounded entirely too smug in saying that. 'Only because I thought it wouldn't have you in it. I am here because I had no choice if I was to retrieve the necklace.'

'Choice? Yes, indeed.' He turned her angry words aside as he walked round the bed to stand before her, the burning heat back in his eyes. 'Choice you are, my love.' He ran his fingers down the soft curve of her cheek. 'The very cream of the lot.'

His soft answer and soothing caress awoke once again tingling answers in places Belle tried to ignore. This betrayal by her own body aroused an impatient vexation. She had foolishly thought that all the quickening fires she had just felt in his arms had been thoroughly quenched by her anger. But she was becoming increasingly aware of the folly of that conclusion. Where his finger touched, she burned. It was a hard fact for her pride to accept. He was capable of scattering her wits in a thousand different directions. She wished she could deny it, for she realised he had a way of affecting her that made her uneasy of future encounters.

He stood before her, his wide shoulders narrowing her world to a dark, limited space. She glanced past him, but quickly dismissed the idea of darting for the door, for she strongly suspected he was as quick as he was strong. Shaking her head, Belle stepped back from him and pressed a trembling hand to his chest to hold him away.

'You have been too long with the military and got too comfortable with the camp-followers to know how to treat a lady. I've heard how soldiers like to dally here and there at their leisure—I can't imagine officers being any different.'

'In some cases your imagination is correct, Belle. After years of soldiering, adjusting to civilian life is not an easy matter, and I, for one, intend to try.'

'And I am not gullible enough to believe in miracles,' she bit back. 'I am not one of your common women. I will not be tumbled between the sheets and left to bear a child in shame. This was a mistake, a mistake you will have cause to regret.' She walked past him, heading for the door.

'A mistake for you, maybe, but not for me. You see, I know you now, Belle. I know how you react to my kiss, to being in my arms. The next time you may not be so eager to leave.'

She whirled in a flare of rage. 'Why, you conceited—buffoon. There won't be a next time. I would see you in hell first.'

Striding towards her, he bent his head, his laughing

breath touching her brow as he chucked her playfully under the chin. 'Your endearments intrigue me, but I did not fight with every measure of skill and wit at my command to preserve my life as well as my company of men on the battlefields of Spain and Waterloo, to have it taken away in peacetime by a mere slip of a girl.'

'The slip of a girl you speak of I left behind in America, my lord.'

'My eyes confirm what you say, Belle,' he murmured, his eyes probing with flaming warmth into hers. 'You are what any man would desire—softly rounded in all the right places, yet slender and long of limb. You have whet my imagination to such a degree that my pleasure would be to throw you back on to the bed and make love to you.'

She stepped back. Behind the pattern of her beautiful face, she was outraged. The red blushes on her cheeks had settled into a dark glow, the flush of sudden battle in her face. Her retreat was necessary to cool her burning cheeks, and to ease to some degree the unruly pacing of her heart. 'Stop it. You should not be saying such things.'

'Come now, Belle, believe me, after surrendering your virginity you will be amazed at the pleasures to be found in the arms of a lover.'

'Lover? Ha!' she scoffed. 'The man I surrender my virtue to will be my husband. It is not something I shall give away in the weakness of a moment in the bed of the vilest of rakes.'

Lance did not seem surprised or insulted. Undaunted, he lifted his brows quizzically, a twist of humour about his beautifully moulded lips. But never had he looked more challenging. 'This is indeed a crushing moment,

Belle! I have been called some names in my life, but I must confess never to have been called—the vilest of rakes.'

Belle saw him struggling to hold back his deep amusement. Then, to her rising dismay, he threw back his head, letting out rich, infectious laughter. 'This has really made my day—"the vilest of rakes".'

'You are insufferable,' Belle cried angrily, her rage pouring out. 'Let me out of this room this instant.'

'You needn't be distressed by what has just happened between us,' he said, no longer laughing, but still quietly amused. 'Making love can be just as pleasurable for a woman as for a man. Are you so fearful of losing your virtue, Belle?'

She thrust her face forwards to deliver her own angry rejoinder. 'With you? Yes!' she answered with a finality that brooked no discussion. 'I will not allow myself to be sullied and then tossed aside by you, leaving me little hope of attracting a respectable husband. Rumours have a way of shattering lives, my lord. No man wants spoiled goods.'

Lance offered her a cajoling smile, appealing to her with all the charm he was capable of putting into play. He had not got to where he was in life without becoming aware that many women he had known had been intrigued and captivated by the smile on his lips.

'I'll have you know that right now you're presenting a definite challenge to me,' he accused, amusement gleaming in his eyes. 'I've never before known a woman who seems to loathe me one minute and the next accept my attentions as you did just now on the bed. Can I not persuade you to relent?'

'You certainly know the right words to entangle a gullible maid's mind, my lord. But I am not gullible and certainly know the risks I would encounter if I allowed myself to be taken in by the likes of you. What woman would willingly invite such disgrace?'

Cocking a magnificent brow enquiringly, Lance peered down his noble nose at her. 'Not all women who know me would consider it a disgrace.'

'Just how many women have you addled with comments of that sort, my lord?' Belle asked snidely. 'If any of them believe you then they must be simple minded. You can say what you like, but any *lady* would be upset to be involved in a conversation such as this. It is hardly a topic to soothe one's nerves.'

His eyes danced as he probed the bright green orbs. 'I'll allow the subject itself wouldn't soothe your nerves, Belle, but the joining of our bodies in the ritual of making love would do wonders for relaxing you. I'd be more than willing to show you.'

'I'm sure you would, but I'm not going to give you the chance. Now please stop it. You are far too persistent for my peace of mind.'

'When I see something I want, I go for it.' He shrugged nonchalantly. 'It's in my nature. At least the men under my command thought so.'

'I'm not one of your men,' she retorted, and had cause to wonder what would follow as his eyes gleamed tauntingly into hers.

'Believe me, my lovely Belle, looking as you do, I would never mistake you for one of them—not even for an instant. None of my men ever looked even remotely appealing to me.' Lance chuckled softly. Devilment shone in his blue eyes as he placed a finger beneath her chin and tilted her face to his. 'Don't be alarmed. Relax. I'm not going to kiss you again. At least not yet.'

Suddenly Belle found herself trying to gather the shattered pieces of her aplomb. His persuasive voice seemed to bombard her very being.

'Just be thankful I've decided to let you leave.'

She met his warmly alluring eyes with a cool stare as she warned him crisply, 'I should jolly well hope so. If you lay one hand upon me, my lord, I'll scream the house down. That much I promise you.'

'In which case, I shall comply with your wishes. Your presence in my bedchamber would take some explaining to my guests.'

Belle now had cause to regret her impulsive decision to come to his house. It was the kind of bad behaviour she had indulged in when she was a child—too hasty to jump in, too stubborn to draw back before it was too late, and suffering regret afterwards. There was more than just regret this time, however, much more.

She flung her head backwards so that more of her hair was loosed from its pins, coiling down her spine, so gloriously a shade of rich brown, now as dark as night. Her chin jutted dangerously and her eyes flashed.

'How noble of you,' she uttered sarcastically. 'If you know what's good for you, you will never lay hands on me again.'

Her lips curled back over her teeth in a snarl, and Lance thought she was like an animal on the defensive. Dear God, she was a magnificent creature, but heaven help the poor devil who got landed with her as a wife. He liked his women quick-tempered, spirited and with fire in their veins. It made for a satisfying and exciting relationship, but Belle Ainsley with her bull-headed stubbornness would not only need a husband as strong-willed as herself, but with the patience of a saint.

'As to that, Belle, I shall make no promises. Who knows what will come from our association? I will tell you now that I consider my independence of great importance. I am not necessarily anxious to give it up immediately now I have returned home, but I may just decide to forget the promise I made to myself to remain a bachelor and take you to wife just to show you what delights can be had between a married couple.'

Belle glowered at him and spoke with derision. 'What subtle ploys you practise, Lord Bingham. If you think to get me into your bed with your liberal use of the word *marriage,* you will find I am not as gullible as you think.'

Lance laughed outright. 'I get the message, Belle, so continue with your parties and concentrate on finding a husband—which is what the Season is all about. I've seen the many smitten swains following at your heels. I would think you'd find it difficult to choose among them. Although I can almost pity the man you eventually settle on. The poor man won't have a moment's peace.'

'Like you I am in no hurry to wed, and Grandmother is not putting pressure on me to do so. I have only recently come to England and I am testing the water, so to speak. I am quite happy with my single state.'

'Ah, but you will be caught and settle down to connubial bliss with one of your suitors ere long.'

Angry and humiliated beyond anything she had known in her life, as she watched him turn to retrieve his discarded jacket, Belle vowed to make him regret in a thousand different ways that he'd tampered with her. Her eyes settled on a small table where he had put the pouch and the smile that tempted her lips was one of cunning. Starting with the necklace.

So, he thought he had outwitted her, did he, by telling her some lame story about it belonging to his own grandmother? How easily she had swallowed it. How gullible she had been, but no more. She would not give him his victory. While picking up the pouch, which she slipped into her pocket, she grabbed hold of her hat, dropping it. She bent to retrieve it, and, turning round, Lance halted abruptly, for he found himself confronting a very fetching derrière stuck up in the air.

He emited a low groan with the gnawing hunger she aroused in him, for he had never seen anything quite so stimulating as those snugly bound buttocks, for the tight trousers left nothing to the imagination. Tempted to go to her and slide his arm around her waist and pull her back to him, to forget all logic and again sweep her down on to his bed, he halted, prone to wonder if he was having another lewd fantasy involving this precocious young woman, and it came as no surprise to him that she had sharply awakened his manly cravings like none other before. He stepped back as she straightened up, having retrieved her hat.

Aware of the pouch in her pocket, unaware of Lance's lewd thoughts, her smile turned to one of triumph at her own cleverness. It was the perfect payback. Pulling her hat down over her ears, tucking her wayward locks beneath it, she turned to the door.

They were descending the stairs when Belle's worst nightmare was realised. Rowland Gibbon emerged from the dining room without bothering to close the doors behind him. Some of Lance's guests followed him into the hall. Cursing softly, Lance immediately took Belle's arm and was already pulling her back up the stairs in an attempt to forestall a calamity, but too late. Rowland had

seen them. He let out a loud gusto and started towards
the bottom of the stairs, his heels clicking on the black-
and-white tiled floor.

'Ha! What's this, Lance? Trying to hide from your
guests. I won't have it. Already Lady Marlow and the
other ladies are feeling quite bereft and have sent me
to find you.'

Realising the futility of trying to escape, Lance and
Belle made a final descent of the stairs.

Rowland's eyes shifted to Lance's companion,
whom he thought to be a youth hanging back. Rowland
raised an enquiring eyebrow. 'And who have we here?'
he asked, bending over to peruse the face under the hat.
He turned to Lance with a grin. 'So, you had another
engagement. Are you not going to introduce me?'

'You've already had that pleasure.'

'I don't think so—although the lad does seem
somewhat familiar.' Without more ado he snatched the
hat from Belle's head, drawing a shocked gasp of furious indignation from her. Rowland uttered a soft
whistle when her hair cascaded about her shoulders.
His exclamation was one of disbelief and he chuckled
softly. 'Why, 'tis no lad I see before me.'

The guests let out a collective gasp, and a few giggles
came from the maids of the house, who had stopped in
their tracks to gawp at the youth who had a definite
feminine air about him, only to be shooed away by an
irate butler.

'Leave it, Rowland,' Lance uttered through his teeth.

Rowland wasn't going to let it drop. With Belle's
identity revealed, he turned his incredulous look on
Lance and back to the slender, black garbed figure.
'Good Lord! If it isn't Miss Ainsley!'

Belle felt physically ill and glanced towards Lord Bingham's guests. She recognised several of them as being elite members of the *ton*. The expressions on their faces ranged from amusement to icy condemnation. Knowing there was no help for it but to brazen it out, in a defiant gesture she thrust out her chin and squared her shoulders.

'As you see, sir,' she replied coolly. 'Please don't ask me to explain what I am doing here dressed like this. You would not believe it.'

Smiling broadly, Rowland laughed. 'I might. I shall certainly enjoy hearing it.'

'Miss Ainsley took the opportunity of me being otherwise engaged to steal into my house to retrieve the necklace I took from her last night,' Lance told him, careful to keep his voice low. It was bad enough that his guests had witnessed Belle coming down his stairs with him attired as she was, without providing them with her reason for being in his house.

Comprehension dawned in Rowland's eyes, quickly followed by astonishment. 'Ah, she did?'

'Indeed. My disguise didn't deceive this clever young lady and she must be complimented on her success. She was about to walk off with the necklace when I returned home unexpectedly and took it back.'

'Did she, now? Then she is to be congratulated, but I'm sorry you got it back. I would have been in order to demand my money back, for I would have considered I'd won the bet.'

Belle frowned, but what Sir Rowland was implying didn't sink in immediately. Until she saw Lance cringe.

'Take no notice of what Rowland says, Belle.'

But as if he hadn't spoken, she said, 'A bet? Am I to understand last night, when you posed as a highwayman and put me through hell, was all about a bet?'

'It wasn't like that.'

'It wasn't?'

'No,' Lance assured her. 'I told you, I was simply retrieving my own property.'

'That's what you told me,' she flared. 'But now I am not inclined to believe you.'

'It's true. Believe me.'

'And the bet?'

'Was merely a reaction to Rowland's scepticism.'

Belle glanced at Sir Rowland to see him somewhat shamefaced now. 'You mean he didn't believe you would succeed?'

'I didn't,' Rowland said. 'Not for a minute.'

Belle didn't reply immediately. All she could think of was Lord Bingham and his friend laughing together at her when they'd made their bet. As the colour mounted high in her cheeks and warmed her ears, the people crowding in the doorway became a blur.

'Well, I'm glad you had some fun at my expense—enjoying yourselves enormously, I don't doubt.' The look she turned on Lance was murderous. 'You accost me in the early hours—at gunpoint, I might add—you steal my grandmother's necklace, scare me half out of my wits by threatening to shoot me—and all because you had money riding on it.' Moving to stand before him, she thrust her face close to his. 'My God! My breaking into your house was nothing compared to that, you—you animal. I hope you enjoy your winnings.'

Turning on her heel, she strode past him, past a stupefied butler, who was standing with his mouth agape, her only thought being to get out and away from her tormentor and his astonished guests as quickly as she could.

'Belle, wait. Your grandmother?'

She spun round. 'What about her?'

'She will have to be told.'

'I don't think so—you see, there is nothing to tell.'

'Wait.'

'Go to hell,' she bit back, whirling round and hurrying to the door, unable to say more because she couldn't get any more words past the lump in her throat.

Lance followed, but she rushed out of the door before he could stop her. With her coach waiting down the street, she was inside and on her way home within moments.

Lance stood in the doorway, watching her coach disappear.

After ushering the guests who had watched the whole scene back into the dining room and closing the door, Rowland came to stand beside him and casually remarked, 'I take it she didn't know about the bet?'

'Of course not.' Lance spun round. 'Do you see *stupid idiot* written on my face, Rowland?'

He shrugged. 'Why should it matter to her if we made a bet? You won, don't forget—and besides, Miss Ainsley's intrusion into your house was not the action of a respectably reared young lady, now, was it?'

'She came here for all the right reasons.'

'Well, I think you've come out of it pretty well. You have the necklace and two hundred pounds.'

Frowning, Lance closed the door. Something puzzled him—Belle's parting remark about her grandmother. She had nothing to tell her, she had said. Why would she say that—unless…?

Lance looked at Rowland. 'Wait here.'

'Lance—what…?'

'Wait.'

Rowland watched his friend bound up the stairs two at a time. Not a minute passed and he was back.

'Well?' Rowland asked, unable to hide his curiosity.

'She's taken them.'

'Taken what?'

'The diamonds.'

Rowland smiled, his face almost comical in its disbelief. 'Do you mean to tell me that the delectable Miss Isabelle Ainsley has outwitted you?'

'This time, Rowland—and it will be the last. When I get my hands on that green-eyed witch, I'll…'

Rowland could clearly see that Lance's pride had suffered a grievous blow. 'You'll what?'

A smile flickered into Lance's eyes as he shot a wry look at his friend. 'I haven't made up my mind yet. But whatever I decide, she won't like it.'

He stood and looked at the closed door through which Belle had disappeared, thinking of her in his arms, of her soft warm body curving to him, of her long, lovely limbs entwining with his. The hot blood surged through him and he chuckled to himself, amazed that one young woman could make him feel like this. He was worse than any rutting stag in her company.

In helpless misery Belle leaned back against the upholstery inside the coach, her heart filled with dread in anticipation of the condemnation she would ultimately receive from her grandmother. Had her departure from Lord Bingham's house not been witnessed by his guests, she could have returned the diamonds to their rightful place and her grandmother would have been none the wiser.

She was confident the coach driver and the two footmen wouldn't say anything about being held up. They were terrified she would accuse them of being irresponsible. After all, they were supposed to be taking care of her granddaughter. They were armed and should have been prepared for such a thing happening.

As it was there was nothing for it but to tell her grandmother everything. There would be no redemption for her, she knew that. People were too quick to judge and condemn. She had already tarnished her reputation with her liaison with Carlton Robinson when she had known no better, and there were those among the *ton*— ladies mostly, who saw her as an American upstart who outshone their own daughters, and deeply resented her popularity among London's eligible bachelors and therefore reducing their chances of making a good match—who would take vindictive delight in her downfall. In their eyes she was a shameless wanton.

As for Lord Bingham, she could not see her actions reflecting on him, she thought bitterly. If there was a scandal, she doubted he would be embarrassed by it. The man was a complete and utter scoundrel and she hoped never to set eyes on him again—and yet she did wonder how he would react when he discovered she had taken back the necklace. She could only hope that he would concede defeat and not pursue it, but deep down she knew he wasn't the kind of man to let it drop.

Her grandmother arrived home the following afternoon feeling much better, but insisted on going to her room to lie down, summoning Belle to follow her up.

From her bed where she was sitting propped up against a mountain of pillows, the dowager countess looked at her granddaughter perched on the edge of a chair next to the bed. 'Did you enjoy yourself at Carlton House the other night, Isabelle?'

'Yes, very much,' Belle answered, putting off the moment to tell her of the awful thing she had done. 'I always enjoy parties and the Prince Regent excelled himself.

The countess's gaze became pointed. 'Are you feeling well, Isabelle? You are very pale.'

'Yes—I am quite well. I—I didn't sleep very well last night.'

'Then you must have an early night. I must say that I would have preferred you not to have had anything to do with Lord Bingham. I sincerely hope he has not approached you since?' The countess noticed that a bright pink had swept into her granddaughter's cheeks, a sure sign that the girl was guilty about something. 'He has, hasn't he—the scoundrel.'

'I—I happened to encounter him yesterday after visiting you. He—he rode part of the way home with me.' She quailed at the look that entered her grandmother's eyes—a mixture of disappointment, hurt and anger. 'I'm sorry, Grandmother. I know you asked me not to have anything to do with him, but I—I couldn't avoid him.'

The countess rested her head against the pillows and closed her eyes, deep in thought. 'That man is too persistent,' she murmured at length. 'I have decided we shall leave for Wiltshire earlier than I intended. I would like to think that at Harworth Hall you will not be so easily available to him. Unfortunately that may not be the case. The Ryhill estate borders Harworth Hall, so unless our neighbour remains in London—as I sincerely hope he will—then there is every chance that the two of you will meet some time. Hopefully it will be later rather than sooner, and in the meantime Lord Bingham will have found himself a wife.'

Belle fell silent. As relentlessly as she had tried to thrust that blue-eyed devil from her mind, regretfully he was still very much in residence. She remembered what it had felt like to be in his arms, how his kiss had made her forget everything but the two of them, how he had sent her emotions spiralling upwards, her passion mounting until she feared for her sanity. In fact, it was something of a shock to her that she was just as susceptible to his absence as she was to his presence.

It seemed far fetched to think that one man could move her to such extremes, yet when she compared her joy at the feelings he had awakened in her to the strange, inexplicable yearning that presently thwarted her mood, what else could she put it down to?

Anger stirred inside her, anger at her response to his seduction, at the betrayal of her body. Damn him, she thought. How dare he do this to her? And now her grandmother had told her his home in Wiltshire adjoined Harworth Hall, and she found herself in the vexing position of how to avoid him in the future. What could she possibly do to save herself now that he looked like some godly being sent to earth to play havoc with her mind and her heart?

Unable to stop her mind running off in a dozen different directions, she got up and went to the window and stood looking out. Her back was ramrod straight, her hands clenched by her sides.

'Isabelle? What is it?'

With a worried, haunted look, as though she carried a burden too heavy to bear on her young shoulders, she turned and looked at her grandmother, meeting her questioning eyes. She would have to tell her everything. It could not be avoided.

Chapter Five

Belle thought her grandmother was going to have an apoplectic fit as she hesitantly told her of everything that had transpired from the night Lord Bingham had played highwayman. Her eyes never moved from her grand-daughter's face. She seemed unable to speak, to form any words, from between her rigidly clamped lips. When Belle had finished speaking she remained for a while in contemplation of her clasped hands. Belle respected her silence, stifling her painful anxiety.

At last the older woman raised her eyelids and looked at her and Belle shivered at the anger and disappointment in her eyes.

'I am deeply shocked, Isabelle. Deeply so.'

'Grandmother, I am so sorry.'

'Sorry? Isabelle, what you have done is outrageous. Among other things, to enter the house and the bed-chamber of any man, never mind a practised seducer, was disgraceful. Do you know what you have done? No decent man will have you now. Did he touch you?'

Growing increasingly alarmed by her grandmother's

anger and distress, Belle actually considered telling a lie, but the increased colour in her face told its own story.

'So, he did.' The Countess's voice was low and shaking. 'You foolish, foolish girl. The answer is written all over your face.'

'Grandmother, please don't upset yourself. It was my fault. I—I should not have been there.'

'At least you have got that right. You may not understand the enormity of what you have done, but he knows. He is just like his grandfather—uses women for his own amusement and then discards them. I will not let Lance Bingham do that to you. He has to do what is right.'

'Oh, please,' Belle burst out, having no idea what her grandmother meant by that. 'He did nothing so terrible. It was just a kiss, nothing more than that.'

'It was enough,' she said, with biting, icy calm. 'Do not forget that you are already treading on thin ice in society's eyes because of your liaison with Carlton Robinson. Another scandal will ruin you completely. Your reputation was shattered the minute you entered Lord Bingham's house, destroying any chance of your making a decent marriage—and to add to the shame your wantonness was witnessed by the elite of London society. You were seen coming down the stairs together, so everyone will have correctly surmised that you were with him in his bedchamber. No other man will have you now. As soon as the scandal breaks—indeed, I shall be surprised if it hasn't already—you will be blacklisted. We have to go and see him, you do realise that, don't you?'

'I would rather not see Lord Bingham ever again,' Belle mumbled miserably.

Her grandmother smiled thinly. 'You have no choice—wretched girl. I'm surprised that after all the trouble he went to to get the diamonds, he could be persuaded to part with them.'

'He wasn't. I mean—I took them back when he wasn't looking. He told me they belonged to him—but I didn't believe him. Is it true, Grandmother?'

'Yes, it is true, and if I had been aware of what had occurred, I would have let him keep them. You should have let me deal with it. What were you thinking?'

'What is the story behind the diamonds?' Belle asked. 'Will you not tell me?'

'Never mind that now. What is important is how we are going to extricate you from this sordid affair without complete ruin to your reputation.'

The countess knew the lengths the *ton* would go to ostracise Isabelle—and there were many who, regarding her as an American upstart who gathered men around her like flies, would enjoy slating her. Those who were anxious for their own daughters to make good marriages were jealous of Isabelle's burst into society, putting their own darling daughters in the shade. It wasn't just her beauty that drew the attention of single males. There was a vibrancy about her, a sparkle that was absent in many of the newly launched débutantes. Now they would have enough fuel to cinder Isabelle and turn to ashes any infatuation that London's bachelors might have felt for the girl.

The countess prided herself on being realistic and a moment's thought made her understand that what she was about to do was the right thing for Belle—and it was borne out of the fact that she refused to let history repeat itself. The countess had been treated very badly by Lance Bingham's grandfather, Stuart Bingham. She still felt the pain of being jilted and the humiliation that almost ruined her reputation that followed, and she didn't want this to happen to her granddaughter. The diamonds—a Bingham family heirloom—had been given to her on her betrothal to Stuart Bingham. When he had broken the engagement and asked for them to be returned, as a form of punishment she had refused and had kept them to this day. Perhaps now was the time to give them back.

Lance Bingham was handsome and so well mannered that resorting to posing as a highwayman to get back something that by rights belonged to him, one could hardly believe that in doing so he had done anything wicked. He was so like his grandfather with that merry twinkle in his eye, that soft smiling curl to his mouth, the way he spoke. She had noticed the way he had taken Belle on to the floor at Carlton House, the way he had looked at her. Who could help it, and the idle thought occurred to her that here was a man whom Belle could not get the better of. He might be the one person who could tame her wild and rebellious granddaughter. Perhaps it was time to forget all the old grievances after all.

Lance was in his study when the butler came to inform him that the Dowager Countess of Harworth and Miss Isabelle Ainsley had arrived and that the countess insisted on seeing him.

The word *insist* caused Lance's eyebrows to snap together into a frown. 'Show them into the drawing room,' he said shortly. 'I'll see them in there.'

Keeping her eyes straight ahead of her, Belle followed reluctantly in the wake of her grandmother. The butler swept open a pair of carved oaken doors and stepped aside to admit them into the drawing room, a comfortable, tastefully furnished room.

Belle's entire being was engulfed in mortification, her misery increasing a thousandfold as she sat stiffly on the edge of her chair across from her grandmother and facing the fireplace. She couldn't help remembering the last time she had been in this house, and knowing how furious Lord Bingham must have been on discovering she had taken the diamonds when his back was turned, she dreaded the moment when she would have to confront him and see what she knew would surely be contempt written all over his features.

She was not wrong. The man who strode in moments later, his tall frame clad in impeccably tailored dark blue trousers and coat and white shirt and neckcloth at the throat, bore little resemblance to the laughing man she had met at Carlton House only four days ago. Today he was an aloof, icy stranger who gave her no more than a cursory glance before focusing all his attention on the stately woman who was watching him closely.

'This is an unusual occurrence, Countess, for an Ainsley to step over the Bingham threshold,' Lance remarked coolly. 'Not that I don't welcome it, you understand. In my opinion it is high time that whatever grievances there have been between our families in the past were left there. However, you could have spared yourselves the embarrassment of this visit. I had every intention of calling on you later.'

'Then I have saved you the trouble,' the countess replied stiffly, her purple turbaned head erect and her gloved hands folded upon the jewelled head of her cane. Having lived with her dislike of the Binghams for many years, she was too carefully schooled in good manners to show it.

'Nevertheless it is good of you to take the time to call at this unfortunate time. Can I offer you refreshment?'

'No, thank you. I have not come here to make polite conversation,' she stated ominously, looking at Lord Bingham intently.

He crossed to the fireplace, draped his arm across the mantel and turned, regarding his visitors with a cool and speculative gaze. His gaze lingered on Belle, who was watching him with a cool reticence. He could not help but admire the way she looked. Her overall appearance was flawless and he was quickly coming to the conclusion that she would set the standard by which all other women would have to be judged, at least in his mind.

Her garments were in the height of fashion, and her slender form complemented them perfectly. The high-standing collar and the waist of her short, cropped jacket gave something of a military flare to the dark blue creation of soft wool. A dove-grey silk stock flecked with darker threads was wound about her slender throat and the skirt was in a contrasting paler blue to the jacket. Her glorious hair had been smoothed back from her face and caught up at the crown in a heavy coil, upon which sat a dark blue hat, which matched her jacket. Several feathery curls had escaped the confines of the style, lending a charming softness to her creamy skin, and the appeal in her large, silkily lashed green eyes was so strong that he had to mentally shake himself free of their spell.

'No, I thought not,' he replied in reply to the countess's remark.

'I recognise that I must lend all my support to my granddaughter at this time,' the countess went on. 'She has told me of everything that has transpired since the two of you met at Carlton House and how you forcibly removed some valuables from her person and terrified my servants. I don't like primitive behaviour, Lord Bingham—especially when it threatens a member of my family.'

'I saw something that belonged to me and I took it back.' He flicked his brows upwards mockingly. 'Primitive behaviour,' he stated quietly. 'However, it proved to be a pointless exercise since your granddaughter took them back.' His eyes swung to Belle. 'Is that not so, miss?'

Belle stiffened her shoulders and met his gaze direct. 'Yes. I saw the opportunity and I took it.'

'I expected better of you, Lord Bingham,' the countess remarked. 'Your actions were those of a feckless youth—not a distinguished military officer.'

'I agree absolutely. And for what it's worth I regret what I did. I should have approached you over the matter.'

'Yes, you should. However, it's too late for that, which is most unfortunate. I am not here to question what prompted a man of your standing and experience to behave like a halfwit. It is done now and we have to try to make the best of it.'

Lance ignored her reference of him being a halfwit. To argue the point would be stupid and serve no purpose. 'Why are you here, Countess?'

'Because by your actions you have compromised my granddaughter.'

'I disagree. Your granddaughter compromised herself the moment she entered my house,' he said, not in the least perturbed. 'So,' he said, going to sit in a large winged chair, propping his right ankle on his left knee and steepling his fingers in front of him, 'am I to believe that your conscience smote you and you have come here to do the right thing and apologise for breaking into my home?'

'My conscience has nothing to do with it,' Belle snapped, clamping her lips together when her grandmother shot her a stern look of displeasure.

'Then do you mind telling me why you are here?' he demanded, his dagger gaze pinning Belle to her chair.

'My granddaughter in her naïvety came to your house to retrieve something you took from her by force—at the point of a gun, I understand—something valuable she believed was mine. In return you ruined her.'

Abandoning his nonchalant manner and sitting forwards, Lance sounded ready to explode. 'I did what?' he ground out ominously.

'You attempted to seduce a young lady of good breeding in your bedchamber.'

'I did not invite her into my bedchamber. She came of her own volition,' Lance reminded her forcefully, preferring to ignore what she said about seduction since it was true.

'When you found her you should have seen to it that she left your house discreetly and not under the watchful eyes of society and your servants. I have a moral code, Lord Bingham, and you publicly breached that code by exposing her to scandal.'

'If anyone can make a scandal out of a woman leaving my house—although I feel that I must point out that at the time your granddaughter far more resembled a youth than a respectable young lady—then they need their minds examining.'

'Not when that young lady is my granddaughter.' The countess gave Belle a withering look. 'Lord Bingham's remark leads me to assume you were wearing those appalling breeches you brought with you from America. This is worse than I thought. You have given society enough bait to feed off until the next Season. I recall telling you to dispose of those wretched clothes when you arrived.'

The severe rebuke caused Belle to lower her eyes and mumble, 'I'm sorry, Grandmother. I forgot.'

'What she was wearing is insignificant,' Lance remarked.

'Insignificant! A respectable young lady wearing breeches may seem insignificant to a practised seducer like yourself, Lord Bingham, but Isabelle is nineteen years old with high hopes of making a good marriage and you have ruined her.'

'You know, Countess, I find it amazing,' Lance drawled with some amusement, 'that nearly everyone who knows me is half-afraid of me, except a handful of my friends, you, madam, and your granddaughter. I can only surmise that courage—or recklessness, call it what you will—is passed through the bloodline to her. So,' he finished with a mocking grin, 'I will give you leave to take me to task in my own home if it will make you feel better. What is it you want from me?'

The countess looked at him, her piercing eyes alive with anticipation. 'You may not like what I have to suggest—indeed, I don't like it myself, yet I can think of no other way at present to stop the gossip that will surely ruin Isabelle.'

'Say what's on your mind, Countess. I am listening.'

'There are many kinds of persecution that are not readily apparent, such as the whispered conjectures, the gossip and subtle innuendoes that can destroy a reputation and inflict a lifetime of damage. I can think of only one possible arrangement that can hold sway over that to be adequate enough to protect her. I am suggesting that you marry my granddaughter.'

Lance was taken aback; his face became livid with anger. 'What? Marry your granddaughter! Have you gone mad?'

'I can assure you that I am not,' the countess stated firmly.

Lance struggled to calm his temper. The suggestion that he marry Belle Ainsley was almost too much to bear. When he next spoke his face was a taut mask of controlled fury. 'Forgive me, Countess. Since your suggestion is not what I expected,' he uttered drily, 'I must take a moment and consider the possible repercussions that may occur because of it.'

Pushed beyond the bounds of reason by her grandmother's words and shamed to the depths of her being, Belle sprang from her chair. 'No,' she cried, managing to drag her voice through the strangling mortification in her chest. This was worse, much worse than she had dreamed it could be. Her glance skidded from her grandmother to Lord Bingham. 'Please believe me, I knew nothing of this. The idea of our marrying is ludicrous. I don't want to marry you.'

Lance's eyes jerked to Belle's and his face became a cynical mask. 'You're absolutely right,' he mocked sarcastically, remembering another time and another face—Delphine's face, a face that still wrenched his damaged heart. Also that of a child he couldn't bear to look at because it reminded him of the woman its arrival into this world had taken from him, reminding him of the guilt that continued to torture him and would not let him be—the guilt of abandoning Delphine in her hour of need. 'It is ludicrous and I don't want to marry you either. And yet all this time I've been harbouring the delusion that all girls yearn to snare wealthy and titled husbands.'

'I am not like other girls,' Belle bit back.

'I sensed that from the moment I met you,' Lance remarked in a bland drawl.

Belle heard the insult in his smoothly worded agreement, and she almost choked on her chagrin. 'Then that's it. We won't wed.'

'Sit down, Isabelle,' her grandmother ordered with icy calm, turning her determined gaze on Lord Bingham once more when her granddaughter, humiliated to the very core of her being by his unkind words, had obeyed. 'And I would appreciate you addressing my granddaughter with more respect, Lord Bingham.'

Lance allowed a meagre smile to convey his apology. 'After many years as a soldier, Countess, I'm afraid I shall have to relearn the art of gallantry.'

'I dare say there was not much call for it in your encampments. It is with considerable distaste that I feel I must ask this of you. I am doing it for Isabelle's sake. If it were not for the slur you have placed on her virtue, I would put the matter from me and have done with it. Since no decent man will want to marry her now, you will have to do the honourable thing and marry her yourself. I think it's the least you can do. Her birth is as exceptional as yours. She is your equal, so you can have no objections to her suitability.'

A muscle twitched in Lance's cheek as his angry glare took in the two people staring at him. Why did he have this feeling that he was caught in a trap? 'No objections?' he bit back, his face turning positively glacial. 'I have plenty.'

'Yes,' the countess scathingly replied. 'I thought you might.'

'And so has your granddaughter if the look she is giving me is an indication of how she feels.'

'Isabelle will fulfil her part of the bargain.'

'Even though she might thoroughly loathe me?'

'She will do the honourable thing. She may be as averse to marriage as you are just now, but I believe that will change when she realises the seriousness of the situation—and she does not loathe you.'

'No?' Lance questioned, glancing at the beauty who looked fit to burst with fury. 'We have just listened to her vehement protests. If I discerned anything in her manner, then I'm willing to wager that you would never get her to the altar.'

'You are too free with your wagers, Lord Bingham,' Belle broke in scornfully, 'and I do not care for them. I shall no doubt suffer from the wager you made with your friend Sir Rowland Gibbon for a long time to come.'

'In case your granddaughter didn't give you the full facts, Countess, I shall enlighten you. The reason why I decided to retrieve the diamonds was due to a wager laid down by my good friend,' Lance explained. 'He did not believe I would succeed. I am happy to say that I won the wager, before your granddaughter took it into her mind to enter my house to steal them back. What will you do if I refuse to marry her?'

'Then I shall have to consider having you charged with armed robbery and even go so far as to include attempted seduction.'

'That is ridiculous,' Lance responded with cold sarcasm. 'To openly accuse me would only broadcast throughout London the very scandal you find so damaging to your granddaughter. I will not marry her and that is that.'

'For that I thank you,' Belle retorted with angry sarcasm, ignoring her grandmother's sharp eyes that were telling her to be quiet. 'I think I would rather be ruined in the eyes of the *ton* before consenting to be your wife.'

The eyes he turned on her were hard and a jeering grin showed startling white teeth against the swarthy skin. 'I am glad we are of accord, Belle. *If* I ever decide to take a wife it will be in my own way, with the woman of my choosing, and not when a woman is holding an axe over my head, which is precisely where all my manly instincts rebel.'

'An axe,' she repeated innocently.

His mood was mocking, cruel and angry. 'You know perfectly well what I mean. I don't like being forced. It goes against the grain—my grain.'

'So you intend to go merrily upon your way and not right the wrong you did,' the countess said coldly. 'You should have known what the consequences would be of dallying with an innocent, respectable young woman in your bedroom—that it could affect your life in a most permanent fashion.'

Lance looked at her long and hard, refusing to be moved. He was a man who had made his own choices for most of his life, and as much as he yearned to appease his manly appetites with Belle Ainsley, how could he, like some lapdog, blandly accept this elderly woman's will without yielding his mind?

'As far as I am concerned, Countess, I have done no wrong. Had I done so, I might have even married your granddaughter if she had acted as if she desired marriage to me. It is an unfortunate occurrence, I grant you.

'I do not feel committed to marry her, and to come here and threaten me was most unwise. Do exactly as you have threatened and have me publicly charged and brought up before the Court for armed robbery if it will make you feel better. But do not forget that in order to punish me you will destroy your granddaughter and your own good name. Is that what you want?'

'What I want is fair play, Lord Bingham.'

'In that we are in accord. I am certain that when your society has chewed over the incident, in time, when another scandal hits the scene, it will blow over and be forgotten as they get on with slating someone else.'

His arrogant calm and the recollections of her own ill use at his grandfather's hands brought the countess to her feet, shaking with wrath. 'How dare you refuse to give the respectability of your name to Isabelle—to take advantage of her and then to simply cast her off the way your grandfather…' She halted, breathing heavily as she struggled to bring her anger and her emotions under control. When she next spoke her voice had lost its strength under the strain and at the possibility of opening old wounds.

'Forgive me. This has nothing to do with the past. It is about Isabelle and saving her from ruin. You kissed her—and, yes, I know you found her in your bedchamber, but that did not give you the right to lay your hands on her.'

Suddenly Belle, who had remained a silent observer during her grandmother's outburst, went to her and took her arm with concern. 'Please do not upset yourself, Grandmother. I am sure all this can be sorted out in a calm and reasonable manner.' Drawing herself up straight and squaring her shoulders, looking more like Miss Isabelle Ainsley than she ever had, she fixed Lord Bingham with a level stare.

'I can understand your reticence to marry me, Lord Bingham, and you know I have no more desire to marry you than you have to marry me. We will take our leave of you now, but before we do so I feel that I must say that your behaviour from the very beginning has not been what I would expect from a man of your standing.'

'You are absolutely right and I apologise for any distress I may have caused to you and the servants who were with you that night on the road. For what it's worth, I had no intention of harming any of you.'

'Faced with a masked highwayman with a pistol pointed at us, we weren't to know that. As far as I am concerned the matter is closed.'

'Not quite,' her grandmother said. Taking a velvet box from her reticule, she placed it carefully on a table to the side of Lord Bingham. Slightly puzzled, he looked from the box to her. 'The diamonds, Lord Bingham. The time has come to return them. It will be a relief to be rid of them after all these years. They have been a permanent reminder of a time that is painful for me to remember.'

'You didn't have to hold on to them, Countess.'

'Pride, Lord Bingham. It was pride that made me hold on to them—which you should know all about. I will ask you for the last time. Will you reconsider your decision and marry my granddaughter?'

In the same tone of voice in which he would have shoved away a hand offering a box of sweetmeats to him, he said, 'No, Countess, certainly not.'

The countess understood that his decision was irrevocable. She had lost. 'Then if you will excuse us, I will not waste any more of my time. Come, Isabelle.'

The countess swept out of the room, followed by her granddaughter. A deadly calm had settled over Belle, banishing everything but her shame and humiliation. There was nothing she could do. Her grandmother's arguments had slid off him like a smooth, frozen block of ice. Her grandmother could not compel a man to marry her granddaughter when he neither loved nor desired her and when his self-interest could be served as well by some other solution. Pride alone might perhaps constrain him.

She looked squarely at Lord Bingham as he held the door open for her to pass through, and as she met his gaze her small chin lifted and her spine stiffened. Lance saw her put up a valiant fight for control—a fight she won—and she looked as regally erect as a proud young queen as she followed after her grandmother, a dark blue hat on her head instead of a crown.

Only the ragged pulse that had leapt to life in his throat attested to Lance's own disquiet as he stared after her with mingled feelings of regret and concern. However, he was relieved he had escaped from the dilemma and seized on his own instinct that the dowager countess was not serious in her threat to have him charged. He had also mentally listed all the reasons why he was reluctant to marry again—why he should not sacrifice himself on the altar of matrimony with Belle Ainsley.

But as he had stared at the proud young beauty before him, he could not put from his mind that by his own actions, if the scandal did indeed hit society like the explosion of a thousand guns, he would have inadvertently, but effectively, destroyed her future. If not for his damnable pride, he might have broken his guise of stoic reticence and agreed to marry her. He'd be wiser by far to test the susceptibility of his own heart where she was concerned before he severed his association with her completely.

The simple truth was that he was strongly attracted to Belle Ainsley and she was far too beautiful for any man to turn his back on. Though his eyes saw the door through which she had just passed through, her face was imprinted all over it and the force of his feelings astounded him. He was quite bewildered by the emotion he felt in his heart. He couldn't really describe what he felt for her because he didn't have any words. All he knew was that he felt strange, wonderful, different from anything he had ever expected to feel or would ever feel again. It was as if he had spent his whole life waiting for her to be there, but marriage to her was out of the question.

On leaving Lord Bingham's house, something inside Belle, some bright and hopeful light that shone brighter whenever she thought of him, faded and winked out of existence. But out of sheer pride she held herself tightly together around the emptiness, not wanting to betray the desolation she felt.

Belle thought she could not feel any more humiliated than she had on her last encounter with Lord Bingham at his house, but she soon discovered she was mistaken. He continued to remain a popular figure at any event. This was not so for Belle. In every well-to-do house— above and below stairs—there was a hunger for a bit of scandal. Those that had been present to witness her disgraceful escapade gossiped, and what they had to divulge about her visit to Lord Bingham's house and the time she must have spent in his bedchamber, was liberally embroidered and flew like a forest fire from house to house.

From that time onwards no callers, no entertaining billet doux which she usually received from her admirers, and which she generally enjoyed reading as a flattering diversion, arrived at the house in Hampstead. Belle could not have imagined the effect it would have. Reluctant to go out, for the first few days she remained secluded within the house, needing somehow the security of the solid walls around her. But despite her self-imposed seclusion she had no doubt the whole of society knew what she had done and that she would have to face everyone soon.

Having abandoned her decision to go to Wiltshire, for she had no wish to be seen to running away from a situation that would confirm what everyone believed, the Dowager Countess of Harworth decided to sit it out. To Belle's surprise her grandmother was sympathetic to the way she was being treated and not even her influence could persuade people to change their minds. In the eyes of the *ton* she had broken all the rules governing moral conduct. She was unfit company for virtuous young ladies and gullible heirs, a shameless wanton soiled and used.

Belle dragged her thoughts from the memories of the handsome, blue-eyed man who haunted every moment of her days and nights, and despite the despicable way he had treated her, she was unable to dismiss her hungering guilt at having actually enjoyed the things he had done to her. She was unable to blot out of her mind the exquisite sweetness of the moments she'd spent in his arms, the memory of his passionate kisses, of his whispered words of passion, for they kept returning to torment her, and she couldn't prevent it.

* * *

Not to be defeated—and by no means having given up on Lord Bingham doing the honourable thing by Isabelle—the countess persuaded Belle to attend a function she had been invited to before the scandal became public—a ball at Lord and Lady Schofield's house in Mayfair.

Belle shuddered at the thought of what might happen. 'I cannot do it. I cannot face everyone.'

'Yes, you can. You won't be alone. I shall be with you and you have spirit enough to withstand what everyone will put you through. If you are seen out and about, it will help stem the gossip until the next unfortunate young lady falls from grace and they will lose all interest in you.'

And so Belle gave in.

Less than half an hour in the crowded ballroom, she was painfully aware of the extent of her disgrace. It was the first time since she had come out into society when she was not surrounded by admiring beaux. Those friends and acquaintances who did not wish to distance themselves from the influential Dowager Countess of Harworth were polite and courteous, but didn't hesitate to cast scathing glances at Belle. She responded mechanically to the few cold greetings addressed to her. It seemed to her that the sun had gone out and that life tasted of ashes.

Heads turned, and she couldn't fail to notice the censorious way people looked at her and whispered behind their fans. They had plenty of reasons to criticise her and she hated them all, loathed every prying eye. They were all strangers, brittle, sophisticated strangers, who resented her intrusion into their select society and who were relishing the mortifying situation in which she now found herself.

Determined to put on a brave face and keeping her head high, in a state of consuming misery Belle stood on the side of the dance floor, watching the dancers whirl by, while drowning in humiliation and making a magnificent effort to pin a smile on her face and avoid the malicious eyes that made her skin burn. Nothing of what she saw penetrated her thoughts, for her mind moved like a disembodied wraith through everything but the quandaries she faced. Afraid she would lose her slender thread of control and the tears shining in her eyes would find their way down her cheeks, her grandmother never left her side.

From a distance, witnessing Belle's humiliation at first hand, believing he had had a hand in her downfall by exposing her at Lance's house and mortified by it, Sir Rowland Gibbon left to seek out his friend at his club, to take him to task for feeding a beautiful young woman to the wolves, for in his opinion that stupid wager had been the beginning of her fall from grace.

Striding into the gaming room of the dimly lit exclusive gentleman's club, which was not lacking for wealthy occupants willing to wager enormous sums of money on the turn of a card, Rowland found Lance just finishing an unsuccessful game of faro. On seeing his friend he stood up, the expression on his face dour.

Rowland laughed lightly. 'For a man who is usually lucky at cards, Lance, you have a remarkably sour look on your face.'

An ironic smile twisted Lance's lips. 'Tonight isn't a good night. As you know I normally find cards a pleasurable occupation, but tonight my concentration is elsewhere. Come and join me in a drink.'

The two men left the card room and seated themselves in two comfortable armchairs. Lance nodded to a footman to bring two drinks to their table.

After a few minutes of companionable silence, Rowland said, 'I've just come from the Schofields' ball in Mayfair—a splendid affair as usual.'

'Then why aren't you still there?'

'I came to seek you out. The Dowager Countess of Harworth has taken it upon herself to defy the whole *ton* and introduce Miss Ainsley back into the ranks, which, considering what I witnessed tonight, is no mean feat. The object is to try to brave it out, but I don't envy the beautiful Belle.'

With a grimace of annoyance, Lance leaned back in his chair and picked up his glass. 'What has this got to do with me, Rowland?'

'It has everything to do with you,' he pointed out, trying unsuccessfully to keep his voice blank as he crossed his legs in front of him.

Lance stared icily at his friend. 'In what way?'

'Belle Ainsley has been given the cut direct from half the *ton*. It seems grossly unfair to me that while she is being ostracised so severely, the unprincipled reprobate who brought so much unhappiness into her life should be enjoying such good fortune when her future looks so bleak.'

The glass in Lance's hand froze halfway to his lips. 'You exaggerate, Rowland. Miss Isabelle Ainsley is a beautiful young woman who is proving to be the biggest success of the Season.'

'That was before she encountered you. Ever since it

became known that she spent some time alone with you in your bedchamber, it's been public knowledge that she's used goods.' Rowland watched with grim satisfaction as a muscle began to twitch in Lance's rigid jaw. 'It is a brave thing she is doing—showing herself in the face of so much hostility. Think yourself fortunate that the countess didn't bring a charge against you for highway robbery. As a result of everything you have done, Miss Ainsley is at the mercy of the *ton* and will probably have to leave London and live in shamed seclusion in Wiltshire.'

'Come, Rowland, you exaggerate.'

Rowland looked at him askance. 'You really have no idea, do you, Lance?'

'With the Season winding to a close, in the two weeks since I last saw her, apart from going to my club, I've immersed myself in business matters, for I fully intend leaving for Ryhill within days. And also,' he added with contempt, 'among what is amusingly called polite society, matters that concern you personally are never discussed openly—only behind one's back. How is she bearing up?'

'She isn't—if what I have just witnessed is anything to go by. The first time I saw her, her sparkle almost knocked me off my feet—but now that sparkle lacks lustre and she is just going through the motions. She will undoubtedly find it hard to forgive you for the transgression against her.'

Lance had given little thought to how Belle must be suffering the *ton*'s rejection. Silently cursing himself, he tossed down the contents of his glass as if he wanted to wash away the bitterness of his friend's verbal attack. He didn't try to defend himself. How could he? What

Rowland said was true and it brought home to him his own cruel treatment of that beautiful young woman.

Thoughts of his father came to mind. As his only male offspring, his father had sought to share his wisdom he had gleaned from his own experiences, teaching his son not merely with words but through example. Above all he had shown him the true meaning of duty and honour, which Lance had put into practice many times in his military career and his daily life—the same duty and honour that had been absent in his treatment of Delphine, but which he must apply to dealing with this situation of Belle.

As so often of late and to his absolute chagrin, he found himself once more beset by visions of her. He remembered how she had looked when he had come upon her in his room, the golden candlelight on her creamy skin, her softly curling hair about her face, and his thoughts brought to mind how those sweet and gentle arms had felt about his neck, and how her subtle body had curved into his own.

Though he had once thought himself immune to the subtle ploys of women, even though he had known her for such a short time, he had begun to think he would never be free of Belle. From the very beginning she had stirred his baser instincts. Yet much as she ensnared his thoughts, he found his dreams daunting to his manly pride, for whenever she flitted through them like some puckish sprite, he felt more like a slave than a conqueror. Although he'd have greatly preferred to limit her constant assaults on his thoughts and his poorly depleted restraint, he was beginning to suspect that, in comparison, standing firm against Napoleon's forces had been child's play.

He was caught in a trap, and unable to think of a means of escape from this dilemma that had presented itself, he felt the noose of matrimony tighten inexorably around his neck. If he married Belle, he would not come out too badly. But for now he was furious that by his own behaviour he was being forced into making a decision that was thoroughly distasteful to him, and not having the upper hand.

'The way I see it,' Rowland went on, 'you have done her a great disservice. You have no choice except to rescue her from what she is suffering now. There is no lack of beaux at the ball, but not one will partner her. Good Lord, Lance, the lady could not be blamed if she took it into her head to hate you for this.'

An indescribable expression flashed across Lance's face as he slammed his glass down and surged out of his chair. 'I don't intend to give her the opportunity,' he replied in an implacable voice.

'Now what?'

'To the Schofields' ball, but before that I shall recruit as many unattached males from the club who will be utterly delighted to partner Miss Isabelle Ainsley at the ball. I must also stop at my house to change into my evening clothes, and arriving at the ball I will speak to the Dowager Countess of Harworth. '

'Really?' This would be worth seeing and Rowland, determined not to miss such a momentous occurrence, shot after him. 'I'm coming with you.'

Latecomers to the Schofields' ball were still coming through the door, the butler's monotone rhythmic tones rising above the noise. *Lord and Lady Hazelwood. Sir Thomas and Lady Mortimer. The Earl of Ryhill...*

Belle's eyes opened wide and she blanched, not daring to look at the man who was the architect of all her troubles. There was a dread, sick feeling in the pit of her stomach, yet in her heart, pounding heavily, bloomed an odd sense of elation.

'I would like to leave,' she said to her grandmother in a furious voice.

An odd quiet was sweeping over the room as heads turned to stare at the new arrival, and after they had had a good look, turned to look at Belle with raised brows. She knew exactly how their collective minds worked. They were eager to see what would happen next. Would Lord Bingham acknowledge her—or would he cut her dead?

Having no wish to wait and find out, she said, 'I cannot possibly stay now.'

The countess read what was written on her granddaughter's face. 'Don't even consider leaving,' she stated quietly but firmly. 'Get a grip on yourself and see it out.'

Looking towards the door, Belle felt her legs begin to tremble and a gasp rose in her throat, for clad in black evening clothes and wearing an expression of mild amusement, was Lord Bingham, the Earl of Ryhill. Her shock was superseded by a feeling of unreality as she watched him prowl the outer limits of the dance floor like some sleek, powerful panther.

Lance stood on the sidelines, a solitary, brooding man looking with a bored expression on his handsome face at the scene before him, and then he saw the tawny-haired goddess and his heart lurched. Though he made every effort to resist her appeal, he could feel the meagre store of his resolve waning. At times like these, he had cause to wonder why he had refused the Dowager Countess of Harworth's offer of her granddaughter's hand in marriage, for the only person he was punishing was himself. He couldn't imagine the virtuous Belle being tormented by cravings of the magnitude he had recently been suffering. But marriage? God damn it! He didn't want to get married, not to anyone. Never again.

Belle was looking at him, pale and stricken and very lovely—and furious. Seeing how the fashionable set shunned her and whispered about her, he was angry, but managed to appear superbly relaxed and smiled slightly before turning to speak to an acquaintance.

It was difficult for him not to cut a way to her side, but if he was going to make things right for her it was important to play out a charade and appear casual. Since he couldn't stop the gossip about his relationship with her, he had set out to turn it about, to ensure the attention was directed in a way he wanted it directed. He knew everyone was watching them both, positively bursting for a firsthand *on dit* about his relationship with her and what actually had happened between them when they had been alone together in his bedroom.

He mingled with the throng, giving a nod here and pausing now and then to shake hands and speak with an acquaintance, but all the while never losing sight of Belle. His eyes followed the undulating sway of her gown that flowed and shimmered in glistening waves about her long legs.

Another waltz was starting when Sir Rowland Gibbon suddenly appeared by Belle's side.

'Come, Miss Ainsley, dance with me.'

He led her on to the floor and danced her into the midst of the twirling couples, and the fact that Sir Rowland Gibbon was championing her was immediately remarked upon. Swallowed up by other dancers,

Belle breathed a sigh of relief. She was safe for the time being, but then a humiliating thought occurred to her and she scowled up at her partner.

'I have been an outcast all night and suddenly you ask me to dance. Did you want to dance with me by any chance, or did Lord Bingham tell you to?'

Rowland grinned down at her, his face very boyish and amiable now he had bowed to Lance's pressure and shaved off his beard. 'Lance has much to thank you for. He regrets what has happened to you and wishes to make amends. He has asked me to tell you not to worry and that everything will turn out right.'

Belle's eyes widened with shock. 'Amends?' She shook her head at the sheer absurdity of what he was saying. 'He can make as many *amends* as her likes, but he cannot escape the fact that because of him I am well and truly ruined. As far as I am concerned, I want nothing more to do with that arrogant Earl. I would appreciate it if he would keep as far away from me as it's possible for the time we are here.'

Chapter Six

Of course Lance had no intention of doing any such thing. A flamboyant young lord who had been drinking heavily latched on to him, and following his gaze as he watched Sir Rowland Gibbon dancing with Belle, he remarked, 'Miss Isabelle Ainsley is a beauty, is she not? But then you would know, wouldn't you,' he uttered with a leering grin, 'having had her all to yourself—in your bedchamber. You must have come to know the lady—intimately.' Showing his lack of polish—and also his inability to hold his drink—he gave Lance a nudge and a knowing wink.

Lance nodded without changing his expression, and taking a glass of wine from a tray raised it to his lips. 'Do I?' he said in an amused tone.

The gentleman snorted with surprise and disappointment. 'You mean you don't?'

'That is precisely what I mean.' Then he automatically added a proviso to forestall further gossip. 'However, I count myself fortunate to be on friendly terms with all the Ainsleys.'

The gentleman heard that with some surprise. 'You don't say? But I thought your two families were…'

Lance lifted his eyebrows with some amusement. 'What? At daggers drawn? It is nothing but lamentable nonsense and people should learn to separate the rubbish from the truth. Over the years there has been a gross lack of understanding. Don't believe a word of it.'

'But you were alone together, and you did compromise the lady?'

Unable to deny it since everyone knew Belle had spent time with him alone, instead of throwing a punch as he was sorely tempted to do, Lance said, 'The whole of London knows it to be true—but it was a ruse of mine to get her alone.'

'And?'

'And nothing. I lured her to my house with the promise of returning some property I had taken from her. It was not through want of trying on my part. Miss Ainsley—who is a paragon of virtue and a finer example of refinement you couldn't hope to meet—would have none of it. I succeeded in getting her alone, but she soon gave me my come-uppance and left. I'm here tonight in the hope that she'll accept my apology and look on me with more favour.'

'Perhaps she will,' the lord chuckled. 'Nothing as fickle as women, eh?'

And so saying he left to impart this new bit of information to his friends, that the beautiful Miss Isabelle Ainsley had repulsed the powerful Earl of Ryhill and that particular bit of information was far more interesting than that he had seduced her.

Standing aside, Lance watched with satisfaction as the story was circulated and within no time at all male heads

turned to look at Belle with renewed interest and speculation, and several hesitantly presented themselves to the
dowager countess and requested she introduce them to
her granddaughter. While remaining curious at this
change in direction, she was more than happy to oblige.

However, everything was explained when Lord Bingham had arrived and requested to speak with her alone,
telling her that he had come to stem the gossip about
Miss Ainsley. Seeing the sense of his words, that they
combine forces to dispel this nonsense that was in danger of ruining her granddaughter completely, she had
agreed. When he had left her she had been a quiet observer of his movements.

It was with a sense of unreality that Belle danced
with these gentlemen who had lost their aversion to her.
She smiled politely and listened to their comments, but
her only real feeling was that she was no longer ostracised. She even danced again with Sir Rowland, and was
not aware when he looked at Lance or of the moment
when Lance tipped his head that Rowland danced her
on to the wide stone terrace, where he left her with the
excuse of going to get two glasses of champagne.

A man came on to the dimly lit terrace and a voice
said, 'At last. I was beginning to think I would never get
you alone.'

Shock stiffened Belle's body. For a split second, her
feet rooted to the ground, then abruptly she turned away
from him. 'Go away. I have no wish to speak to you.'

He moved slowly towards her and took her arm.

Belle could feel fury bubbling up inside her. 'Let
go,' she snapped and jerked her arm. She would have
fled back inside, but he held her fast. Her voice broke
with the anger she felt. 'I said let go.'

'Easy, Belle,' he said, releasing her arm. 'You and I have a matter to discuss.'

Spinning round, she glared at the handsome, forceful, dynamic man standing before her. He looked powerful, aloof and disgustingly self-assured. 'Anything we have to say has been said. After everything that has happened, how dare you feel you have the right to approach me? How dare you try to manipulate me as if I am yours to direct— just as though you have a perfect right to? Now go away.'

Even in the meagre light, her unparalleled beauty proved a strong lodestone from which Lance could not drag his gaze. Quietly, he said, 'Will you calm down and listen to what I have to say?'

Belle did her best to hold in the resentment she felt, to be dignified, as a lady of her class would be, but it was very hard and her expression was icy. 'Nothing you can say can undo what you have done to me.'

'I would like to try.'

'And I suppose this was your doing—getting your friend to bring me out here?'

'There is nothing untoward in that, Belle. I merely wanted to talk with you privately for a few moments. After all that has happened, I thought it especially needful tonight.'

'Why tonight?'

Lance bent his head, considering how best to approach the subject. 'Personally I don't care a damn what people think of me, but no matter what you think, it is not my wish to cause more gossip that will hurt you.'

Her face working with the strength of her emotions, which had, for the moment, got the better of her, reluctantly Belle gazed up at him. In the dim light his eyes shone softly down into hers. His words, spoken quietly and with gravity, made her wary. 'It's a little late for that. You must have seen how I am being treated in there. They might as well have tarred and feathered me and tied me to a lamppost.'

At any other time Lance would have laughed at the image her words conjured up in his mind, but now he would not insult her by doing so, for the strain of what she had gone through—was still going through—was there on her lovely, troubled face for him to see.

'You have been treated harshly. You did not deserve that. For what it's worth I'm sorry and would like to put it right.'

'Ha,' she scoffed. 'What are you all of a sudden— some kind of wizard? All those partners. You made them dance with me, didn't you?'

'They were easily manipulated.'

Belle was so humiliated by his answer that it took her a moment to reply. 'Have you any idea how humiliating it is for me to know that?' she fumed.

He shrugged nonchalantly. 'It needn't be. Those men wanted to dance with you. They are not nearly as malicious as their female counterparts and were looking for any excuse to lead you on to the floor. I provided them with the answer.'

Gazing at the cool, dispassionate man standing before her, looking so powerful, aloof and completely self-assured, Belle managed a nervous little laugh and said sarcastically, 'Not only are you an accomplished soldier on the field of battle, my lord. You also appear to have a gift for strategy and subtlety on the dance floor, too.'

'I do my best,' he replied, ignoring her sarcasm. 'There is also a rumour circulating that I was the one who pursued you, that I was responsible for you being in my bedchamber, and that you evaded my advances.'

'And who started this rumour?'

'I did. So far most people in there are starting to think you might have been wrongly maligned.'

'I can't argue with that.'

Lance's eyes glowed with the reflected light of the lanterns as he watched her unrelentingly for a lengthy space, heightening Belle's tensions until she could hardly stand the suspense. Rather than leave herself open to his unyielding stare, she turned her head away.

'I think I should go back inside. Grandmother will be wondering where I've got to.'

'Come and dance with me. I have no doubt the tongues will wag even harder, but let them. This time they will wag to a different tune.'

'I'm supposed to be evading you, remember,' Belle retorted cuttingly. 'What will everyone say when we suddenly appear and take to the floor?'

He grinned. 'They'll see how weak you are and can no longer resist my manly charms.'

She looked at him coolly. 'Don't flatter yourself— and don't you think you should seek my grandmother's favour first?'

'Somehow I don't think your grandmother will raise any objections, and will be happy to combine forces if it stills the gossip.'

'You mean I'm not completely ruined?'

'Not if you marry me.'

Belle paled, unable to believe what he had said. Her anger stirred. 'Marry? I think you've taken leave of your senses. I recall you telling me in no uncertain terms that you didn't want to marry me,' she said with cold, quiet dignity, lifting her chin and stiffening her spine. 'In fact, you made it bitingly clear that you didn't want me for your wife.'

'That was then. This is now. I've changed my mind,' he said flatly.

She frowned, giving a hard, sceptical look. 'Changed your mind? As easy as that? Why? Is it pity or guilt that has prompted you to ask me—that has prompted you to do the honourable thing?' she demanded.

He shook his head, knowing she would suspect this—and as proud as she was, her pride would make her oppose him. 'Neither. I care enough about you to be hurt by the dreadful way you have been treated by society. You do not deserve that.'

'No, I don't—and I thank you for your concern,' she remarked with heavily laden sarcasm. 'Whether it is genuine or not means little to me. Your honourable nature is to be applauded, but you don't have to feel under any obligation to marry me.'

'I don't.'

Belle's chin lifted even higher at his suddenly chilling tone. 'I told you I didn't want to marry you. Have you, in your arrogance, assumed that I have changed my mind?'

'It has been known for some women to do so,' he stated rudely.

'And I recall telling you I am not like most women.'

'I know that too.'

'So we won't marry.'

Lance stared at the scornful young woman who was regarding him down the length of her pert nose and felt a glimmer of respect that she would dare to take him to task over what he was offering, which was to her advantage. 'On the contrary. I have already spoken to your grandmother. It is settled.'

His smoothly worded statement made Belle almost choke on her chagrin. 'You have done this without consulting me first? How dare you do that? You had no right. None whatsoever.'

'I had every right,' he said coldly. 'Your grandmother was the one who approached me, remember. Do not forget that in order to punish me she threatened to have me publicly charged with highway robbery and attempted seduction.'

'She would not do that. She was bluffing.'

'Maybe she was, but it is a risk I am not prepared to take. Do me the justice to admit that we were both responsible for the circumstances to bring about a union between the two of us, so that now it's a question of that union being a success. It is in both our interests. It is obvious that in marrying me—'

'It is not obvious at all,' Belle cut in irately. 'In marrying you I do not make a love match or even one I could possibly approve of. I might even say I make a forced marriage. Would it be a great surprise to you if I told you that the feelings you inspire in me, far from resembling love, rather approach a feeling of anger?'

Lance did not seem surprised or insulted. Undaunted, he lifted his brows quizzically, a twist of humour about his beautifully moulded lips. 'I can imagine,' he said, shrugging his shoulders in a way that Belle hoped was casual, but at the same time she was filled with pain. But why should she care whether he loved her or not? He was offering her a life line, to enable her to hold up her head in society and not have to listen to the slights and slurs, the whispers and jeers. Why should she care about the rest?

'I ask you to put aside your feelings and see marriage to me as a way forwards. Otherwise...'

'Otherwise?'

'You'll be dreadfully unhappy.'

Belle's face hardened, and she said through clenched teeth, 'Because of you, I have already been unhappy. I have no intention of starting all over again.'

'It needn't be like that. You won't find me a cruel husband—and you'll find me generous, I promise you.'

'That is not what I mean,' Belle burst out a little hysterically. 'You expect me to be grateful for your generosity and that I should submit to you accordingly. You speak of marrying me as if you're discussing a—a business arrangement—without any feeling or emotion, without even a pretence of...'

'Of what, Belle? Of love?' As he held her gaze his features noticeably hardened. 'You have just told me that a union between the two of us will not be a love match, so I assume you have no illusions about that,' he sneered at her coldly. 'Love is a word that is so overused it loses its meaning and force. It is a word used to manipulate idiots. I am sure you will agree.'

Hearing her words quoted back at her with such frankness, Belle stepped back and turned away from him, wrapping her arms around her waist as she thought about what to do, knowing he was waiting for her answer. He obviously didn't want to marry her—in fact, she suspected he must have thought hard for some way out of marrying her, for he seemed to dislike her intensely, but as he had shown when they had been alone together, he desired her too. Then again, perhaps she was only trying to fool herself into believing it.

Unable to see her face, Lance moved to stand behind

her. Now he had made up his mind to marry her, he could not understand her reticence. Was he not doing her an honour by consenting to make her his wife? How dare she argue and defy him? How dare she challenge him?

'Well? How far have you got in making your decision?' he asked harshly.

Belle stirred and seemed to wake from a bad dream. 'It's agreed. I will marry you.' She turned and faced him. 'But I want to say that after what you have done and my own aversion to you, I was wounded by your harsh refusal to consider my grandmother's suggestion that you do the honourable thing and consider me for your future wife. Have you any idea how difficult and humiliating that was for her? The fact that it was you who started the whole thing by taking the diamonds, and that disgusting wager with your friend, made your rejection all the more painful.'

'But you do agree to the marriage?'

'Yes. I respect your decision, but I know this is not what you planned or even what you want.'

'No, it isn't,' he stated frankly, 'and I won't pretend otherwise. I made that plain enough when your grandmother came to see me and I take nothing back. My freedom has always been important to me, and I am averse to relinquishing it.'

For a lengthy moment, Lance's deep blue eyes probed the dark depths of hers. He was profoundly aware of the enchanting young woman's body standing close to him and her intoxicating perfume. His entire personality was pervaded by a shrewdness that had never taken principles into account, but only the fluctuations of human nature. He was clever, and he knew that when he held a woman in his arms he was very powerful. There was always a moment when the woman's self-defence yielded before the lure of sensual rapture and he knew how to turn that moment to his advantage. If Belle was to be his wife, then perhaps he didn't have to wait for the wedding night to enslave her. It was a pleasing thought, one he intended to act upon.

'However,' he went on, his eyes suddenly teasing as his hands went to her shoulders and he drew her near, his voice low and seductive, 'I do find myself attracted to you. It just so happens that I want you, Belle—you cannot condemn me for that—and I know you want me. We have wanted each other every time we have been together. You are beautiful, innocent and courageous, passionate and stubborn—and I hope you will forgive my wrongdoings and get to like me.'

Feeling perilously close to tears, Belle dropped her gaze, unable to absorb the amazing revelation that he was actually attracted to her. 'I liked Carlton Robinson when we first met,' she whispered. 'After a couple of days I couldn't stand the sight of him and couldn't wait to be rid of him. It would seem that I have poor judgement in the matter of men. Maybe I should change my mind about marrying you.'

'Belle,' he said softly, 'you have no choice if you want come out of this with your reputation intact. Come, let me look at you,' he cajoled gently, but when she complied by raising her head, his brows gathered in perplexity. The tears glistening in the long, silken lashes were hard to ignore. Laying a hand alongside her cheek, he gently wiped away a droplet with his thumb. 'What has happened is not so bad that you should feel a need to cry.'

Embarrassed because she couldn't contain her

emotions, Belle responded with a shake of her head. 'I'm not.'

'Come now, your lashes are wet. If they aren't tears, then I would have to think it is raining, and yet I cannot feel it.'

Belle recognised the threat of her emotions were about to get the better of her once more and she stepped away from him, away from the gentle touch of his hand on her cheek. It certainly didn't help her composure now to feel a resurgence of the various sensations she had experienced when they had been alone together in his bedchamber. Though sorely lacking experience in the realms of desire, instinct assured her the wanton yearnings gnawing away inside her were nothing less than cravings that Lance Bingham had elicited with what he had done to her that night she had crept into his bedroom.

'I'm all right. It was just a moment of weakness, that's all. It has passed.'

'And you're sure of that, are you, Belle?'

Before she could prepare herself, his arms rose and dragged her to him. And then he was kissing her hair, her cheek, and caressing her lips with his own. His lips moved on hers, the fierceness changing to softness, to the velvet touch of intoxication. An eternity later he pulled his mouth from hers and looked down into her eyes, which were warm and velvety soft.

'That was a mistake,' Belle said desperately.

His lips quirked in a faint smile. 'Then let's make another one.'

As he spoke he took her hand and led her down the terrace steps into the darkness of the garden beyond and away from prying eyes. His tall figure dark against the shadows, with just enough light from the house to see her by, he reached out and pulled her to him. His eyes were like flames of fire, scorching her.

Belle was astounded at her body's reaction to this man. A touch, a kiss, a look, and he could rouse her, and something rose and shouted for the joy of it. Her heart was pounding in her breast and she could feel his beating against hers to the same rapid rhythm. She pressed herself close to him, not with fury but with delight, with something she had felt before when he had kissed her, which she knew was the female in her responding to the male in him. It was madness. She made a sound in her throat and she threw back her head in the exultation of the moment.

'You do want me, don't you, Belle?' Lance triumphed softly, her breath sweet and warm against his mouth as she still clung to him. 'Say it. Your heart beats far too quickly for you to claim uninterest, my love.'

She was dazed, her eyes unfocused with that soft loveliness that comes when a woman is deep in the pleasures of love, her senses completely overruled by this magic that had sprung up between them. Cupping her chin, he began to kiss her face, her eyelids, her cheeks. Her lips trembled as he again claimed them fiercely with his own.

'My God,' he whispered hoarsely, his blue eyes smouldering as he gazed at her upturned face. 'You are the most direct, self-willed woman I have ever met, traits I admire in any woman, but you are also so damn lovely and desirable.' Pulling her down on to a bench, in the semi-darkness, where the light of the moon contended with the glow from the occasional lantern, the sight of her white shoulders, the fragile neck, aroused in him a violent but unfamiliar desire, such as no woman had ever aroused in him. It was not just blind and bestial lust. There was about it a somewhat mysterious, almost sweet and gentle allure.

Covering her mouth with his own once more, his lips moved against hers, his breath on her mouth. His hand caressed her hard nippled breasts and seemed not to want to stop, before sliding carelessly under her gown and over her thighs as he kissed her passionately. His lips touched her cheeks and moved to her throat and Belle shivered involuntarily at their burning intensity and the touch of his hand on her bare flesh. Her conscience told her to fight him, but there was no fight in her and her senses staggered with ecstasy. Her whole being seemed to burst into flame, while delicious sensations overwhelmed her. The feel of him, the smell of him, all combined to transfix her. She hardly noticed the moment when he lifted her off the hard bench and placed her on the cool, soft, sweet-smelling grass.

Clinging together, their world became one of passion and incoherent sound and heat. From the ballroom the strains of music and voices floated on the night air, and overhead an owl screeched, but the lovers were deaf and blind to everything but each other. When Lance raised her skirts Belle caught a flash of her own rounded thighs, pale and lustrous, above her silk stockings. She became aware that she was holding her breath, that her face and breasts were hot as if a fire had burned them. Drawing her breast from her bodice, Lance cupped it in his hand and kissed and sucked it with his mouth. Belle had never been touched there by a man before, and the sensations he created drove her almost out of her mind.

She was conscious of a trembling throughout her body and desired, above all things, to feel his hard, lean body pressed to hers. He carried on kissing her and caressing her, arousing her until thought and feeling, heart and head became a liquid flame. He drew out all her suppressed longings, freeing her passion until she could deny him nothing. She obeyed the passions of her body, caught up in an agonisingly sweet, yet terrible intensity. Lance lay on her and she felt the strength of him as he held her unresisting body close and took her, penetrating deeply. She held him to her as he took his pleasure of her, moaning with pleasure and pain of her own. Entwined, Belle was conscious of nothing but a wild ecstasy as they merged together, each fulfilling the other in the most sublime act of making love.

Lance gloried in the feel of Belle's pliant, firm young body straining against his. It was like a yielding, living substance as she gave all her desire and passion, responding to his inner heat. Her slender arms wrapped around his neck as their mouths fastened hungrily on one another, hers moist and warm. A man well used to the lusty pleasures that were always available to him, Lance had not until he had met Belle held a woman in his arms who was not only young but innocent, untouched and pure, with a serene beauty that delighted him.

Then it was over and for a time Belle had no immediate thoughts. She had nothing but the memory of incredible joy, of something immense that had happened to her, beyond which nothing was comparable. Opening her eyes, she saw Lance's face bent over her. Wanting to hold the moment and feel him close to her, she was disappointed when he moved away and stood up, calmly adjusting his clothing. Belle sat upright, confused, her body still pulsating with heat and the feel of his body joined to hers. She couldn't believe that she had given herself to him because of deeper feelings she did not fully understand.

Lance took her hand and pulled her to her feet. He smiled as she struggled to compose herself, relieved that they were alone in the garden and no one had come to find them.

'Are you all right?' he asked, raising his hand and gently caressing her cheek. He was looking down at her, his gaze penetrating. Her eyes were dark and huge in her pale face, and her skin gleamed like soft silk in the dim light. She was as bewitching as any pagan statue, and she had responded to him not as a girl but as a woman. He was not disappointed. However, his body's almost uncontrollable desire for her had amazed, unnerved and thoroughly displeased him. He would not touch her again until she was his wife.

Belle nodded, lowering her eyes and smoothing her skirts, suddenly shy of him. Even on the brink of surrender she had realised that she was on the point of giving something to him which by rights belonged only to a husband, and yet since Lance was to be her husband, oddly, she found neither shame nor scruples and felt no will to resist. Why not give him what he so boldly demanded, she had thought, what no woman could be sure of keeping once a man had made up his mind to take her by force or cunning?

'Do you feel any regrets?' he asked.

'Yes,' she confessed. 'I—I wish you had waited until—until we are married before you did that. I have been told a woman's virginity should be a highly valued gift to her husband. Should you decide not to marry me, who else will have me now?'

'Once I give my word about something, Belle, I never

retract it. We will be married, and the fact that you are no longer the chaste virgin of a moment ago matters little to me. Personally, I have never particularly prized virginity.' He shrugged with complete indifference. 'It doesn't matter.' He took her hand. 'Are you ready to go back inside?'

'Yes, I think we should.'

As he led her back to the ballroom, Belle wished he hadn't been so cavalier about her lost virginity. She wished it had been more important to him.

Word had spread of Lord Bingham's public defence of Miss Isabelle Ainsley. When she appeared on the dance floor with him, whatever had taken place between the two of them that had created the scandal seemed to have vanished. Observing the Dowager Countess of Harworth's expression of approval as she watched them dance together, those present concluded that a betrothal might be imminent after all. It was a possibility that distressed the lady's other suitors, and no matter how they vied with each other for her attention and argued amongst themselves, it was plain to see that Lord Bingham had prior claim.

On the day the betrothal of the Earl of Ryhill and Miss Isabelle Ainsley was announced in the newspaper, as arranged, Lance rode to Hampstead to discuss arrangements for the wedding with Belle's grandmother.

The dowager countess always kept her emotions under rigid control and in this instance she was feeling a grim and angry resignation towards the marriage of Isabelle to Lance Bingham. Entering the salon where he was waiting for her, as she regarded him she contemplated with bitter amusement this unexpected twist of fate. How had things come to this—her granddaughter marrying into the family she had distanced herself from for fifty years, and all because Lance Bingham's grandfather had rejected her love?

But this was no time to argue over former grievances. The brutal fact was that if this marriage didn't go ahead, then her granddaughter's chances of making a suitable marriage were negligible.

Seating herself in her favourite high-winged chair beside the hearth, with a nod of her head she indicated the chair opposite. She sat quite still, her back ramrod straight, her white head high, but the bitter disappointment of the last weeks had added a decade to her face.

'Isabelle will be in shortly. She's been riding on the Heath and has just returned.' She gave Lance a piercing look as he sat across from her and crossed his long, booted legs, thinking him a handsome devil despite everything. In fact, he was exactly the man she would have picked for her granddaughter, for he was a vigorous, forceful man to keep Isabelle well guarded and safe, especially now. She was a girl who needed firmness, a strong hand to guide her, but with care. 'Of course I would rather it hadn't come to this—you must know that.'

'I do—and no doubt my mother will be uneasy about it when I tell her, although she cannot fail to be taken with your granddaughter. When she has been made aware of the circumstances that have brought our betrothal about, she will agree that I am doing the right thing.'

'I understand your mother does not live at Ryhill?'

'No. She resides at Bilton House—which is where I was raised. As you know—since you are as familiar with the area as I am, it's a mere three miles from

Ryhill—not too far to visit. At present she is in Ireland—County Cork—which is where my sister Sophie
lives with her husband's family. Sophie is expecting her
first child and my mother travelled over to be with her.
When we have arranged a date for the wedding, I shall
write informing her of the event. Unfortunately she may
not be able to get back in time.'

'Like you say, that is unfortunate. You are quite certain about marrying Isabelle?'

'When I left the army I confess that marriage was not
in my immediate plans. However, what is done is done
and let me assure you that when Isabelle is my wife, I will
take care of her and do my utmost to make her happy.'

For the next fifteen minutes they discussed the terms
of the betrothal and the dowry, until the door was flung
open and Belle appeared, drawing their attention.

Belle's cheeks were still flushed from her ride and
her eyes glowed. She marvelled at the tingling rush of
excitement that affirmed Lance's presence, even before
she glanced in his direction. She was aware in that instant of a sudden pang in her breast, a familiar, wild, uncontrollable beat. Something in the brilliance of his
eyes made her catch her breath, and her flush deepened
when she remembered how wantonly she had given
herself to him at the Schofields' ball. She felt her body
heat with passion, and for once she did not care.

As she looked at him, the rush of familiar excitement
caused her to become tongue-tied, affected strongly as
she was by the force of his presence. She was all too
aware of the strong body that had pressed down on to
her own. Emotions swept over her and two spots of
high colour touched her cheeks as she remembered the
intense passion they had shared. Sometimes, at night,

she imagined him in her bed, and her skin would perspire, and a flame would flicker through her to gather in the deep recesses of her body, between her thighs, much to her disgust and rising passion. Her thoughts now were in disarray, desire and reason conflicting.

Warily she watched him rise to his feet with that panther's grace of his that seemed so much a part of him. At this shift in their relationship to that of an engaged couple, she found herself decidedly disarmed and equally aghast at her own shy response to him. But she was not so naïve as to believe his character had reformed in the three days since the ball when she had last seen him.

It didn't help her composure at all knowing that behind that charming mask of refined masculinity there lurked a disreputable rake bereft of any concern for how he used besotted young women for his own ease and pleasure. His kisses and caresses had been lethal in stripping away her resolve, and she realised she had cause to fear for she had become just as susceptible. He had aroused a yearning inside her for a repeat of his attentions, and she fervently wished she could banish the weeks until their wedding to the four winds.

With a growing sense of unreality she watched him move away from her grandmother and start toward her with long, purposeful strides. He grew larger as he neared, his broad shoulders blocking her view of the room, his blue eyes searching her face, the slight smile curving his lips one of arrogance and self-assurance.

'Good morning,' Lance said, his eyes running over her slender figure, clad in the sensuous softness of shimmering green velvet. Recalling the way he had made love to her at the ball, he dragged his eyes from the vee of her bodice and scanned her face for signs that she might have come to regret her decision, but there was no sign of it. Having given her time to reconsider her decision, would she have done so, he wondered, had he not taken her virtue?

'Good morning, Lance,' Belle said, unsure how engaged couples greeted each other. His expression was guarded, his eyes sharp and almost unfriendly as he looked at her. She was the only one who noted it, however, for he had his back to her grandmother. 'I'm sorry I wasn't here when you arrived. I've been riding on the Heath. It's such a lovely day I lost all track of the time.'

'I think some refreshment is in order,' the countess said. 'Ring the bell, will you, Isabelle?'

One of the servants appeared in answer to Belle's summons, then left to fetch a tray of drinks and food.

Cupping her elbow in the palm of his hand, Lance led Belle to a sofa and sat beside her. 'Your grandmother and I have just been discussing the terms of the betrothal.'

'Have you?' Belle found it incredible that he still intended going ahead with the wedding. He had told her he was attracted to her, that he cared for her. At least, she thought cynically, he didn't mouth words of love he didn't feel. Neither had he proposed to her with any show of affection, so she had accepted his proposal in the same unemotional way it had been offered.

'Will it be a large wedding?' she asked; considering Lance's title, his family and her own, she couldn't imagine it being anything else.

'You are the bride,' Lance answered. 'What would you prefer?'

'That it's not too large—if that's all right. I'm afraid I'd find it all rather daunting and would prefer a small affair.'

'Then that is how it will be.' He looked at her grand-mother. 'Are you in agreement, Countess?'

The dowager countess acquiesced with a regal nod of her head. 'Like you said, Isabelle is the bride—although I would prefer the wedding to take place at Harworth rather than here in town. The ceremony would be at the local church—where generations of Ainsleys are interred—the wedding celebrations at Harworth.'

'How long must we be betrothed?' Belle asked. 'A year? Six months?'

'Absolutely not,' Lance said irrevocably. Having already come firmly to the awareness that being within close proximity of Belle aroused every mating instinct he was capable of feeling, despite his aversion to the marriage itself, he was determined their betrothal would be of short duration. 'I wish to proceed with the court-ship with all possible haste.' He glanced at his fiancée sitting rigidly beside him. 'What say you, Belle? Do you have any objections as to the date upon which the testing of our emotions should begin? If you have none, then may I suggest that we start as from today?'

'No, I have no objections—that would be perfect.'

'You have to get to know each other,' the countess countered. 'The rules are strict. At the ball the other night you went to a great deal of trouble to make it seem there had been little but flirtation between the two of you. Unless you go through the appropriate courtship rituals, which Isabelle has every right to expect, no one will ever believe it. Although I am of the opinion that you conquered the highest hurdle that night and every-one will move on to talk about something else.'

'What do you have in mind?' Lance demanded shortly.

'A courtship never takes less than a year, but I will

concede and say six months,' the countess offered, com-
promising, 'of calling on her properly, escorting her to
the normal functions, and so on.'

'Two,' Lance announced flatly.

His imperious tone didn't daunt the countess in the
slightest. 'I suppose if it isn't to be a large wedding, it
could be arranged in two months,' she conceded. 'Now
the betrothal has been announced,' she said briskly,
looking at the newspaper beside her where she had been
reading the announcement before Lord Bingham's arrival, 'I would like to return to Harworth very soon—
next week at the latest—which should give us enough
time to begin preparations for Isabelle's wedding gown.
Then your courtship can be conducted away from the
prying eyes of the *ton*,' she said, reaching for the tea the
servant had just put in front of her.

'I would be honoured if you would both dine with me
this evening,' Lance offered amiably. 'Afterwards I will
be your escort to the Earl and Countess of Sidmouth's
party at Sidmouth House.' His gaze slid to Belle. 'After
all, it is the evening of our engagement and everyone
will expect to see us together. We can use the occasion
to set a pattern for our future—and enjoy everyone's surprise when they realise you really are to be the next
Countess of Ryhill.'

After they had drunk their tea and nibbled on cakes,
with the countess's permission, Lance took his future
wife for a turn about the garden.

After a few moments of strolling along the walkways
in an amiable but somewhat nervous silence, Belle said,
'None of this is easy for my grandmother. Despite her
haughty manner and plain speaking, she is finding it dif-

ficult to come to terms with my betrothal to you—as I am myself.'

'I am very much aware of that, Belle.'

'The reason why she is finding it difficult is stuck firmly in the past. I know that much. You said your grandmother kept a journal. I take it you have read it?'

He nodded. 'It certainly makes for interesting reading.'

'Will you tell me what you know?'

'Certainly. Your grandmother and my grandfather knew each other for many years—the families were good friends and she and my grandfather's sister were close. She always believed they would marry. They became engaged—the necklace was his gift to her, but then my grandfather met my grandmother and fell hopelessly in love with her.'

Belle stared at him aghast. 'Did he jilt my grandmother? Is that what happened?'

Lance nodded. 'I'm afraid he did. Your grandmother tried everything to get him back, but to no avail. In the end she gave up, but refused to return the necklace when my grandfather requested it for sentimental reasons. It was a family heirloom and meant a great deal to the Binghams.'

'Poor Grandmother. Your grandfather must have hurt her terribly.'

'I imagine he did. When she realised it was hopeless, since my grandfather's love for my grandmother was very much in evidence wherever they went, she married the Earl of Harworth, your grandfather, and went to live at Harworth Hall—which was as close as she could get to my grandfather.'

'Are you telling me she didn't love my grandfather?'

'I'm sure she was fond of him and held him in high

esteem, but I think she still carries a candle for my grandfather to this day.'

'I'm glad she decided to give the jewels back— although had she done so sooner, we would not be where we are now.'

Lance looked at her sharply. 'What's this I hear, Belle? Regret?'

'It would certainly cast a different light on everything. There would have been no scandal. You wouldn't have asked me to marry you and we certainly wouldn't be planning our wedding. Admit it, Lance. It's the truth, isn't it?'

'I suppose it is. And would you have turned me down had I asked you anyway?'

'Yes. I'm sorry. Do you mind?'

He looked at her with grudging admiration. This situation must be devastating for her, he realised suddenly, having to support a solution to her predicament without much enthusiasm. 'You've no need to apologise or look so despondent. Don't ever fear telling me the truth—no matter how bad it is. I can accept it and even admire you for having the courage to say it.'

'Thank you.'

'You are correct in saying that we wouldn't be thinking of our future together if you hadn't taken it into your head to wear the necklace to the Prince's party at Carlton House.'

'Yes. Little wonder Grandmother was angry with me. I had no idea how upset she would be, because I didn't know the story behind them. I merely thought they were too beautiful to be kept locked away all the time. At least she returned them to their rightful owner.'

He gave her a wry smile. 'After fifty years, I suppose

one could say better late than never. Do you think she would have done so, had you not brought the matter back into the public eye?'

'I don't know that. I cannot speak for my grandmother. What I do know is that from what you have told me and knowing her as much as I am able to do after such a short acquaintance, she must have loved your grandfather very much.'

'I believe she did, which accounts for her actions and for which—as anyone who has been in love will understand—she can be forgiven.'

'Being aware of your own perceptions on love, which you explained to me so frankly the other night, I am surprised that you have even a modicum of understanding. But I thank you for saying that.'

'Maybe that is why she is so protective of you, and why, after the humiliation she suffered herself all those yours ago, she wanted to save you from the same fate.'

'She is not a devious person and I can imagine the torment that lies beneath her façade of stiff dignity, which is her nature, and none of us can help our nature. Nor is she an ogre. I have full confidence in her ability to be fair minded when it's deserving—which was the case when she returned the diamonds to you—and equally harsh when circumstances compel her to be so—as when she insisted that you should do the honourable thing and marry me. I sense that she very much regrets what happened and her part in it. I can also understand how resentful you must have felt when you saw me wearing the necklace at Carlton House.'

'Yes, I confess I was resentful—and angry—but I also knew that my resentment had nothing to do with you.'

'I have to ask you this, Lance—what of your family?

How will they react when they realise you are to wed a woman from a family they must despise?'

'My mother does not despise anyone. What happened between our grandparents had nothing to do with her. She is fair minded and will not turn her back on you because of who you are. After she has weighed everything up, she will see that we are doing the right thing and accept you as my future wife. To be honest, I think she'll be relieved to end the feud and move on.'

Belle paused and turned to look at him. 'And you, Lance? Will you be glad to move on?'

He frowned, his expression becoming tense, causing Belle to regret having asked the question. It was as though Delphine's ghost stood between them. The picture of the woman who was the mother of his child continued to haunt him, those well-remembered brown eyes daring him to fall into the same dangerous trap in which he had allowed himself to be ensnared not so very long ago, causing him to lose his self-respect and his sanity.

'I accept that things will change when we wed, but as for moving on—well—we shall see.'

Chapter Seven

Lance glanced at her. 'As my wife, you know what will be expected of you?'

'Of course, but I hope you won't expect too much too soon.'

He scanned her upturned face, finally broaching what was on his mind. 'I gather, then, that you didn't enjoy it when I made love to you.'

Belle flushed to the roots of her hair and she averted her eyes, feeling a profound embarrassment. She appeared to consider his question before saying hesitantly, 'It—it was not what I expected—although I found it most—illuminating.'

His eyes narrowed on hers. 'Illuminating? I was hoping for something better than that. Have you ever been kissed before, Belle?'

'That is a secret I'd rather not confess. It is for me to know and for you to wonder about.'

'Few confidences can remain untold between husband and wife. Couples share the most *intimate* secrets—as well as other things.' He gave her a sharp, knowing look. 'And by that you know what I mean, so do not play the innocent.'

Finding it increasingly difficult to meet his gaze, Belle proceeded to walk on, trailing her hands over the flower heads as she went. 'Intimate? Are we to be *intimate* again then, Lance?'

Following in her wake, Lance scowled, watching her skirts swaying jauntily ahead of him. He had the greatest temptation to drag her off the path and into the confines of the shrubs and do more than kiss her, yet he was intrigued by her enquiry. Gently taking hold of her arm, he turned her to face him.

'We were intimate at the ball. Would you like to be intimate with me again?'

Beneath his closely attentive stare, a soft flush heightened on Belle's cheeks. She knew how quickly his passions could be inflamed, and how eager he must be to repeat his actions of that particular occasion, and she also knew she must be wary. Even so, she kept her composure well enough to say, 'I'm sure your disposition will be tested enough during the two months of our betrothal for us to ascertain our compatibility with just the minimal amount of physical contact, so if you intend using your manly charms to weaken my defences again, Lance Bingham, perhaps you should consider that I will not succumb to you again without the lasting commitment of marriage.'

'You will have to get used to it when you are my wife,' he warned, moving to stand dangerously close to her. 'You will have to be available to me whenever I want you.'

Acutely aware of the nearness of his tall, wickedly muscular body, a blaze of excitement and tension leaped through Belle, her reaction a purely primitive response.

She could almost feel its heat and vibrancy through her clothes. Helplessly, she stared up at him, two bright spots of colour staining her cheeks.

His eyes smouldering, Lance stared back at her. 'Consider it, Belle. As my wife you will be at my beck and call day and night. I will take my pleasure of you at my leisure, whenever I want.'

If he was trying to destroy her resistance, he was succeeding. His voice had suddenly grown husky with sensuality, slicing through her like a hot knife through butter. She believed him—the fire streaking through her loins was so fierce it made her tremble.

'Do you enjoy provoking me—and teasing me?' she remarked. 'Are you trying to persuade me to change my mind about marrying you? Is that it?'

He gave her a hard look, his mouth tightening as he stared at the softly heaving bosom and the tantalising mouth. Belle Ainsley might look fragile, but he was beginning to suspect she was as strong as steel inside, and that behind that sweet, beautiful exterior of a genteel lady lurked an impish vixen who was every bit a match for the animal in him. He wouldn't persuade her to change her mind.

'I am merely pointing out to you what you can expect. I would waken all the passion in that lovely, untutored body of yours and make you moan with pleasure—' He broke off, realising his mistake. His strategy had backfired with a vengeance. He had begun by trying to threaten and frighten her into backing out of this marriage he had grudgingly agreed to, and had finished up with his own resolutions threatened instead.

He could feel his body reacting to the image his own

words were arousing. Mentally flaying his thoughts into obedience, he made a fierce effort to control himself and stepped back, looking down at her standing there, wide-eyed and vulnerable and trembling. And lovely. Dear Lord, she was lovely. He wanted her with a fierceness that took his breath away.

The fact was undeniable. He did not want to keep himself in restraint for the next eight weeks. How would he be able to endure having her near without making love to her? He told himself that she was just a woman, and women were all alike, and he had never known one who couldn't be driven from his mind. But Belle was different. She was to be his wife and bear his children. That alone made her different. His inner turmoil turned to self-scorn. He should never have got so close to her. He should have kept his distance.

'I told you, Lance,' Belle said quietly. 'As your wife I shall know perfectly well what is expected of me. I will try not to give you reason to regret marrying me. I promise you.'

'No, you won't,' he stated. 'Don't be concerned that my barbaric display with words will be repeated. Despite my attempts to banish the tantalising memory of making love to you, I find I cannot.' A devilish smile twisted his lips. 'You're presenting a definite challenge to me, so before I weaken and forget myself and sweep you off into the bushes from which you will not emerge without yielding to my animal desire once more, I think I should return you to your grandmother.'

Focusing her gaze ahead of her, Belle was beset with so many conflicting emotions: anger, humiliation, wounded pride, regret. Was it possible to make this ill-fated marriage work when her feelings were so nebulous and chaotic? Yet one stood out clearly—her desire for this man.

She wondered how she was going to get through the weeks of her betrothal, how she was going to withstand this powerful man walking beside her. She knew it would prove far more difficult than she imagined. When she was with him she couldn't breathe without feeling his presence with every heightened sense of her female perception. It would be so easy to allow herself to yield to those provocatively stirring memories he had created when his hands had moved boldly over her body and he had invaded her in the most intimate way, that even now brought blood rushing to her cheeks and a feeling of molten heat flowing through her and into her loins so that she could think of nothing else.

Later, extremely nervous about appearing in society for the first time as Lance's fiancée, Belle was suffering from a severe fit of nerves. She took special pains with her appearance, knowing she'd be dashing the hopes once and for all of others who might have had their hopeful sights on Lance as a possible husband.

A pale pink taffeta creation that bared her shoulders sublimely was what she chose to wear. It was bejewelled with tiny seed pearls and other diminutive beads that shimmered in the light. She wore no adornment at her throat, for the garment needed none. Her hair was drawn back smoothly from her face, the shining tresses intricately woven into a weighty mass above her nape. The fact that she had spent so much time fashioning her coiffure attested to her desire to win her future husband's approval.

She tried to tell herself she was marrying Lance

because she had no choice, that it was the only way out of an impossible situation, but as she closed the door of her bedroom to go downstairs, she admitted that wasn't entirely true. Part of her *wanted* to marry him. She loved his handsome looks and his lazy smile. She even liked the brisk authority in his voice and the confidence in his long, athletic strides and the way his eyes gleamed when he laughed, and the way his lips felt on hers.

There were so many things she liked about him, she thought bleakly, and there were so many things about him that she had yet to find out. She had no illusions about what Lance felt about her. He was attracted to her, she knew, but beyond that he felt nothing for her. She, on the other hand, was in serious danger of falling in love with him. But he had told her he didn't want her love and would scorn her for it.

When they arrived at Lance's house, for a moment he stood before her drinking in her beauty in quiet appreciation. Belle accepted his slow, exacting scrutiny as an unspoken compliment, for the warmth of those deep blue eyes had intensified significantly by the time they reached her shining head. She gazed at the dangerously impressive figure of the unpredictable Lance Bingham, attired in evening black and white that made him look overwhelmingly male.

Lance favoured them with a glinting smile, but Belle noted his manner was guarded and reserved. 'Good evening,' he said briskly. 'Welcome to my home.' He looked at Belle. 'Spare me just a moment, will you, Belle?' He looked at his butler. 'Show the dowager countess into the drawing room. We won't be a moment.'

Excusing herself, Belle followed him into his study.

'I won't keep you long,' he promised, reaching into a drawer of his large carved desk and taking out a small velvet box. Without another word, he took her hand in his and slid a ring on to her finger. Belle gazed at it in wonder. A cluster of large emeralds were surrounded by shimmering diamonds.

'Lance, I—I never expected... It is the most incredible, beautiful ring. Thank you.'

'It is an engagement ring—what a man gives to his future bride. It is customary.' His lips curved in a smile as his gaze settled on her lips. 'You can thank me with a kiss.'

He stepped closer, forcing Belle into nerve-racking proximity with his powerful body, and slowly lowered his lips to hers. He saw her mouth part to welcome his, which captured hers in a long, hungry, thorough kiss, crushing her hard against him. Leaning up on her toes, she slid her hands up along his hard chest and twined them around his neck, letting her fingers slide through the soft hairs at his nape, while he explored her mouth with heady delight, his kiss attesting to his ravenous greed, draining Belle's mind by his ardour and her body's helpless response to it.

When he finally lifted his head, she stared into his smoky deep blue eyes, trying to understand why his kisses always had this shattering effect on her.

Lance stared down at her with an odd expression of bemusement and self-mockery on his chiselled features. 'I can see I shall have to give you jewels more often to get a response like that from you. But for now my gift comes with a dire warning, Belle. Do not kiss me again like that until after we are married, otherwise I will not be held responsible for the consequences.'

Belle already knew how easily he could be carried away by his ardour, which would lead him to behave in an unspecified way. He was telling her he had no wish to lose his head and she was feminine enough to feel a surge of satisfaction because her nearness and her kiss could so affect this extremely experienced man. She also knew of the dangers of getting too close to him, for she would be unable to resist him if he plied her again with his persuasive wooing. He could steal her will away with no more than a gentle kiss.

She smiled coyly up at him. 'I have your meaning, Lance, and will be only too happy to oblige.'

He scowled down at her. 'Eight weeks, Belle, for eight weeks, and then you can prepare yourself for my assault.'

At dinner the three of them conversed amiably. No one seeing them would believe that theses two families had been anything but friends for the past fifty years.

Afterwards they attended the Earl and Countess of Sidmouth's ball in Mayfair. It seemed as if everyone in London was there, and every pair of eyes seemed to shift to them as their names were announced. Having read the announcement of the betrothal in the newspaper, heads turned, fans fluttered and whispers began.

No one looking at Belle would have guessed how nervous she was. For a moment while Lance paused to greet an acquaintance, she stood beside her grandmother at the top of the steps leading down into the ballroom, looking down into the sea of nameless faces. Then Lance suddenly appeared by her side and held out his hand. Belle placed her hand in his and he tucked it possessively in the crook of his arm.

Lance felt it tremble, and, bending over her, murmured, 'You're nervous, aren't you? I can tell.'

'Terrified,' she amended, pinning a smile to her lips. 'Everyone is looking at us.'

'Belle,' he said severely, but with a dazzling smile for the benefit of the onlookers, 'you are the young woman who brazenly entered my bedchamber and threatened to break my hands if I dared to touch you.'

Belle stared at him askance. 'Did I really say that?'

He grinning down at her. 'Every word. So do not dare turn cowardly now.'

Her mouth suddenly dry, Belle glanced around at the curious faces, some craning their necks better to see her. 'I'll try not to,' she replied, 'but it won't be easy. Don't they know that it's impolite to stare?'

'Probably not. Ignore them,' Lance quipped, unlike her completely impervious to the stir they were creating. When the countess was approached by an acquaintance and invited to sit with her, he took two glances of champagne from the tray of a passing footman. His bold admiring gaze swept over Belle's face, and then he lifted his glass and gave her a subtle toast.

It was all sweetly poignant, and Belle, beginning to relax, no longer cared a whit about any other reason for being there other than it was to celebrate their engagement. It seemed to take an age for them to reach the dance floor, because they were interrupted at every step by someone insisting on a friendly word.

They partnered only each other, waltzing with effortless ease, and in his arms Belle glowed and sparkled and reigned like a young queen. Lance's recent kiss, the husky sound of his voice, the way he held her in the dance, they were like sweet music playing through her heart. He was daring and bold and passionate, and Belle had no objections, but through it all she felt a certain amount of unease, for she sensed Lance was being like this for her benefit, and that behind that smiling façade he remained guarded and resentful of being drawn into a situation he might have cause to regret.

'You look radiant tonight, and very beautiful,' he said, studying her upturned face closely. 'You appear to be happy with the situation, Belle.'

'I am—very happy—but I am also apprehensive,' she confessed.

'You are? Why?'

'Because I'm afraid it might all go terribly wrong.'

'And why should it do that?'

Her gaze fell from his and she looked at his frilled white shirt front. 'I'm being silly, I know, but it's a feeling I have.'

'This is what you want, isn't it—marriage to me?'

She raised her eyes to his. 'Yes—of course.' She meant what she said, but the apprehension that occupied a small corner of her mind would not go away. 'But— is it what you want, Lance?'

He looked away from her, his face guarded. 'Of course,' he replied, his answer brusque, as the strains of the waltz died. 'This is the last social event we will attend before I have to leave for Ryhill and you for Harworth. Will you mind leaving all the glamour and sparkle of the Season behind for the solitude of the country?'

'Not really,' Belle replied quietly, disappointed by his unconvincing response to her question, but in no mood to take him to task over it just then. 'I shall be happy to go. Besides I am looking forward to seeing Harworth.'

'And Ryhill—of which you shall be mistress of very soon.'

'I know—and thank you, Lance.'

His broad shoulders lifted in a shrug. 'Then since the dance has ended, I think it is time for us to leave.'

'Yes,' Belle replied, realising he was uncomfortable with her gratitude.

'Might I suggest that, if your grandmother would care to leave for Harworth earlier than planned, we could travel to Wiltshire together?'

'You needn't put yourself to so much trouble. Besides we have things to do for the wedding before we can leave for Harworth.'

'As you wish.'

After he escorted Belle and the countess back to Hampstead, when her grandmother went inside the house Belle said a quiet goodnight to Lance. He stood looking down at her a long moment, and after kissing her lightly on the lips—which was more like a duty kiss than of the passionate kind she was becoming accustomed to, Belle thought with a surge of disappointment—he turned on his heel, walking with long strides back to the carriage.

Belle followed his tall, powerful form with her gaze until he had climbed in and told the driver to move on. Her expression was wistful, her yearning for him written on her face. Tears welled in her eyes and a tight ache in her heart. Deep down she knew Lance didn't want to marry her, but she hoped, with all her heart, that all that would change when they reached Wiltshire and they had the time to get to know each other better.

At present it would appear that the passionate interlude they had shared had done nothing to change their relationship. What had been a devastating experience for her had meant nothing to him at all. She blinked back the tears. She had had been stupid to confuse physical desire with love. Just because a man made love to a woman with such fierce intensity didn't mean his heart was engaged.

In the days that followed, Belle had little time to think of Lance as she was swept into preparations for the wedding, her wedding gown being of prominence to all else. Her grandmother took charge of everything, and Belle couldn't help smiling at the return of her grandmother's familiar autocratic manner—it was vastly preferable to the wounded and worried woman the scandal had made of her.

In the midst of all the preparations, Belle did take a moment to consider her situation. How had it come to this? she wondered. At the beginning of the Season she had made her début on the London scene with no other thought in her head than to enjoy herself, and if she met a man she fell in love with then so be it. And because she had no experience of men like Lance Bingham, being gullible and blind to everything but the devastatingly handsome man she'd met at Carlton House, she had been drawn to him in the most inexplicable way, but not in the way she had imagined it.

The truth was that before he had taken up his military career, Lance Bingham had the reputation of being a notorious rake with a well-deserved reputation for profligacy. Did men change all that much? she wondered. Countless women fell in love with him all the time, and she was just another one of his victims to fall prey to his fatal attraction. He was twelve years her senior, which in the beginning had made her even more wary of his appeal. What could a naïve young woman do to fortify herself against the persuasive charm of a man of experience? Certainly a few moments in his presence could make her flustered despite the handsome young aristocrats who gathered around her, each vying for her attention. But in retrospect these eager gallants seemed hopelessly immature when she had met a more worthy subject with whom to compare them.

However, she must not forget that Lance was not marrying her from choice and that their marriage was one of great inconvenience to him. He did want her— at least physically—his lustful wooing left her in no doubt of that. And the whispered overtures he had had plied her with when he had found her in his bedchamber, coaxing her to yield to the delights to be found in his bed, of how he would like to introduce her to the more erotic rudiments of being a full-fledged wife, quickened her own hunger now that he had given her a taste of what to expect. But was it any different to what he would say and do to any other attractive woman?

In the days that preceded her wedding, Belle was content to settle down at Harworth. It was an extensive, splendid estate, the Tudor house with additions in various styles added through the years. There was a constant stream of friends and neighbours of her grandmother, who came to call to wish her well. Only Lance stayed away and she was deeply hurt and disappointed by this. On the odd occasions when he did escort her to formal events in the neighbourhood, his polite attentiveness could not be faulted, but beneath his handsome façade he was cool and guarded and she felt she could not reach him. It gave Belle the uneasy feeling that she was marrying an absentee stranger.

He was a man any woman would be proud to have for her husband—or lover. Belle fought the memory that thought aroused. She tried not to think of when he had made love to her. Sometimes she forgot for a while the incredible wanton things they had done, and the mention of his name would send them rushing back. Yet he seemed to have dismissed their moment of shared passion so easily. If it had meant anything at all to him he wouldn't be avoiding her like this.

She tried to appear unconcerned about his absence, even going so far as to make excuses for him, saying how busy he must be at Ryhill, having only recently taken on his inheritance and the heavy responsibilities this must entail. But deep inside her she was profoundly hurt and more than a little angry by his absence during these days before their wedding, which they should be spending together and getting to know each other better.

The closer it got to the wedding, more often her heart seemed torn asunder by two choices, both of which at different times seemed rational. One was driven by a growing desire to become Lance's wife in actuality, the other, based on the fear of entering into a loveless marriage, to abscond. Yet when she mused on the latter option, knowing she was soiled goods and no other man would want her, a miserable emptiness settled on her heart, leaving her feeling drained, and she'd find herself struggling against an assault of tears, both strong indications of his effect on her and her reluctance to leave him. In spite of the precautions with which she had sought to fortify herself, it was a hard fact for her to face knowing that her fascination with this man had deepened in the short span of time she had known him.

* * *

Despite the reticence he felt toward his forthcoming marriage to Belle, she would have been surprised to know how Lance, who was determined to hold her at bay for as long as possible, found his gentlemanly forbearance surely strained. Belle was far too beautiful and alluring for him to nonchalantly endure her nearness and not make love to her.

In a quest to put some distance between them, he limited the time he spent with her. Even when he was forced by the demands of protocol to conduct himself in social good manner and escort his fiancée to functions that required their attendance as a couple, he sought to remain distantly detached. He conversed with her when compelled, and then briefly, a contrivance which allowed him by dint of will to maintain his gentlemanly forbearance.

On the morning of her wedding day Belle was unable to dispel her feeling of despondency. Today she was going to commit her entire life into the keeping of a man who did not love her. Every instinct for self-preservation that she possessed warned her not to go through with it, not to marry Lance. She couldn't help comparing her own situation with that of her grandmother, how she had been forced to live without the love of her life and had married someone else—her grandfather. Had they been happy? She hoped so, but all her life she must have felt she had settled for second best.

Second best! This was where the difference lay. Second best did not apply to her, for there had been no one else before Lance. He was the first man to stir her emotions and set her body aflame with desire. She wasn't sure she liked the way her heart was inclined to race when she recalled the occasion when they had made love, when he had spoken smooth endearments into her ear, for it made her realise how vulnerable she was to his charm. The powerful persuasiveness that he was capable to launch against her womanly being could reap devastating results, for what defence had she against a man adeptly skilled in the art of seducing women?

It was these thoughts that persuaded her that she wanted Lance to be her husband. She wanted to be made complete by him, to become a part of him, to know him as she had never known a man before—and perhaps with the knowing, for both of them, would come love.

The weather was warm and heady with the intoxicating scents of flowers wafting on the gentlest of breezes. With the sun's radiance in evidence, it was perfect. With time to spare before they were to leave for the church, alone with her grandmother, Belle hesitantly brought up the subject of the diamonds—the diamonds Lance had given her to wear on this special day—believing that if they did not speak of it, there would always be some unease about it.

'Lance told me about the necklace, Grandmother. Why did you not tell me that you were engaged to his grandfather?'

The countess turned her head away, gazing out of the window, and Belle said quickly, 'I am sorry. You needn't tell me if it will upset you to speak of it.'

'It's not that,' she said, slowly returning her gaze to Belle's face. 'I know how very sensible and understanding you are, but it was all so long ago now that I often wonder if I understand it myself. '

'But you loved him.'

'Oh, yes. I loved him with all my heart and soul. We were to be married and I loved him and he cut me out of his life for someone else when he was the only thing worth living for. He had given me the diamonds on our betrothal. You know the rest.'

'That you did not return them.'

'Afterwards I hated myself more than I hated those diamonds. I wanted to give them back, but I felt if I were to do that, my humiliation would be total. So they remained in the box until you took it upon yourself to wear them.'

'I should not have done that. It was unforgivable of me. My stupidity hurt you, and for that I am sorry.'

'Don't be. It's too late for self-recrimination now.' She smiled softly, reaching out and gently fingering the diamonds that had been the cause of so much controversy. 'They are exquisite, are they not? I'm glad Lance thought you should wear them today. There could not be a more fitting occasion. You—are quite taken with Lance Bingham, are you not, Isabelle?'

She sighed. 'He is handsome and manly, with the most persuasive smile.' Her eyes suddenly clouded. 'However, I—confess that I have had my doubts about marrying him. Why, on waking this morning I asked myself if I was ready for all of this. I almost got cold feet and considered calling the whole thing off—but—when I weighed everything up, I realised that marrying him was the sensible thing to do.'

'Have you fallen in love with him?'

'In all honesty I don't know how I feel. He—he makes me feel things I have never felt before. I like being with him. I like it when he smiles and laughs and tells me I look nice. I—have come to care for him deeply.'

The countess smiled and, taking Belle's hand, squeezed it gently. 'There you are, then. If it isn't love you feel now, it soon will be. I believe Lord Bingham is quite taken with you, too.'

Belle had no idea what Lance's feelings were where she was concerned, for she still felt a profound disappointment and hurt that he had not come to see her as often as she would have liked. When he kissed her he made her feel that he wanted her, but that was desire, and desire and love were worlds apart.

'How can you know that? Has he said so?'

The countess chuckled softly. 'No, not in so many words, but I have eyes in my head and I have seen the way he looks at you. If he felt nothing for you he would never have bowed to propriety and agreed to marry you. I can see you are like me after all—and he is so like his grandfather. And who knows? There may come a time when we shall have cause to bless those diamonds that have been the cause of so much discord.' She got to her feet and straightened her spine, smiling at the young woman she had come to care for very much. 'Now come along, Isabelle. I think we've dawdled long enough. We have a wedding to go to—or has it slipped your mind?'

The roads around the village church were snarled with curricles and carriages that had disgorged their passengers. The little church was full to overflowing with the local aristocracy garbed in silks and fine brocades, and friendly villagers lined both sides of the path, all come to witness this union between two of the most notable—if not always friendly to each other in the past—families in Wiltshire.

More nervous than she cared to show, in an ice-blue

gown of incredible beauty and extravagant expense, Belle took a footman's hand to be helped from the carriage. There were so many people, all strangers, yet they were all wishing her well.

In the vestibule Daisy fussed about straightening her train and adjusting her veil. When all was as it should be, Belle placed her trembling fingers on Rowland's arm, glad that he had agreed to give her away, there being no male influence in her life.

When she paused before she began the endless walk down the aisle, where all eyes were focused on her, that was the moment when the enormity of what she was about to do hit her. Panic shot through her and she asked herself why she was doing this, telling herself that it wasn't too late to turn and run, that she could escape, but her legs were already carrying her towards the altar, to where the minister stood, the marriage book open in his hands. Rays of sunlight slanting through the mullioned windows caught the diamonds glittering in her hair and her veil.

Rowland must have sensed her fear, for he smiled sideways at her and murmured, 'Take heart, Belle. The parson knows the difference between the last rites and a wedding ceremony.'

Smiling nervously up at him and taking reassurance from her grandmother, who was in the front pew where she should be, her heart began to lose the battle against terror—until her eyes focused on Lance. Dressed in a splendid suit of midnight blue and a pristine white cravat, he stepped into the aisle and waited for her to reach him. With his face partly shadowed, he looked so tall and powerful and dark—as dark as her future.

Belle was unable to quell the sudden ache that his

grim expression aroused in her or the sorrow she felt when she remembered her girlhood dream of how she wanted her wedding day to be. How different this was. Her dream had been to go to her future husband with a heart bursting with love and joy. Instead there was only fear and dread and regret. But somehow she managed to keep her own expression cool and serene as she relinquished Rowland's arm and took her place beside Lance Bingham.

As the music soared, unaware of the moment when Belle had almost taken flight, Lance turned to look at her. To some degree his attempts to treat her impersonally and keep her at arm's length had helped, but on seeing the perfect vision walking slowly towards him, provocatively beautiful in her flowing ice-blue gown and gossamer veil, it was tantamount to being hit with a sledgehammer in a most vulnerable place, dispelling some of the gloom of his marriage ceremony from his heart.

It was with a feeling of intense pride that his intense blue gaze locked on to hers, and when she was in front of him, and before his features settled back into their grim lines of cynical indifference, briefly his eyes smiled down at her, and he said, 'You look extremely beautiful, Belle.'

The compliment was just what Belle needed to bolster her courage. Her heart swelled ready to burst as Rowland put her hand in Lance's, and she felt his long, strong fingers close firmly round her own in a reassuring grasp. If she had any remaining doubts about marrying this man, they were dispelled in that moment, and as they turned to the minister and she took her place by his side, she knew that with or without Lance's love, this was where she would remain for all time.

Everyone listened in breathless silence as the wedding ceremony was conducted. In muted, trembling tones, Belle replied to the questions the minister presented to her. The firm, deep voice of Lance echoed hauntingly in the stillness as he too made his responses, his voice deep and resonant echoing through the church, promising to love and cherish her, and endowing her with all his worldly goods. And then it was over and these two proud and beautiful people were pronounced man and wife.

'You may kiss the bride,' the minister said.

Lance turned and looked at her, his eyes gleaming with something that was so intense and so terrifying that Belle stiffened when he drew her towards him and his arms went round her, encircling her. Bending his head, he claimed her trembling lips in a long drawn-out kiss that brought a frown of disapproval to the minister's brow and a smile to the lips of all those present. Then he released her and took her arm. After signing the documents that made their union legal in the eyes of the law as well as God, with the sound of congratulations ringing in their ears, Lance led his bride down the aisle and out of the church.

Everyone was there to see Lance's shiny black carriage drive off, swaying gently along the road towards Harworth Hall. It was drawn by four prancing chestnut horses in magnificent silver harnesses. Two coachmen mounted in green velvet livery sat proudly erect in front.

Belle sank almost breathless with relief into the deep luxurious upholstery and looked down at the broad gold band which Lance had slid on to her slender finger—a bold statement, she thought, telling the whole world that she belonged to him.

When Rowland, in jovial mood, had leaned into the carriage and told him to go directly to Harworth, Lance had laughed, which went a long way to relaxing Belle. It was the first spark of humour she had seen from him in a long time. She cast a glance at her new husband as the carriage left the church and found his eyes assessing her. But then she caught the ironic flicker in his eyes and realised that perhaps nothing had changed. Trying to hide her disappointment, she turned away.

Seated beside her, Lance sensed her tension and her inner sadness, and realised, as if for the first time, just how difficult she must be finding this situation. This was her wedding day, the most important day in a girl's life. She was leaving everything that was familiar to her in order to face a new way of life at the side of a husband who, through his restrained manner and avoidance of her, he thought with a twinge of regret, must have given her the impression that he didn't want her.

Suddenly and without pausing to question the reason why, he wanted to make things easier for her, to show that he was willing to give their marriage a chance. Having a wife would be a great benefit to him at Ryhill. And Belle was undeniably lovely.

'I meant what I said in church, Belle. You look lovely,' he uttered quietly, taking her hand and holding it in a firm clasp. His tone held an odd note of pride, and perhaps awe, that made her turn her head to him. With the dappled shade of light playing across her creamy skin and wisps of hair escaping from their pins caressing her cheek, she was the most beautiful woman Lance had ever laid eyes on. Whether due to the gently curving bosom beneath the confines of her gown, the satin softness of her skin, or the rosy blush that infused her

cheeks, brightening her eyes until they seemed to glow
with a brilliance of their own behind the thick, sooty
lashes, or the way her lips were softly parted, his attention was firmly ensnared, such enticements being too
much for any man to ignore, much less one who had
found himself hard pressed by a lengthened abstinence
and ever-goading passions.

Something in his chest tightened. When she lowered
her eyes he placed a gentle finger under her chin, compelling her to meet his gaze.

'Kiss me, Belle.' His senses alive to the elusive
perfumed scent of her, and unable to resist the softness
of her lips, he drew her close. Wordlessly she offered
him her lips. Her kiss was tentative at first, as if she
needed time to reconsider what she was doing, but when
his mouth opened over hers, as his heat flowed into her
she seemed to relax a little.

Taking her in his arms, covering her mouth with his
own, he kissed her long and deep. It was the first since
they had left London. Tonight was their night, when he
would truly make her his wife in every sense, and his
blood stirred hotly. Already he was mentally undressing and kissing her, caressing her with his hands and
mouth until she was wild for him.

Having kissed her to near insensibility, he raised his
head and looked at her flushed face. 'Was that to your
liking, madam?'

'Mmm. It was so nice I wouldn't mind if you kissed
me again.' She leaned forwards to steal another. Her
husband readily accommodated her, this time making
it far more sensual as his tongue slipped inwards to
explore further. She moaned against him, and when he
released her lips she pleaded for more.

'You're insatiable, my love, but I dare not continue lest I arrive at our wedding breakfast in a state of embarrassment.'

A shy but mischievous smile curved her lips. 'I've never kissed a man before in an open carriage. I feel almost wanton.'

'Kissing—or anything of an intimate nature—is not wantonness when it's between a couple who has been bound by marriage. It is an honest desire—and right now I want you with a craving that will not be appeased by a mere kiss.'

'Do you really want me, Lance?' she asked, a slightly anxious frown creasing her brow.

Now that he was no longer kissing her and he could think more clearly, Lance realised how much he did want her, that no power on earth would persuade him to cast her out of his life—and to reassure her, he kissed her again.

The wedding breakfast was quite splendid. The Dowager Countess of Harworth had spared no expense. When the guests had all arrived and made their way up the grand staircase, which was flanked by footmen standing stiffly at attention in blue-and-gold Ainsley livery, beneath a huge chandelier in the ballroom decked with summer flowers, Belle stood beside Lance while the butler, in a stentorian tone, announced each individual.

Belle was assisted into her chair at the table by her husband.

The meal was a splendid affair, and when the endless toasts offered for the bride and groom's health were over and the musicians struck up the first waltz, to the sound of hearty applause, blended with laughter, Lance led his bride on to the dance floor.

Relieved that he had lowered his guard at last and hoping it would continue, a sigh of relief slipped from Belle's lips as he swept her smoothly around the ballroom, continually turning in ever-widening circles until the faces of those who watched became an indistinct blur beyond his broad shoulders.

'How are you feeling now?' Lance enquired softly.

Belle laughed, evidencing not only her relief, but her pleasure at being able to dance for the first time with her husband.

'Better. I was worried about Grandmother.'

'I thought you might be—but she looks as if she's enjoying herself.'

'I'm sorry your mother couldn't make it back for the wedding. I look forward to meeting her.'

'She is impatient to meet you. My sister has been delivered of her baby—a daughter—and Mother is on her way home.' He looked at her upturned face, a teasing smile twitching at his lips. 'You dance divinely, wife. You are as light as thistledown in my arms.'

'I feel as if I'm floating on a cloud.'

A wicked, devilish grin stretched across Lance's lips. 'I hope that's the way you will feel when I make love to you—later.'

Before she could reply to his *risqué* remark, he had spun her round so that her feet almost left the floor. For Belle, nothing existed beyond her husband's encircling arms and the endless glitter of blue eyes that held hers captive. They spoke in muted tones—an intimate sharing of comments about the wedding. There was a warm, underlying excitement within Belle that Lance had kindled with his earlier kiss—a promise and a tingle of anticipation of that moment when she would be alone with him.

Lance was completely entranced with the soft eyes that glowed with a shining lustre that radiated her happiness. Feeling immensely blessed to have found such devotion, and very much aware of her pliant body moving with his, as if their minds were joined in secret accord, he was impatient to whisk her away from the celebrations to Ryhill, for it was only there that they could be assured of adequate privacy.

Chapter Eight

It was close on midnight when they bade family and friends goodnight and left for Ryhill, half-an-hour's drive away. When they arrived, welcoming lights shone from the windows. Climbing out of the coach, before she knew what was happening, Lance swept Belle up into his arms and carried her laughing into the house, where he set her to her feet.

'Welcome to Ryhill,' he said, kissing her lips. 'Countess.'

She giggled, returning his kiss. 'How very grand it sounds. It's going to take some getting used to. I've only just got used to being addressed as Miss Isabelle.'

There was only Masters, the butler, to receive them. Having endured an agonising abstinence and wanting nothing to hinder his union with his wife, Lance told him to go to bed.

With a knowing smile Masters was happy to oblige.

Lance pulled his wife close. 'Would you like a drink—or would you like to see our bedroom?' he invited with a teasing smile.

Belle's eyes shone as they swept over her handsome husband, and her lips curved in a sensual smile as she looked into his lusting eyes. 'Only if you'll come with me.'

'You don't think I'd let you go without me, do you?' he answered her with a chuckle. 'And the way my mind's been working all day, it may be another week before I allow you to leave.'

He whisked her up the stairs to the master bedroom. Reluctant to release her, he kicked the door closed with his foot, glancing round quickly to make sure Belle's maid had done as he instructed and not waited up for her mistress. If there was undressing to be done he would do it himself.

With all his self-control, his breath came quickly and his heart beat high in his throat as he gathered her into his arms and grasped her tightly to him. 'Alone with you at last. I've wanted you for so long, hungered for you. For too long I've tried to avoid kissing you the way I've been yearning to for fear of where it would lead us. To put it bluntly, Belle, I'm almost starved for your kisses and all the other temptations I found myself facing whenever I was near you.'

Recalling the time he had made love to her and all the glorious things he had done to her, Belle grew heady with anticipation. Nothing he had done to her since had come equal to that exchange.

'Is that the reason why you've been avoiding me of late?'

'You noticed?'

'How could I not? It made me wonder if you would go through with the ceremony—that you might have had second thoughts and come to regret your decision to marry me after all.'

'I'm sorry if I gave you reason to think that. I did have reservations about our marriage—I told you that at the beginning—but now it is done I accept it.'

'Then you don't mean to avoid me any longer?'

'Just try to keep me away. I want our marriage to work, Belle, and I can see no reason why it shouldn't.'

His eyes looked down into hers and Belle saw he was sincere. Her lips curved in a gentle smile. 'Then what are you waiting for? Please, Lance—wait no longer.'

Looping her arms around his neck, she drew his head down to hers. His mouth eagerly sought hers and their bodies strained together hungrily. When they pulled apart, she kicked off her shoes and stepped back to slip out of her dress, tossing it over a chair. Raising her petticoat to reveal her long, sleek legs encased in silk stockings, held in place by white ribbons above her knees, she unfastened the ties. Suddenly she glanced at her husband. Had she issued an invitation to ogle the sights, he couldn't have been more eager to respond. With his shoulder leaning against one of the ornate posts of the huge bed, his expression was one of admiration. Already he had stored within his memory diverse views of her—this one he would install as the most tempting.

Ensnaring his gaze, Belle felt her lips curve in a smile. 'Didn't anyone ever tell you that it's rude to stare?' she teased, seeing where his gaze was fastened.

'I can't help it. The sight of you enslaves me. I've never seen so much perfection wrapped up in one woman.' When she bent over to remove her stockings, providing him with a generous view of her ripe, creamy breasts, he halted her. 'Leave them on.'

Making a pretence of being shocked, she giggled. 'Really, you have the strangest quirks, Lance Bingham.'

'You'll have a lifetime to become familiar with them, but I prefer to be about more serious pleasures now.'

'And what would they be?' she queried with her head tilted to one side and a provocative smile on her lips.

'I'll show you.' When she raised her arms to let down her hair, he relinquished his stance. 'Here, let me.'

His fingers freed her hair, which cascaded down her spine in a silken mass. His hungering eyes swept over her alluring form in a long, lingering caress. Then he was lifting her in his arms and carrying her towards the bed, where he stood her on her feet. They were both hit by a frenzy to undress completely—apart from Belle's stockings—and in naked splendour they caressed each other, Lance covering her body in greedy kisses, before tumbling her on to the bed.

Soon Lance's mouth was tracing over his wife's body, claiming a soft peak, his hand searching out the secret softness of her, and the fires of passion in Belle rose higher still, sweeping away her restraints until they blended with his in an erotic exchange that left them both heady with desire.

Lance's naked body covered hers and the probing of his maleness she willingly accepted. Then his narrow hips were passing over hers in long leisurely strokes. Deep within her, Belle could feel a heat overflowing her womanly ardour.

Luxuriating in the joy of being one with her, and consumed by her womanly warmth, Lance was thoroughly engorged with lust. A hot, pulsating flame quickened Belle's blood as his movements became more concentrated and increasingly forceful, igniting her fervour. Soon their passions were soaring out; Lance's control shattering and his own reservations shattering with it as he claimed her fully and filled her with the urgent desire he'd been keeping so tight in check since his first possession of her that moonlit night in the garden of Schofield House.

It was only when his shuddering release was over that he remembered why he had harboured any reservations at all. And by then, he couldn't find the will or the energy for regret. Their gasps were finally silenced, becoming soft, blissful sighs of contentment.

They lay in each other's arms, kissing, touching and whispering, Belle already luxuriating in her new wifely state. She existed in a warm glow. Never had she felt so happy or felt the way she felt now for another human being. But what did Lance feel for her? He wanted her body, that was clear—but desire and need were not love. Whatever interpretation she put on it, she was greedy to savour it all again. This time Lance made love to her in a most physical way, snatching her breath in a fierce ardour and forcing every pleasurable sensation that could be wrenched from her.

Everything outside that room had ceased to exist for her, for it was all here in her husband's encompassing arms. The intensifying hunger within her became almost insatiable, driving her to a kind of wildness that had her digging her nails into the flesh on his back. Then she caught her breath as pulsing waves of bliss washed over her. Feeling a feverish warmth filling her, she welcomed it, clasping her husband's tautly flexing body as he relaxed against her and rolled on to his side, taking her with him.

'The way you make love leaves my head in a whirl,' Belle murmured with a trembling sigh, resting her cheek on his furred chest.

His hand slid over her breast, causing her to catch her

breath at the scintillating shock of pleasure he elicited as the tips of his finger passed over her nipple.

Lance was certain he had never experienced such exquisite fulfilment. He also knew he wouldn't have traded his freedom for what he had now. Belle was different from any other woman, a delightful creature in her innocence, and he could imagine that with a little more tuition from him, she would enslave his mind so completely that he'd willingly yield her anything.

'You're beautiful, my love,' he murmured huskily.

'I recall you telling me that the joining of our bodies in the ritual of making love would do wonders for relaxing me. How right you were. I feel as if I could float away. It's the same feeling I experienced when you made love to me before—only this time, as your wife and in your bed, it was so much better.'

'And your reputation is no longer in question. Now you are my wife, it will be more pleasurable,' he breathed as his hand slid down her smooth belly.

The gentle breeze stirred the curtains, the sun's rays illuminating the figures within the bed. Belle lay back on the pillows, wrapped in Lance's arms, her limbs entwined with his. Her eyes were closed, and a dreamy, contented smile curved her lips.

Lance was aroused from sleep by servants' voices outside the room. His movements roused Belle and she rolled closer, reaching out a hand to caress his lean, muscular ribs. Wanting nothing more than to remain in bed, but aware of the lateness of the hour, he swung his legs over the edge of the bed and sat up. Belle laughed happily and, springing up, embraced him from behind.

'What's this? Deserting your wife already?'

He smiled as he felt the softness of her breasts on his bare back, delighting in the feel of them. 'Absolutely not, my sweet,' he said, thrusting his arms into his robe. 'I shall go below and summon breakfast and instruct your maid to attend you.'

'Don't be long,' she told him, padding with unashamed nakedness across the carpet to her dressing room, where a large tub of scented water awaited her. 'Ooh, how lovely,' she gurgled happily, realising Daisy had let herself into the dressing room by another door so as not to disturb her mistress and her husband. 'I'll have a bath while you're gone.' She cast a playful, seductive look over her shoulder. If he could not declare his love for her, at least she could humour and tempt him. 'You can wash my back if you like.'

He grinned, tossing the robe aside, the temptation to join her at her toilet almost his undoing. 'Minx. You know how to tempt a man. Besides, it's large enough for the two of us. It would be a shame to waste the water.'

He took her in his arms, thighs and belly touching, feeling the thrust of her breasts against his chest.

'Let's get in the water,' she said, eager to get on with the process.

They soaped and lathered each other, teased and kissed. Belle was becoming more sure of herself now, sure as she had never been when she had climbed into bed with him last night, when it had been Lance who had dictated, who led the way. She had been a novice then, happy to follow, and because he was a good teacher, she had learned from it and now there was no need for him to guide, to provoke, to demand. But Lance continued to set his own pace, gathering her into his arms, wet and slippery, and then back to bed.

* * *

It was mid-morning the following day and Lance and Belle were in the drawing room, drinking coffee. Belle glanced to where Lance sat reading his newspaper. She couldn't believe that she was his wife. Wife. A glow warmed her at the thought. Perhaps now she would have the chance to prove to Lance that he hadn't made a dreadful mistake in marrying her. Perhaps their relationship would be different now that he had accepted their marriage.

Ever since he had decided to marry her, for most of that time he had existed in a state of smouldering anger over being forced to wed her. Letting her gaze wander to the window and the long curving drive beyond, she gave a wistful sigh. She was falling in love with him—or had fallen. It was the only reason she could think of for the excited quivering feeling that assailed her whenever she was in his presence. Happiness, joy, delight were welling in her, filling her because this handsome, vital man belonged to her, every glorious inch of him. She had been attracted to him from the start, to his strength, his passion. She was still considering this revelation and reflecting on the tenderness of Lance's lovemaking when she saw a landau was approaching the house.

Lance glanced up from his newspaper and looked through the window, recognising the equipage. 'Good Lord!'

'Who is it?' Belle asked when he discarded the newspaper and got to his feet.

'My mother.'

His announcement had Belle shooting out of her chair. She was sorry that Lance's mother had missed their wedding and she was looking forward to meeting her, but because of the past and not sure how she would be received, she did feel a certain amount of trepidation.

'Oh, dear. I wish I'd known she was going to call.' Her hand went to her hair. 'I must look a sight.'

Aware of her nervousness, Lance took her hand and gave it a reassuring squeeze. 'Don't be nervous. She won't eat you. And you look wonderful.'

'I feel terrified,' Belle confessed, without taking her eyes from the equipage in the drive, seeing a woman alight after a few moments. 'But what if she doesn't like me and resents me for snaring her son?'

'I'm sure she'll do nothing of the sort. Don't worry. She'll love you, you'll see.'

Unfortunately Belle did not share Lance's confidence.

When Lance's mother swept into the hall, they were both there to greet her. Lance left Belle's side to enfold the older woman in his arms, expressing his delight at seeing her.

'Mother, it's wonderful that you're back. I hope your journey was uneventful.'

'It was. I returned late yesterday. Naturally I was eager to meet my new daughter-in-law,' she said, looking past him to the nervous young woman, 'so I came straight over.'

Lance held his hand out to Belle, urging her forwards with a reassuring smile.

'Mother, may I present Belle—my wife. Belle, this is my mother.'

'I am very happy to make your acquaintance, ma'am.'

Elizabeth Bingham, with light blue eyes and grey-streaked dark hair, was reserved and considered Belle for a long, uncertain moment before she gave a quick, worried glance at her son. As if with decision, she sighed and took Belle's hands in her own.

'Welcome to Ryhill, Belle—and please call me Elizabeth. I'm happy to meet you and delighted to have you in the family. I can't tell you how sorry I am that I missed your wedding—but we have plenty of time to get to know each other and you can tell me all about it. How are you settling in at Ryhill? You're not finding it too daunting, I hope.'

'I must confess that it's not what I'm used to. Since coming to England I've lived with my grandmother so I have no experience about running a house—but given time and application, I shall soon learn.'

'I have every confidence in you, Belle, and I shall be glad to help in any way I can. The servants are extremely competent, so I am sure you'll soon get used to running such a large house. What a beautiful name you have.'

'Actually, my name is Isabelle, but everyone—except Grandmother, that is—calls me Belle,' Belle explained.

'I may call you Belle?'

'Of course you may. I would like that.' Belle was completely taken with the easy friendliness of this attractive woman and accepted the feeling as mutual as Elizabeth's slender fingers squeezed her own before releasing them.

Elizabeth studied the dark green eyes regarding her solemnly from beneath a heavy fringe of dark lashes, and finally managed a smile. 'I am well pleased that you and Lance are married. It's time he settled down. You must find living in the country so very different from London—and a big change from America, I am sure.'

'Very much so.'

'I can imagine your marriage to Lance has drawn much attention hereabouts; in fact, it all happened with such speed that I cannot believe it. One minute you are unattached, Lance, and the next you aren't and announce that you are to be married in just a few weeks. Everything happened so fast. I suspect there are a lot of disappointed young ladies hereabouts.' She smiled at Belle. 'Whenever he comes home he always sets all their hearts aflutter with dreams and aspirations of securing him for themselves.'

'Then they'll all be disappointed,' Lance said, smiling proudly at his wife of forty-eight hours. 'I am well satisfied with the wife I have. I want no other.'

'And I approve your choice. Belle is charming and I know we will become good friends.'

'Come,' Lance said, sliding his hand to the small of Belle's back, where it rested comfortably. 'Let's go into the drawing room, where we can have some tea while we catch up on everything. I'm eager to know all about Ireland and Sophie—and about my new niece.'

He was about to propel his wife towards the drawing room, only to be halted in his stride by his mother's next words, spoken sharply.

'Your niece? Your niece is doing nicely, Lance. Would that you could show the same interest in your daughter.'

For a moment a deathly hush fell upon the hall. The word *daughter* caught Belle's blurred attention. She stared with dazed shock at her mother-in-law. She wanted to ask her what she meant by that remark, but the grim expression on her face as she looked at her son made her wary.

'I take it you have told Belle about Charlotte, Lance? I sincerely hope so, because this is where she should be.'

'Charlotte?' Belle asked, bemused. Her heart contracted. Slowly she turned to look at her husband, so distracted by her own rampaging emotions that she never noticed the sudden hardening of his face or the way he faced his mother, as if he were bracing himself to meet a firing squad. 'Lance? What is this? Please tell me.'

For a man usually so mentally astute, Lance was too stunned to move.

'This is no place to discuss the matter. I think we should go into the drawing room,' Elizabeth said, going ahead of them into the room and closing the door when they were all inside. Before entering the house she had sat for a moment in the landau, gathering her courage for what she had come to do. She shrank from the pain she must confront, and the hostility she might encounter from her son. 'Lance has a daughter, Belle—a daughter he clearly forgot to tell you about.'

'I didn't forget,' Lance ground out—his face was white, taut with rage. 'If you don't mind, Mother, I would prefer not to have this discussion.'

'No, Lance, I don't suppose you would,' Elizabeth said, clearly determined to stand her ground. 'You never do. It is true to say that you seem to forget your daughter exists half the time. I'm sorry, but that's the way it is. Little Charlotte is so sweet and so exactly like you, more every day. She is your responsibility and of course she must come to you. She can't stay with me. It isn't right.'

From across the room, wildly Belle looked about her, her mind already realising what her heart couldn't bear to believe. She could not bring herself to go to him. Suddenly her knees went weak. Reaching out for the nearest chair, she sank into the seat. Her insides had gone cold with dread. She waited for Lance to tell her the child had nothing to do with him, but he didn't.

'Lance—is this true?' she asked when she could find her voice. 'Do you have a—a daughter?'

He looked at her, his face hard and cold. 'Yes, I do.'

No slap on the face could have hurt so much. A sudden weight fell on Belle's heart at what was happening. She was stunned, bewildered, and a thousand thoughts raced across her brain and crashed together in confusion. There was no room in her heart or her mind for anything but this vast disappointment, which had already become an aching pain.

'I'm so sorry, my dear,' Elizabeth said, feeling sympathy for this young woman who had married Lance in ignorance, and anger towards her son for withholding from her an important part of his life. 'I don't like doing this and I certainly did not intend distressing you, but you have a right to be told. While in Ireland Charlotte contracted a fever and was quite poorly. She had us all worried for a time. I couldn't bear it if anything should happen to her while she is in my care. So I made up my mind to return her to her father—where she belongs.'

'How old is Charlotte?' Belle asked, her throat so constricted she could hardly get the words out.

'Nine months,' Elizabeth provided.

In wretched disbelief Belle looked from her mother-in-law to Lance. 'Nine months? But—she is still a baby.' She swallowed convulsively. 'Lance—how could you do this—to your daughter—and to me? Is—is there something wrong with her?'

'Charlotte is a perfect child, Belle,' Elizabeth assured her. 'She is beautiful, warm and loving—and she needs her father.'

'And her mother?'

Lance's face twisted and darkened. 'Her mother—

my wife—is dead,' he bit out. Pushing a hand, which had a curious tremble in it, through his thick hair, he took a step back, his face quite blank now. 'And now I would be obliged if we could speak of something else.'

'And I will not be so easily put off,' Belle was quick to retort, trying not to think of the woman—dear God, his wife—who had died such a short time ago, a woman who had borne him a child—a woman he must have loved and whom he still mourned. The thought was so immediate, so dreadful, that she didn't even want to think about it, for she could not bear it. She felt as if she had awakened from a glorious dream to a nightmare. 'Your mother is right. You should not have kept this from me. It was cruel and despicable. How did you think I would react when I found out—unless you didn't intend for me to find out and you planned to send the daughter you have so clearly abandoned to live somewhere in obscurity?'

Lowering her eyes, Belle smoothed the skirts of her gown with a hand that shook. Her dejection was caught by Lance. The muscles worked in his cheek as his jaw tightened and he turned and strode to the window. With his rigid back to them, his shoulders taut, he thrust his hands into his pockets.

Belle got up quickly. 'Please excuse me,' she said to Elizabeth, trying to keep her voice from trembling. 'I would like to be by myself for a while.'

Wishing she could find some words of comfort and support, but knowing there was nothing she could say just now that would help Belle, feeling that she must come to terms with all this on her own and that the questions would come later, Elizabeth gently touched her arm. 'Of course. I understand. Come to me when you want to talk.'

When Belle reached the door, Lance spun round. 'Belle—wait…'

She turned ferociously. 'Let it be, Lance. Enough. I have had enough for now. I don't think I can hear more.'

She went out and closed the door. She had learned many things since leaving her home in Charleston. Now she learned another, too. Anger was a great hardener, and it was this that helped her to walk across the hall and up the stairs to the room she shared with Lance.

Resting her back against the hard wood of the door, she looked at the bed, feeling a great urge to go to it and drag the covers off and rip them to shreds. Lance had not disputed the truth of what his mother had divulged, and offered no explanation. Belle wasn't physically hurt by this or wounded, yet inside she was bleeding.

Her cherished hopes were cold and dead, like a corpse, and could not be revived. She thought of Lance—her love—and all the feelings and emotions he had created were blighted and crushed, trust and confidence destroyed.

In her wretchedness she held herself tightly, her arms locked about her body. She had married Lance in the full knowledge that he didn't love her—and now she knew why. It explained so much. He had been married before. He'd had a wife who had been dead for just nine months. Deep in the recesses of her woman's heart, Belle had sensed there was something, and yet she had not recognised what it was. How could she?

That he had married her at all had made her happy. She believed he did care for her and that his fondness was growing into something deeper and stronger. Their loving in the privacy of their bed had delighted her, and it had seemed satisfying to her husband. She had been encouraged by it and believed they were putting down the roots of their marriage, when all the time he was a grieving widower who—she assumed for just then she could see no other explanation—must have loved his wife so much that he put the blame of her death on the birth of his child. What other explanation could there be for him to abandon her like that?

And what of his dead wife? Had he given to her what she wanted—his whole inner self a man gives to the one woman he loves? She, Belle, had given him her heart, though she supposed he was not aware of it. She had given him her trust—and that he had just broken. In fact, she had given him the sum and substance of herself, who had loved no man until him.

In the drawing room Elizabeth was about to leave, thinking it best to leave the newly married couple to talk, to sort out the whole sorry mess.

'Belle must be feeling quite wretched, Lance. Would you like me to go to her?'

He shook his head and turned to look at her. 'No— leave her. It's best that I go. We have to talk.'

Elizabeth went to him and placed a kiss on his cold cheek. 'Yes, you do. It is something you should have done before you married her. Don't hurt her further, Lance. She appears to be a strong and sensible young woman. She'll weather this—and I can only hope she will come to forgive your deception.'

When Lance entered the bedchamber it was to find Belle gathering toiletries and brushes from her dressing table.

'Going somewhere?'

Belle swung round at the scathing tone of her husband's voice. If she had expected him to fall on his knees in remorse for having deceived her, the moment she saw his face, as hard as a granite sculpture, it was obvious he would do no such thing. He didn't bother to come into the room, but instead remained in the doorway, his shoulder propped against the frame, his arms folded across his chest.

'I am moving to another room for the time being. I will get Daisy to move my clothes later.'

'You're what? Just like that?' he said in an awful, silky voice. Although Lance was willing to concede he had treated her badly, he had not expected anything like this, and nor was he going to allow her to deny him the physical side of their marriage. 'After two days of marriage, you want to move out of our marital bed?'

Belle took one look at the anger kindling in his glittering eyes and stopped what she was doing. Never had her heart felt so heavy. 'You must realise that this has come as a great shock to me. I need to be alone for a time—to think about what I am going to do.'

'And why do you think you have to do anything? You're staying here with me.'

The authority and the arrogance with which he spoke infuriated Belle. 'And you can go to hell, Lance Bingham. You cannot expect me to ignore your—indiscretion, to overlook what you have done and how it will affect me. I need to be alone for a time in order to think clearly.'

'You cannot separate yourself from me. You are my wife.'

'Then you should have shown me that courtesy,' she threw back at him fiercely. 'Prior to our marriage you should have told me you had been married before and that you had a child. That you didn't was deceitful and despicable.'

'Have you come to hate me in so short a time?'

'I don't hate you, Lance, but I must be given time to think through what I am going to do, how best to deal with this—and ponder on what my feelings toward you are now. In the meantime, with time to myself, I will then be able to determine my desires and hopes for the future without being unduly swayed one way or the other.'

Lance's eyebrows rose in amazement, then dropped swiftly and ferociously into a frown. Shrugging himself away from the door, he moved further into the room. 'Stop this foolishness. I do not like your tone, Belle. There's no need for all this melodrama.'

Belle moved forwards to confront him with her own rage. 'Melodrama? I am many things, but never dramatic. What you like or dislike is of supreme indifference to me just now. What were you thinking? You must have known I would find out some time. You have a daughter,' she said forcefully. 'Did you intend to hide her away from me? Did you really think that I would not find out?'

'I have not hidden her away.' Lance's voice flared with what could have been pain, but his face was black with anger. 'She is with my mother. And there she will remain until I decide what is to be done with her.'

'I think your mother might have something to say about that. What's the matter, Lance? Don't you like children?'

'I do, as a matter of fact, and when we have children of our own I will show you.'

'Children of our own?' she cried. 'Do you think I would even consider having a child by you when you can't even bring yourself to take care of the one you've already got—when you can't bear to look at her?' She spun round only to have Lance's hand clamp about her wrist and jerk her back to face him. 'Don't you dare manhandle me,' she warned.

Lance was confronted with a woman he didn't recognise—a coldly enraged, beautiful virago. Instead of apologising for his transgression, as he'd intended to do when his mother had left, he said, 'You're making too much of this. You are being totally irrational and absurd.'

Belle pulled her arm free with a wrenching tug that nearly dislocated her shoulder, then stepped back, well out of his reach, her chest rising and falling in fury as she mentally recoiled from the violence flashing in his eyes. 'You are a monster, and I am not being irrational or absurd so don't you dare say so. You have deceived me most cruelly, Lance. At this moment I am so angry that I cannot forgive you.'

'Why? For not telling you that I had a wife before you and that I have a daughter? Would it have made any difference to your decision to marry me?'

'I cannot answer that, but it would certainly have affected me.' She continued to face him, knowing it was quite hopeless, but she might as well say what she had to say. It could make matters no worse. 'What I don't understand is why she isn't here with her father—which is where she belongs.'

'She is being well looked after. She wants for nothing,' he stated coldly. 'I make sure of that.'

'Only her father. She has lost her mother. Are you so heartless you would deny her a father's love? To be without one parent is bad enough, but to be denied both because her father blames her for being the reason her mother died is the ultimate cruelty. Have you not thought how much you are failing her—and your first wife?'

The violent colour of his anger drained from his face, and his eyes glittered. 'What? What did you say?'

'That it would surely sadden your wife if she knew of your rejection of her child. Charlotte didn't ask to be born. At nine months old the child has done nothing to deserve your condemnation.'

There was a deep and dreadful silence, a silence so menacing, so filled with the unwavering determination of the two people involved. Lance took a step towards her, but Belle did not flinch. Their eyes were locked together in awful combat. Neither was about to retreat.

'You speak of things you know nothing about.' His face was white and set with rage, his voice shaking with the violence of his emotion. 'How dare you speak of my first wife to me—her name was Delphine and she died after giving birth on the eve of Waterloo—of what her attitude might be, of what she might be feeling? That is an outrage, one you have no right to commit. Damn you, Belle, for saying it.'

'No, it is you who will be damned, Lance Bingham. You and all the other men who take advantage and make a mockery of a woman's weakness—her vulnerable heart. Dear God, what have I done that I must deserve this—that I must endure…?'

'Nothing. You have done nothing at all. What I did was before I met you and has nothing to do with us—with our marriage. That is the reality of it, so you must accept it.'

'That's just the kind of arrogant remark I would expect from someone who knows they have done wrong.' Belle held herself erect and her words were as cold and cutting as a newly polished and sharpened sword. 'I will not accept it since you have a child that is going to play a big part in my life.'

'And I shall see to it that she has nothing to do with you.'

'We'll see about that. Now, since I can see no point in continuing with this conversation, I would be obliged if you would leave this room while I finish collecting my things.'

He was startled. 'What?'

'Either you leave—or I will.'

'Don't be ridiculous.'

'At this moment I don't want anything to do with you. Your attitude towards your own flesh and blood is unacceptable and disgusts me. I confess that I am not sure enough of my abilities as a mother, but I would care for Charlotte as if she were my own.'

Lance's face froze and his hard eyes locked on hers. 'Have a care, Belle. Do not cross me in this. You will not meddle in affairs that do not concern you. There is a line beyond which you must not go. You are almost at that line and you had best be careful you do not step over it.' He spun from her and walked towards the door.

'And Charlotte?'

He turned and looked back at her. His face was expressionless. His eyes were empty, a glacial blue emptiness that told her nothing of what he felt. 'Let's get this settled once and for all. I don't want her. She will stay at Bilton House with my mother,' he said, then, turning on his heel, his composure held tightly about him, he strode from the room.

Unable to move, Belle was unable to bear it. How could she? She turned her head away and stared, blinded and tormented, at the door through which her husband had just disappeared. Her throat ached and her eyes burned, but she would not cry. She held herself steady, resisting the urge to call him back, to let him take her in his arms, to hold her, and comfort her, and for her to soothe his agony with the outpouring of her own love, for this man whom she worshipped. But she could not.

Shortly afterwards she heard the sound of a horse's hooves on the gravel as Lance left to wherever it was he was going.

She didn't see him again that day. He hadn't returned by the time she retired to another room at the opposite end of the house to the one in which they had shared two wonderful nights making love until dawn. As she lay in the soft warmth of her solitary bed, aching for him, her heart felt sad. She had defied her husband—but at what price? She had seen him angry before, but his fury, his amazingly ominous objection to Charlotte being at Ryhill, was beyond anything she had imagined.

But she would stand firm on this. It was up to her to make him see that what he was doing was wrong. He was her husband for better or worse, and she wasn't going to run away at the first hurdle.

Two days, she thought with bitter cynicism, two days they had been married and already that first hurdle seemed a mile high, but it was not insurmountable. It was up to her to see this thing through. She was mistress of Ryhill, and if Lance still loved and mourned his first wife to the exclusion of his child, then she must be patient and wait for his wounds to heal, no matter how much she was hurting. In the meantime she saw it as her duty to bring Charlotte home.

* * *

The following morning Belle awoke late. Her head was aching, but she made herself go down to breakfast, to be informed when she enquired why Lance's place was not set that he'd eaten early before leaving the house. And so on the third morning of her marriage, Belle ate alone, having no idea where her husband was.

Bilton House was not as large as Ryhill nor as imposing, but surrounded by pleasant woodland and profusely flowering gardens, with a small lake where swans and moor hens floated aimlessly upon the tranquil surface, it was charming. When Belle's carriage drew up outside the door, Lance's mother came out to greet her. It was as if she had known she would come at that precise moment and was waiting. She kissed her daughter-in-law's cheek warmly and said how delighted she was by the visit.

'I think you know why I've come,' Belle said gravely.

Elizabeth smiled, walking with her to the door. 'To see Charlotte, I expect.'

'And to take her back with me to Ryhill—if you're in agreement, that is.'

'It is what I want—what I've wanted ever since the nurse turned up on my doorstep with Charlotte in her arms. I was beginning to despair of Lance ever wanting her.'

'He still doesn't—at least, not yet. But he will. He has to. If he could only try to accept Charlotte, she could be a source of comfort to him.'

Elizabeth paused in her stride and looked at her, her eyes dark with concern. 'Belle, I'm so dreadfully sorry if this has caused trouble between you and Lance. It is the last thing I want—and you so recently a bride.'

Belle returned her smile with a confidence that was not convincing to the older woman. 'Please don't worry. I'm sure things will turn out right. Lance is like a bear with a sore head just now, but this thing has to be faced and sorted out if we are to move on with our lives.'

'You're right. Now come inside and we'll have some tea. Then I'll take you to the nursery to meet your stepdaughter.'

They sat in a charming drawing room overlooking the gardens. Drinking tea and making polite small talk, Belle was relieved when Elizabeth suggested the two of them take a stroll in the garden. It wasn't until they were some distance from the house that she invited Belle to sit beside her on a bench beneath a trellised arch with trailing pink roses.

'I am glad for the opportunity to speak with you alone, Belle. I would like to speak to you on a matter other than Charlotte. I am not one for half-truths or evasion. Lance has told me how your betrothal came about, and I confess to being troubled about it at the time.'

An embarrassed flush mantled Belle's cheeks and she looked down at her hands. 'Yes, I'm sure you must have been.'

'I have to confess,' Elizabeth said tentatively, 'that because of what happened in the past between our two families, I can't pretend I wasn't shocked when he wrote and told me the two of you were to marry. I understand it was to salvage your reputation.'

'And my pride,' Belle added on a wry note.

'Lance's also. You have both been foolish. How did your grandmother react to what happened?'

'She was angry—and extremely disappointed in me. When I came to England, my social skills and knowledge about your ways were sadly lacking. Knowing very little of the kind of protocol that rules English society, she put so much effort into preparing me for the Season and had such high hopes for me.'

'The English Season, which is the time when young girls are introduced into society in the hope of securing a suitable husband, can be daunting at any time—but for a girl newly arrived from America, I'm sure it must have been terrifying. But please go on. How did your grandmother react to your behaviour?'

'When she learned of what I had done—and how Lance turned it to his advantage—considering my reputation to be more important than past indiscretions, and with the loss of a great deal of her pride, she insisted Lance did the honourable thing.'

'And she was right to do so. I would have done exactly the same.'

'Initially he didn't want to marry me—I now know it was probably because he was still mourning his first wife, Delphine. It was too soon. I can't blame him for not wanting to form any kind of relationship with another woman so quickly after losing his wife—never mind risk marrying one. To lose a wife on the eve of battle—to be thrown into the fray so to speak right away—I can't think how he's survived and stayed sane.'

'Lance is strong,' Elizabeth replied. 'He's one of the finest, strongest people I've known. I think he takes after his father in that. I realise that you were threatened with harsh consequences if he refused to marry you.'

'Yes,' Belle replied in a low voice, meeting the older woman's eyes directly. 'I compromised myself.'

'In a way, but from what I understand, Lance forced your hand when he took the diamonds.'

'Had I known that by rights they belonged to your family, I would have left well alone.'

'But you didn't.'

'No. Anyway, he did the honourable thing and agreed to marry me to save me from scandal, which would have ruined my reputation completely and devastated my grandmother.'

'I'm looking forward to meeting her—soon, I hope. It is my hope that we can put the whole sorry business of what happened so long ago behind us. But—you do care for Lance?' Elizabeth's concern that his business with Charlotte might have caused a rift in their relationship was evident in her voice.

'Yes,' Belle answered softly, in complete honesty. 'I care for him—very much.'

Elizabeth relaxed. She knew there was probably much more to the story than either Lance had cared to elaborate on or Belle was now revealing and that she hadn't been informed of the details. Nor did she think she needed to be. She knew her son was no saint—his hasty marriage to his first wife attested to that. And she really didn't care. She was just immensely relieved that Lance had married a woman of whom she approved and who cared deeply for her son.

'Well then, that's all right. I wouldn't worry about how you came together. I know my son, and he wouldn't let himself be forced into anything if he truly objected to it. Besides, you are underestimating your appeal. You're so lovely, my dear. Lance probably took one look at you and couldn't resist you.'

Belle smiled. 'Thank you for the compliment,' she said simply, with gratitude for being accepted so unquestioningly.

'He's already more than half in love with you.' When Belle stared at her with wide, questioning eyes, she smiled and patted her head. 'I saw the way he looked at you yesterday when I arrived at Ryhill. No man looks at a woman that way unless he's in love. I hope it works out for you both, Belle, I really do. Besides, I for one will be glad to put that wretched business of the diamonds behind us. I meant what I said. I look forward to meeting your grandmother—it cannot be soon enough.' She paused before saying carefully, 'Now, would you like me take you to see Charlotte?'

'Yes. I—am looking forward to seeing her.'

'She is quite adorable and has everyone eating out of the palm of her hand. Has Lance told you anything about his wife—Delphine?'

Belle shook her head. 'No.'

'Well, all I know is that their marriage was of short duration. That is what he told me. Apparently she was with him in Spain. When the fighting was over they parted. He had no idea she was carrying his child. It wasn't until the eve of Waterloo that he saw her again—she had just been delivered of Charlotte and wasn't expected to live. Lance did the right thing by her and married her.'

'Oh, dear.' Belle sighed deeply. 'He seems to make a habit of *doing the right thing* when it comes to women.'

Elizabeth laughed lightly. 'It does seem like that. I cannot speak for Delphine since I never met her, but where you are concerned, my dear, I really believe he has. Now come along,' she said, getting up and smoothing her skirts, 'I'll take you to the nursery.'

This was the moment Belle had worried about most, seeing Lance's child, his daughter, who would be a constant reminder of the woman he had married before her. Cool, steady, resolute, she tried to appear as though there was nothing out of the ordinary about the situation, though inside she was quaking.

She was aware of Elizabeth's eyes upon her as the nursemaid reached into the crib and lifted Lance's daughter out, holding her with infinite gentleness as she handed her to her grandmother. Elizabeth smiled tenderly at the pretty dark-haired bundle. Charlotte was awake and lifted her face from the hollow of her grandmother's neck and turned her head and peeped at Belle.

Belle's heart did a somersault. It was like looking at Lance. The same startling deep blue eyes and long black lashes. Her hair, a tumble of glossy ebony curls, lay in soft swirls about her small head. She even had her father's tiny cleft in her round chin. There could be no doubt that she was a Bingham and she was beautiful. Belle could not tear her gaze away from the child. She even had the same arrogant set to her baby jaw and the slight lift at the corners of her mouth that Lance had.

Belle was aware that Elizabeth was watching her closely. In spite of her determination to take her meeting of her husband's child in her stride, she felt her heart sink. Then she firmly pulled herself together. Charlotte was part of the legacy she'd inherited when she'd married Lance, so she'd better get used to it. Reaching out, she gently placed her finger in the little hand, smiling when Charlotte's tiny fingers curled round it firmly and she chortled happily.

'Are you all right?' Elizabeth asked, as if worried by her reaction. 'What are you thinking, Belle?'

She managed a courageous smile. 'I am thinking that I have a beautiful, adorable stepdaughter. I can see she favours her father. I confess I have been worried about this moment, and now I can't see why. You must be proud of her.'

'I am. Very proud—as I hope my son will be eventually.'

'You will miss her when she leaves.'

'I shall, but she won't be too far away for me to visit. Now, if you still want to take her with you, I'll instruct the nurse to make her ready.'

Chapter Nine

Belle's arrival at Ryhill with Charlotte and her nursemaid was expected. With great excitement servants were hovering in the hallway, longing to catch a glimpse of the master's child. The master himself had left the house after a hasty breakfast and had not yet returned, so he had no idea his offspring from his first marriage was about to take up residence in the nursery, which the mistress had ordered to be made ready for the young arrival.

The servants knew very little about the new Earl of Ryhill's private life, only that he was a military man and was the old Earl's nephew. They were aware that he had a child by his first wife, now deceased, living with his mother at Bilton House, so it was only natural she should come to Ryhill now the earl had a new wife.

The young nursemaid carried the bright-eyed, happy and gurgling child—who was delighted with all the attention she was receiving—up the stairs to the nursery. Two footmen emptied the carriage of all the paraphernalia that had accompanied the child from Bilton House.

Belle helped the nursemaid, who was thoroughly

devoted to her young charge, settle in. When Charlotte was washed and fed and put down for the night, Belle looked down at her stepdaughter and felt something permanent enter her heart. It was a warm, melting feeling that she supposed all mothers felt when they looked at their offspring. Yet this was not her child—but she was the closest thing to a mother Charlotte had. Whatever the future held, she vowed to get to know the child and to do her best by her. She really was beautiful, a fine child, healthy and robust, and she prayed Lance would come to love her.

When Lance returned later that night and Masters told him of the child's arrival, he was furious.

Belle heard his raised voice coming from the hall as soon as she left her room. After she smoothed the front of her skirt with slightly trembling hands, it was with a mixture of alarm and trepidation that she went downstairs to face the fireworks.

She found him in his study in the middle of pouring himself a drink. He had his back to her. He'd been riding in the rain and had removed his jacket, having flung it over the nearest chair. His white shirt was soaked, clinging wetly to his broad shoulders, and his brown riding boots were covered in mud.

Sensing her presence, he whirled round so violently that he sloshed brandy down his shirt front. He looked directly at his wife as she closed the door, and she felt the need to recoil from the expression in his eyes. They were hard, with nothing in them of the lively warmth, the good humour that had once lit up his face. They narrowed with what looked like venom and his mouth snarled in a cruel twist.

'So, you condescend to join your husband,' he uttered
with a sarcastic bite. 'What you have done is heartless
and arrogant. How dare you defy me? How dare you dis-
regard my wishes and bring that child into this house to
satisfy your own whim?

'It was not a whim and how dare *you* criticise me?'

'What's that supposed to mean?'

'I don't think I have to spell it out, Lance, do you? I
am sorry if Charlotte's arrival upsets you, but she is here
now so you had better get used to it.'

'You're sorry?' he mocked scathingly. 'Sorry for
what? Defying me?'

'Yes, but not for bringing her here—to where she so
rightly belongs.'

'I want an explanation from you—a reasonable explanation as to why you thought you had the right to go
against my express wishes in the matter of *my* daughter.'

'Well, that's a start,' Belle bit back, thrusting her chin
haughtily. 'At least you acknowledge you *have* a daughter.'

Lance's eyes had a terrible blankness in them and
about his mouth was a thin white line of anger. He went
to his wife, standing over her like a hawk over a rabbit,
and Belle was aware that there was some dreadful de-
structive power in him which if released could destroy
her. But she stood her ground, refusing to let him beat
her on the matter of his daughter.

'You will take her back, do you hear me?'

'Take her back where?'

'To my mother.'

'Your mother, like me, is of the opinion that Charlotte is better off here—with her father.'

'Indeed, then we shall have to think of something—'

Belle cut through his words, trying to contain her

mounting disgust. 'Dear Lord, Lance, your attitude to that child is inhuman. What kind of father are you? Have you never enquired about her—asked if she was healthy and whole? Are you really not interested at all? Charlotte is a baby—your baby—and this is her home.'

'I shall have her removed. There are ways and means.'

'Is that so?' Belle thrust her face closer to his. Her eyes had changed from their usual warm green to the cold spark of emeralds. There were spots of red on each cheek bone, and her mouth was as thinly drawn with determination as her husband's. She held her head high with defiance, and for an instant she saw a glimmer of something in Lance's eyes that, had she not known better, she might have called admiration. 'You should know that if she goes, I go, and there won't be a thing you can do about it.'

Lance stared at her in stupefied amazement as she spun round and stalked to the door. 'You? Don't be ridiculous. You are my wife. You are not going anywhere.'

Belle spun round, a savage, spitting she-cat in defence of herself and the child. She strode back to him, thrusting her face close to his. 'Try to stop me. I mean it, Lance. Your behaviour is totally unreasonable and quite unacceptable. If Charlotte goes, I go with her. I swear I will.'

'Your determination to defend my daughter is commendable, but Charlotte is not your responsibility. She is not your child.'

'No, she is yours,' she hissed. 'Accept it, Lance. That she is not of my flesh is quite irrelevant. I have made myself responsible for her since she is defenceless and she has no one else to speak for her.'

'Dear God, you will not do this. I will not allow it.'

'You will not allow? Ha! Your choice of words is disastrous, Lance Bingham. I am not a servant to be ordered about at will. I am your wife. I shall do whatever I please, and you shall not stop me.'

'Will I not? If you do not heed my warning—call it advice, if you like—you will get a taste of what I can do.' Lance's voice was coldly dangerous.

Belle was beyond caution. 'Advice? If I wanted advice,' she retorted, her eyes sparkling with jade fire, 'you would be the last person I would ask.'

His jaw tightened. 'My compliments,' he said curtly, and Belle watched his mercurial mood take an obvious, abrupt turn for the worse. 'You've learned very quickly what it takes to displease me.'

Fixing an artificial smile on her face, Belle said lightly, 'That wasn't too difficult. Before our marriage you found me strong-willed and direct. I even recall you saying how you admired those traits in a woman. Now you're complaining because I am those things. There is simply no pleasing you.'

To Belle's mortification, Lance didn't deny he found her strong-willed and direct.

'We can discuss how you can *please* me when you return to my bed.'

Outrage exploded in Belle's brain. 'How dare you say that?' she said, her colour rising with indignation. He expected her to resume physical relations as if nothing had happened. 'If you thought you'd married a complaisant, adoring female who would rush to do your bidding, you didn't get one.'

'I will.'

Belle tossed her head and turned. 'You're wrong, Lance Bingham,' she said and started for the door.

'Belle, you are my wife,' he informed her coldly.

She stopped and half-turned, her delicate brows arched in feigned surprise, her colour gloriously high. 'I am aware of that,' she replied, and with a calm defiance, she added, 'and much good it has done me so far.' Having thus informed him that she was beginning to regret her position as his wife, she turned and walked across the room, feeling his eyes boring holes into her back. Not until she put her hand on the handle of the door did his low, ominous voice break the silence.

'Belle.'

'Yes?' she said, looking back.

'Think very carefully before you make the mistake of defying my orders again. You'll regret it. I promise you.'

Despite the cold shiver of alarm his silken voice caused in her, Belle lifted her chin. 'Goodnight, Lance. I hope you find time to reconsider your attitude where Charlotte is concerned.' At that moment the sound of a child crying in the upper part of the house could be heard. 'That is your daughter making her presence known. Perhaps she's as reluctant to be in her father's house as he is for her to be here.'

On that note she left him seething. Lance sank down into a chair, dark brows pulled together in a black frown. He would accomplish what he had set out to do, which was to make Belle understand the rules she would have to live by as his wife, and was certain he would succeed no matter how she fought against it. The very idea of being defied as she had defied him by bringing Charlotte to Ryhill, knowing how he felt, was unthinkable. Moreover his body's almost uncontrollable desire for her when he had faced her defiance, amazed him, and thoroughly displeased him, even though he realised her removal from his bed was partly the cause.

A reluctant smile replaced his dark frown. He realised Belle would never be a complaisant wife in her vibrant, feisty spirit, and with those stormy eyes flashing like angry sparks, her cheeks stained an angry pink, he would find ample compensation.

In an attempt to bring some kind of order into the house, over the days that followed Belle carried on as though the acrimony that existed between her and Lance did not exist, hoping that given time the tension would lessen. If the servants wondered at the manner in which the master and mistress treated one another it was not spoken of out loud, but they thought it odd for them to be at loggerheads after just two days of wedded bliss. There was no contact between them, no touching of hands as there had been at the beginning, no soft glances nor exchange of affection.

Charlotte was an easy, engaging child and everyone who came into contact with her was drawn under her spell—everyone, that is, but her father. Taking a genuine interest in the child, Belle spent a great deal of her time in the nursery, so that she and Charlotte could grow slowly used to one another. She would watch her crawl about the rug and sit before the fire with her on her lap, holding her carefully, liking the feel of the plump, sweet-smelling body against her own, her cheek resting on her ebony curls and listening to her baby talk. She sang soft lullabies to her to get her to sleep, and fully weaned, fed her custard and eggs and boiled milk, for the woman who had wet nursed her in the beginning had left to take up another position.

Determined not to keep her hidden away, on one occasion when Belle had carried her out into the garden, she saw Lance watching from the window of his study. She looked at him, hoping to see some sign of pleasure, of emotion, even sentimentality, but there was nothing visible on his face. It was quite expressionless, and then he turned away.

A heaviness centred in Belle's chest whenever she considered the days ahead. Instead of the tension easing, it only seemed to grow. She had driven Lance away, and this filled her with pain. But her own unfulfilled yearning for him was worse. She knew what it was like to be pleasured by a considerate and tender lover, and her discovery had marked her physically—a hot, restless longing that had her twisting and turning in her lonely bed night after night.

She wished they could share their thoughts and aspirations and truly talk together, instead of relying on the coldly constrained words that usually passed for conversation between them. She wanted to reach out to him when they were together, to have him possess her. She did love him—so very much—why else would she be experiencing this painful yearning? She was finding it harder and harder to retreat into cool reserve when she was near him, especially when memories of his kisses, his caresses and how it felt to wake in his arms, kept spinning around inside her mind.

But she could not bring herself to go to him. The only thing that could put things right was for her to take Charlotte back to his mother, and this she would not do.

Belle swept into the dining room, the skirt of her rose-pink gown swirling about her. Though she had been doubtful about the colour, Daisy had persuaded her to wear it, telling her the colour gave her a fragility and vulnerability her husband would find attractive. The neckline was scooped low and showed more of Belle's cleavage that she considered suitable for a quiet evening at home, but nevertheless she agreed to wear it, knowing that in his present state of mind, it would have no effect whatsoever on Lance Bingham.

And she was right. His deep blue eyes looked somewhere over her smooth, white shoulders as he handed her a pre-dinner glass of sherry, careful not to touch her hand.

She smiled at him. 'Thank you, Lance.'

He merely nodded curtly, his eyes still retaining their total uninterest, as though she were a stranger, so she was surprised when he said with cynicism, 'The colour becomes you—rose—but not without thorns, eh, Belle?'

'Please don't start, Lance. I hoped we could enjoy our meal together without arguing.'

'I have no intention of arguing tonight,' he said, sitting down and crossing his long legs. Reaching for a newspaper, he immersed himself in its contents, paying her no attention—it was as if she didn't exist.

With an ache in her heart, Belle looked at him admiringly. His athletic frame was resplendent in midnight-blue jacket and trousers, his shirt and neckcloth dazzling white. The flame from the candles turned his skin to amber and darkened his eyes to that of the night sky. His dark hair was still damp from his bath and curled vigorously in his nape. He was a vigorous man, and she thought of his smile, how his teeth would gleam in a bold smile.

Belle's young heart beat rapidly in her chest. No wonder she was so much in love with him.

'Have you made arrangements for us to go the picnic tomorrow, Lance?' she asked in attempt to break the uneasy tension that hung in the room.

Lance jerked his head up, lowering the newspaper. 'Picnic? What picnic?'

'At Sir John Bucklow's house. You can't have forgotten. It promises to be a lovely day. I'm looking forward to it.'

He raised the newspaper and continued to browse. 'That's too bad, because we aren't going.'

'Oh?' Belle said. 'That's a shame, for you will miss a splendid day out.'

Lance dropped the newspaper into his lap. 'I don't think you heard me, Belle. I said *we* weren't going.'

'I know. I heard you, but I have no intention of disappointing my grandmother and your mother. We have arranged to meet them there—to introduce them to each other.'

'Why?' he drawled with bitter irony. 'So we can play happy families?'

'It's about time, don't you think? I haven't seen my grandmother since our wedding, and I would like to see her. She has told me the Bucklows' picnics are most delightful and it promises to be a lovely day.'

Lance looked at her steadily. 'I am not going and I refuse to let you go alone.'

'Do you mind telling me why?'

'Because I'm in no mood for a picnic. When your grandmother and my mother meet, they can come here.'

'But it is arranged.'

'Then I will *unarrange* it. Is that clear enough?'

'Quite clear,' Belle told him. She was crushed, but when she looked at him and found him observing her pained reaction with cynical amusement, as hurt as she was, she became quietly angry and felt anything but meek or sad. So for no viable reason, Lance didn't intend to go the Bucklows' picnic, but she did. She knew she would be playing with fire and that she might anger him to the point where he would explode with rage, but she would continue to stoke the fire of his emotions—either fury or desire, for she was sure that one of them would eventually drive him from his stony silence.

When the food was brought in, seated across from Belle, after one mouthful, Lance put his fork down with a grimace of distaste.

'You don't like the salmon mousse,' Belle ventured to say calmly.

He shoved his plate away. 'Not tonight.'

'Would you like something else? I'm sure cook has something—some consommé, perhaps?'

'I do not want consommé.'

'Then—perhaps some—'

'Leave it, Belle,' he snapped. 'Why all the questions?'

'I was only trying to tempt you with something else.'

His furious gaze shot to hers. Tempt? she said. There was only one thing she could tempt him with and it wasn't his damned dinner. 'I'd rather you spared me the wifely concern.'

His sarcastic reply nettled her. His continued determination to punish her was beginning to get on her nerves, but it was pointless to attempt a discussion when he was in such a foul mood.

Lance suddenly threw his napkin on the table and stood up. 'I'm going out. Enjoy your meal.'

Alone, Belle put down her fork and sighed. She glanced around her at the beautiful room, at the candlelight gleaming on the tableware, shimmering on crystal glasses, and suddenly everything seemed so futile.

On the other side of the door Lance stood rigidly still, his hands clenching and unclenching as he tried to bring the onslaught of his fury under control. His breathing was harsh and ragged, his expression so incensed, so bleakly embittered by what Belle was doing to him. She was so damned lovely that it required all his self-control to be in the same room with her. Night after night he lay awake in his empty bed, trying to find an explanation for every unexplainable word or action on Belle's part.

Her determination to have her own way over the child, the way she had faced him in outrageous mutiny as she had reproached him and defended Charlotte, had thrown him off balance; he had not expected her to react so strongly to him having been married before and producing a child from that marriage. And to have to sit across from her at the dinner table when she looked so unbearably beautiful, so young and vulnerable despite the seductive allure of her gown, to smell the intoxicating scent of her so that he almost lost his resolve and dragged her into his arms, almost destroyed his sanity.

He didn't know how long he could stand this living arrangement. Perhaps if they weren't living under the same roof he could find some relief from his agony. His heart and mind understood the harsh reality that Belle would have nothing to do with him while ever he continued to have nothing to do with his daughter. But his body tormented him with the same insatiable desire for her he'd always felt.

Deciding to take up an invitation issued by a friend and close neighbour earlier to partake of a game of cards at his home with a group of others, he left the house. He would welcome the diversion, and by dawn he would manage to drink himself into near oblivion.

* * *

On the morning of the picnic the sun caressed the land in a warm glow. Thinking she would be going with Lance in the carriage, Belle had arranged to meet her grandmother there mid-morning. Hoping Lance would have changed his mind and would go after all, Belle was deeply disappointed when he failed to put in an appearance. Having second thoughts about going in the carriage, she donned her riding habit and took one of the horses from the stable.

Belle had been gone half an hour when Lance arrived back at the house, having spent the night at his friend's house. The night had been a total disaster and he was not in the best of moods. No matter how much he'd drunk or how much he'd tried, he had been unable to concentrate on the game or the jovial masculine conversation of his friends. The annoying fact was that he'd been unable to dispel all thoughts of Belle from his mind.

He was beginning to think he had married a witch, a witch who had got under his skin like thorn with barbs. It was unbearable to have her there and it hurt like hell to pull her out. His mind kept wandering to the night before and how she had looked in that rose-coloured dress, with her charms displayed in fabulous wantonness. What the hell was she trying to do to him? His hands had ached to touch her, to feel her soft skin next to his, and his desire had been almost beyond bearing. Desire and lust. He told himself that that was what he felt for Belle—desire and lust—but deep down inside him he knew it was more than that, much more.

She had been disappointed when he'd told her he had no intention of taking her to the picnic, as if he were doing it to torture her—which made him ask why he had done it. Was it to hurt her, to spoil her pleasure? Hell, he had no rational reason for not going and it was inconsiderate on his part to ruin his mother's and Belle's grandmother's plans to become acquainted at the picnic.

Without more ado he bathed and dressed and went in search of his wife, but failed to locate her. Being told by Masters that she had already left for the picnic, Lance absorbed this with stunned disbelief. Turning on his heel, his face glacial, he headed in the direction of the stables.

Belle arrived early at the Bucklows' residence. Carriages, curricles and horses were scattered in the copse where the picnic was to be held, with men and women dressed in their finest clothes, the women parading about holding brightly coloured parasols. Some of the guests were on horseback, ready for the start of the ride across country before the picnic commenced.

Seeing her grandmother already ensconced beneath a large parasol, Belle left her horse tethered to a post and went to sit with her. Not having seen her since the wedding, she was relieved to find her sitting alone. There were things she had to tell her that would both upset and shock her, but she had to be told before Lance's mother arrived.

Belle smiled and kissed her grandmother and they exchanged pleasantries and discussed the wedding, but the troubled look in her granddaughter's eyes did not deceive the dowager countess. Something was wrong, very wrong, that was obvious.

'You look troubled, Isabelle. Is something worrying you? You are happy at Ryhill, and your husband is treating you well, I hope?'

Belle sighed. 'There is something you should know, Grandmother. Something has happened—something that Lance should have made known to me before I agreed to marry him.'

The smile on the dowager's face faded when she saw the unhappiness in her granddaughter's eyes. Her mouth went dry and her heart began to beat in heavy, terrifying dread as she prepared herself for the worst. 'Tell me.'

It didn't take Belle long to recount everything that had occurred since her marriage to Lance. She spoke calmly, telling her of how Lance had been a widower when they had married, how she had fetched Charlotte from Bilton House and that the child was now living at Ryhill, where she belonged.

The dowager was not at all pleased by this latest crisis. 'I am shocked—deeply so. Your husband should not have kept a matter of such importance from you. You should have been told. Of course you are angry—justifiably so. But how has all this affected your relationship? Are you…?'

'Estranged?' Belle smiled and shook her head. 'No. Things are strained between us, but I am confident that everything will be resolved. Lance is suffering very badly. He cannot bring himself to accept his child. It seems grossly unfair that he should blame Charlotte for her mother's death, but he is battling with himself to accept her. I am sure of it. He no longer mentions her going back to his mother, so I am hopeful that it won't be long.'

'For your sake I sincerely hope you are right. The scandal that brought the two of you together will be as nothing compared to this. You have had an immense shock, a terrible disappointment, but you are an Ainsley and will bear it well. If you had known any of this before you agreed to be his wife, would it have made any difference to your decision?'

'No, I don't think it would. Lance is a good man, a fine man…' She fell silent, unable to say the words she wanted to say. But her grandmother's astute mind had already picked up on what she had been about to say.

'And you love him.'

Belle nodded, meeting her gaze calmly. 'Yes. I do. I love him very much, and I will do all I can to help him get through this.'

'Then I can only hope he is deserving of your love.'

When her grandmother stood up to acknowledge an acquaintance, Belle's attention became distracted when she saw the daunting figure of her husband astride his horse in conversation with a group of gentlemen across the copse. Jolts of shock and panic shot through her. His eyes were levelled on her like a pair of duelling pistols, impaling her on his gaze, leaving her in no doubt that he intended to seek her out at the first opportunity and berate her most severely for defying him again.

But, strangely, she was encouraged by his arrival, encouraged because on being informed that she had left for the picnic, he had cared enough to come and look for her. Belle slanted a long, considering look at him as he sat his strong, well-muscled hunter. Attired in a dark green coat, gleaming brown-leather riding boots and a pair of buckskin riding breeches that fit him to perfection, in her opinion he was by far the most attractive man present.

She watched him as he talked and joked with lazy good humour with those in his group. He looked completely relaxed as he dismounted some distance away from her. His horse shied slightly. As if wishing to restrain it, he ran his hand down the sleek neck, showing that the beast belonged to him and that he knew how to make it obey. Looking in her direction, he began to lead his horse to where she stood.

Unfortunately, he was too far away to reach her before there was a blast on a trumpet heralding the start of the ride. Beneath Lance's glower, Sir John Buckley, who had eyes for no one but Belle, rushed forwards. He bent and clasped his hand to receive her dainty foot, then raised her up. After seating herself and placing a knee about the pommel, taking the reins in a practised grip and completely avoiding looking in Lance's direction, Belle laughed and urged her mount into an easy canter across the fields with the rest of the riding party.

To be so ignored, angered beyond bearing, leaping up astride his own horse, Lance sent the huge black stallion thundering after her, his huge hooves sending clods of earth flying. A race ensued and Belle, with light-hearted abandon, followed the others through the trees and along winding paths, her mare holding her own until they reached open fields and she could stretch her legs to their advantage. They galloped on, Belle urging her mount over any obstacle in her path with a fearless abandon that had Lance filled with admiration one minute and furious that she could be so reckless the next.

When the pace became less hectic and the exhilarated riders slowed their mounts to a sedate walk back to the copse. Lance rode towards Belle, but, to his fury, the overzealous John Buckley was there before him and chatting to her amiably.

Belle was happy to converse with the young man about the pleasant countryside, when a sudden awareness swept over her. One moment she was thoroughly occupied with learning about the different landmarks, the next she was oblivious to everything but her heart gathering speed and the certain, inexplicable realisation that Lance was close at hand.

The perception was quickly confirmed, when his cold voice said, 'If you don't mind, Buckley, I would like a word with my wife.' His eyes raked them both, considering each of them, increasing Sir John's discomfiture by no small degree.

Even though there had been no slightest hint of impropriety, Sir John stiffened apprehensively and stammered, 'I—I beg your pardon, Bingham, b-but Lady Bingham expressed an interest in her surroundings. I was just…'

'Then I shall be happy to familiarise her with them myself.'

Sir John fell back, and, after excusing himself, rode away.

One quick look at Lance's face convinced Belle that he was absolutely furious with her. Not only were his eyes glinting like shards of ice, but the muscles in his cheeks were tensing to a degree that she had never seen before.

'Your skill is exceeded only by your common sense, Belle,' he reproached severely. 'Did you have to take those jumps? You could have broken your neck.'

'Really, Lance, there's no need to get all hot and bothered about a few measly hedges and fences. I've ridden harder courses than that and jumped obstacles twice as high. And you should not have spoken to Sir John like that—making him think you were jealous…'

Lance squinted in the sun's bright glare. 'Damn it, Belle, I *am* jealous.'

His simple acknowledgement confused Belle so completely that for a moment she could find nothing to say. To feel jealousy one had to care. As usual, his tall, hard body radiated strength and vitality, but his dark blue eyes held a dangerous glitter. A winsome smile touched her lips. 'Why, Lance, you really are quite terrifying when you're angry—and jealous.'

'I'm jealous of any man who claims even a moment of your time when that moment could be spent with me,' he snapped unreasonably, his thigh brushing hers as their horses bumped together. The unexpected contact made him acutely conscious of the celibate life he had led since she had deserted his bed. He was hungry for her and could hardly restrain himself from reaching out and dragging her from her horse into his arms and finding the softest grass on which to lay her. 'Was it too much for you to wait and ride with me? It was my intent. Or have you come to regret our marriage and want rid of me?' The fact that she might, cut through his heart like a knife.

Belle gasped, astounded that he should even think such a thing, let alone voice it. 'Be assured that despite everything that has happened lately, I have not. Nothing could be further from my mind. I was merely enjoying myself and couldn't resist riding off. I couldn't help myself.'

'Just like you couldn't help yourself when you defied me yet again and came here when I expressly told you the picnic was off. Your flagrant disobedience in coming here without me deserves retaliation.'

Belle looked at him with considerable amusement. 'Retaliation? Goodness! How interesting. How will you do that? Will you beat me—lock me in my room and starve me? What?'

Unmoved by her humorous account of the punishments he might mete out, Lance scowled darkly. 'Don't be ridiculous. I don't know what is going on in your mind, Belle, but I cannot imagine giving you up. Indeed, the very idea of you being pursued by another man rankles sorely.'

'That is not what I want either, Lance,' she answered softly, truthfully, in an attempt to placate his ire. What he said confused her, for it was in complete variance to his behaviour of late. Unhooking her leg from the pommel, she slipped off her mount with an easy grace.

'Of late you have been avoiding me as if I carried some contagious disease,' he growled, also dismounting, and cursing the lack of privacy they had. 'Indeed, my dear wife, if I did not know differently I would say you protect your virtue more adroitly than any chastity belt ever could. I am both puzzled and concerned at the way you are behaving.'

'How am I behaving?'

'You are cool and unresponsive.'

He towered over her, his overpowering physical presence so close that Belle felt dizzy. An ache lodged in her chest. His accusations were true. But how else did he expect her to behave? Her grandmother had taught her to be a lady, to exhibit restraint and proper decorum, even in the most trying circumstances, and her upbringing made it impossible to be other than cool when she was upset. Bleakly she glanced up at him. She truly was deeply in love with him. Why else would she be experiencing this painful yearning? She was finding it harder and harder to retreat into cool reserve when she was near him.

'Do you not agree that I have justifiable reason to be cool and unresponsive?'

'Absolutely not.'

She could not bring herself to melt towards him, not

when he had made no move to approach his daughter and only seemed to want her, his wife, for the physical pleasure her body could bring. Not when he would satisfy only her wanton need and not the ache in her heart. Yet she felt a strange, satisfying contentment that her nearness could affect him even in the company of so many.

'If we are not together as much as you would like us to be and it upsets you, Lance, then I apologise. Perhaps if you were at home more—with your family'

'Stop it, Belle. I know what you're saying and nothing is changed.'

'I'm sorry.'

Lance wasn't willing to be denied. Taking her arm, he drew her into the shade of a large beech tree, out of sight of prying eyes.

'I'm sorry if I've made you angry,' she said. 'I didn't mean to.'

'You did, and it matters to me. A lot, in fact! I recall you saying that there was nothing you wanted more than to be married to me. You sure as hell have a funny way of showing it.'

Belle was overwhelmed by his sarcasm. 'You are foolish if you imagine that because I have withheld myself from you, that I want no part of you. If you do, then you are both blind and witless,' she said quietly.

He scowled at her darkly. 'Am I?'

'Yes.'

Placing a finger lightly under her chin, he tipped her face up to his, his anger of a moment earlier dissolving when he looked into the depths of her eyes and saw pain. 'I'm sorry, Belle. We haven't got off to a very good start, have we?'

'We could start again with you telling me about

Delphine, and why you married me when you were still mourning her loss.'

Pain clouded his eyes. 'I could, but it won't change anything.'

'You mean it won't change how you feel about your daughter.'

He nodded.

When Belle saw the taut line of his jaw and how his expression had hardened slightly, her mouth went dry and her heart began to beat in heavy, terrifying dread as she sensed that again he had withdrawn from her. 'I know you are a very private person, but I am your wife. If you cannot open up to me, even if it is just a little bit, then it bodes ill for the future.'

'You are right. You should know about Delphine— and why I married you. When your grandmother suggested we should wed, I was repulsed by the very idea of having my life laid out and being forced to commit to something I had not thought of myself. Yet much as I wanted to rebel against it, I found myself wanting you.' His eyes suddenly twinkled with amusement. 'Besides, your grandmother was not above forcing an appropriate response in a wedding ceremony by surreptitiously holding a gun directed towards my head,' he said, chuckling softly, forcing a smile to Belle's lips at the vision of this tall, broad-shouldered man standing in wide-eyed alarm before her much smaller grandmother.

Belle's heart soared and his confession brought a smile to her lips, but the grim expression that suddenly appeared on his face gave her a sense of unease and made her wary.

'I also wanted you to be quite sure that marrying me was what you wanted. Marriage is a great step. I realised how fast things were happening, that you'd scarcely had time to draw breath since that night at Carlton House.'

'It was my entire fault, despite my grandmother blaming you, for what happened. It was down to me. I stole into your house, into your bedchamber. It was unfortunate that you had half the *ton* dining with you that night and to witness my indiscretion.'

Lance looked at her and his expression softened as his conscience tore at him. 'The blame was all mine. If I hadn't taken that damn necklace in the first place you wouldn't have been driven to what you did. I had no reservations about making you my wife. There was nothing I desired more than that. But you might not have been so enthusiastic about having me for a husband if I had told you about Delphine—that I'd been married before and had a child.'

'But why should it mean anything? Plenty of people marry twice. There is no shame in that. Your wife was dead—in the past. She couldn't pose a threat now. Could she? When, Lance? When did the two of you marry?'

'On the eve of Waterloo. Shortly after Charlotte was born.'

'You were only recently a widower. That much I have learned. I don't wonder you were against marrying again so soon after Delphine. Did—did you love her very much?'

He turned a glacial stare upon her. 'Only a woman would ask such a question.'

'A wife would want to know if her husband's dead wife was still a threat,' Belle replied coolly. The harshness of his voice told her that whatever feelings he'd had for Delphine had left scars, as yet unhealed. She had revived painful memories for him and she regretted her curiosity.

His voice was mocking when he eventually spoke. 'Aren't you going to ask me who she was, and how long we had known each other? Women always want to know everything.'

'If you want to tell me, you will.' She turned her head and looked at him. 'You spent many years as a soldier in Spain. I already know that. You must have known many women on your travels. I don't mean to pry into your relationship with Delphine.'

Lance was drawn by the sincerity in Belle's gaze. He felt his resistance waver. 'In truth, I don't know what I felt for Delphine. It was—complicated.'

'Was she very beautiful?'

'In an exotic kind of way. She was an actress. I met her in London at the theatre where she worked. She was happy and vivacious. We got together and when I went to Spain with the army she followed me. I knew nothing would come of our relationship. She understood that—but she always lived in hope. I was in Paris with the conquering army when I sent her away, believing I would never see her again. She didn't complain or try to persuade me to let her stay. She just accepted it—which was her way.' His voice hardened. 'It wasn't until the eve of the battle at Waterloo—when she was on her deathbed, having given birth to my child—that we were reunited. She knew she wouldn't survive the birth and came to Belgium to find me—to ask me to look after the child. There was a priest. We were man and wife for no longer than ten minutes.'

'You didn't know about the child?'

For a long moment his gaze held hers with penetrating intensity. 'Had I known, I would never have sent her away. Had I not sent her from me, she would have had the care she needed and she would never have died.'

'And for that you blame yourself—and Charlotte.'
The intensity of his stare was so profound that Belle
thought he was about to admit what she had said, then
he turned his head away.

'Damn you, Belle. Too often for my peace of mind
you get beneath my guard, under my skin. I shall have
to keep a tighter rein on my tongue in future.'

'I don't mean to. I'm sorry. No more questions.' And
there wouldn't be. Belle had her answer. By not replying
to her question he had given her the answer. He had sent
Delphine away from him. He would not have done that
had he loved her. The Lance Bingham she knew
wouldn't have allowed anything to stand in his way.
Clearly he blamed himself for her death—and Charlotte
was a constant reminder that he had failed Delphine.
That was why he couldn't bear to look at her.

'Thank you for telling me about Delphine, and I
promise I will try not to be too hard on you in future,'
she said, as they got to their feet. The look she gave him
accompanied by a teasing smile hardly portrayed the
emotions she was struggling with. Every time they were
together she was aware of a potent sense of longing inside her. It was a desire so strong that she wanted to cry
because she had made it her endeavour to detach her
heart from him until he could accept that Charlotte was
his daughter.

At that moment her horse, which had wandered off
to nibble a tuft of long grass, disturbed a brightly coloured cock pheasant, causing it to fly up in indignant
alarm. Belle jumped and immediately Lance's hands
came to steady her.

'Oh, the bird startled me,' she breathed, knowing her
tension came far more from Lance's gentle grip on her

arms than from the bird's quick flight. He seemed to be aware of the intimacy of the moment as well, for something flickered in his eyes and his gaze dropped to her mouth. He was close. So close that she could smell the clean, fresh scent of his cologne. So close she wondered with a sudden thudding of her heart if he meant to kiss her. But disappointingly he released her.

'I think it is time we sought out your grandmother. My mother will have arrived and will be wondering where we've got to.'

Knowing how difficult it was for her grandmother to receive a family she had distanced herself from for many years had troubled Belle from the start, but now she saw there was no need when she saw her chatting amiably to Lance's mother beneath the shade of the parasol. Such was Elizabeth Bingham's kindness and compassion, that when she had taken the older woman's hands in her own and smiled as she assured her how delighted she was to meet her at last, skilfully dispatching the past with a graciousness that was irresistible, after fifty years the ice was broken.

'I see the two of you have met,' Lance said, greeting his mother with a light peck on the cheek.

Elizabeth smiled at them both. 'It's good to become acquainted at last.' She turned to Belle, putting a hand on her arm. 'I am so ashamed of myself, my dear, for speaking out so soon about Charlotte,' she said, having made up her mind to speak openly about her granddaughter in front of Lance. He must be made to realise the child was a part of his life and accept it. 'How has she settled in at Ryhill?'

'Very well,' Belle answered. 'She is an adorable child and so engaging. Already she has everyone eating out of the palm of her hand.' Everyone except the one person the child should be closest to, she thought sadly, looking at her husband's face, which was quite expressionless. He did not show even the slightest interest in the conversation about his daughter, but Belle now knew that was not out of coldness. It was out of fear, fear that if he stopped blaming Charlotte for Delphine's death, the full force of that blame would be laid on him.

Chapter Ten

Finding himself on the same landing as the nursery and not quite knowing how he had come to be there, after pausing for an indecisive moment outside, hesitantly Lance pushed open the door, unprepared for the scene his eyes beheld.

The nursery was filled with bright sunshine pouring through diaphanous white curtains. It was a warm, balmy day. Some of the windows had been opened and curtains gently stirred in the slight breeze. The silence of the house weighed heavy. Pictures of flowers and birds and fairies hung on the floral-papered walls, and shelves crammed with books and baskets of toys were everywhere. A clockwork rabbit along with a big brown teddy bear sporting a shining red bow round its neck had been left on the bright blue carpet, and an assortment of dolls were propped up in the window bottom. There was a colourful doll's house in one corner and a child-size table and four chairs in the other, and set at right angles to the hearth, two comfortable easy chairs. The previous occupant of the nursery must have been female, he realised, and as Charlotte developed she would get much pleasure from these toys. For a moment he was distracted from his purpose by the homely tranquillity that protected the child's young life.

The room where the nursemaid slept was through a door adjoining the nursery. The door was slightly open so the nursemaid would hear her charge when she woke from her nap.

It was to the crib in which the child slept that Lance directed his gaze. She was lying on her back, her hands on either side of her face, her chubby palms open. She had kicked away the covers so her baby legs were bare. Not wishing to alert the nursemaid of his presence and careful not to wake the child, curious to get a closer look, he edged closer to the crib and looked down.

He was totally unprepared for the feelings and the emotions that almost overwhelmed him. As memories of her birth assailed him, remembering how he had held her in his arms shortly after her birth, and the promise he had made to Delphine that he would take care of her, he gulped at the air, trying to drag it into his tortured lungs, fighting for breath, for control. He had failed Delphine miserably. How could he have ordered this child out of his life, abandoned her to whoever was prepared to take her?

Not having seen her since her that night, he had no particular feelings for her, beyond holding her—in part with himself—responsible for Delphine's death. The servants were forever singing her praises, telling him how delightful she was, and on occasion he had seen her with Belle or the nursemaid and watched her crawl about the lawn and heard her baby laughter and some-times heard her cry. From such a distance she had made no impression on him, but here, alone with his daughter for the first time, he accepted that she was his responsibility and his heart was stirred with a sense of pride in her infant beauty.

The fan of her dark lashes shadowed her plump, rosy cheeks. Her rosebud lips were soft and pink and slightly open. Her head was covered with a mass of glossy ebony curls, and her eyes—he couldn't see her eyes. What colour were they? he wondered. Did she have his blue eyes or Delphine's brown? Suddenly he was overcome with shame and remorse and a terrible guilt ripped into his heart. This child was flesh of his flesh, and yet he did not know the colour of her eyes.

He thought of how he had berated Belle—Belle glowing and strong, protective and loyal, with a will of burnished steel as she had stood up to him. He had ordered her to take the child away—anywhere, as long as she was not within the vicinity of his sight. In her compassion and understanding, defiant and brave and with blazing eyes she had defied him. She had subjected him to the most massive dose of guilt, coercion and emotional blackmail that he had ever seen anyone hand out.

Fiercely and strongly she had been challengingly ready to defend his child, throwing his scorn back in his face.

In the headlong strength of her mind and body, in the sweet kernel of her heart, now he could see her clearly he knew that he loved her. She had succeeded in breaking down all his defences and he could not bear to lose her. Her smile warmed his heart, her touch heated his blood. The unpredictable young woman had the power to enchant him, to amuse and infuriate him as no other woman had ever been able to. He wanted to have her by his side—and in his bed, to feast his eyes on her and hold her, and to know the exquisite sensation of her slender, voluptuous body curved against his. She stirred his heart which he had thought to be dead, and she stirred his blood to a passion that given a chance would be everlasting.

Reaching into the crib, he touched one of the soft cheeks with the tip of his finger. The child stretched her tiny body and yawned. Something stirred in Lance, growing quite dramatically into an emotion he did not at first recognise but which, when he'd studied it, he was certain he would find gratifying. And then her eyelids fluttered and opened a little in sleep before closing once more, not yet ready to wake. But the man responsible for the brief disturbance in his daughter smiled to himself, a satisfying, jubilant smile that warmed his heart.

Charlotte's eyes were blue, just like his own.

Lance was unaware that his wife, coming to check on her stepdaughter, had paused in the doorway. Belle saw Lance leaning over the crib and her first reaction was one of alarm, until she saw his face. Her breath caught in her throat and hope stirred. There was a softening to his features as he looked at his child. Was this the awakening of a father's love for his child, or a long-delayed sense of responsibility? Was he suffering guilt at the way he had kept the child away from him since birth?

Not wanting to disturb this precious moment, without making a sound Belle stepped out of sight.

Later, when Charlotte had woken from her afternoon nap, with the little girl propped up and taking note of everything she saw, Belle wheeled her along the garden paths in the baby carriage, which had wheels and a handle to steer it. She took her to the paddock behind the stables to see her husband's horses. Charlotte, wide eyed and wondering, began to rock excitedly in her carriage as one of the horses craned its neck over the fence to take one of the sugar lumps Belle always carried in her pocket as treats.

When Charlotte squealed with delight and held up her arms to be lifted out of the carriage, Belle picked her up and settled her quite naturally on her hip, the well-fleshed legs straddling her waist. The horse nudged its head against them and together they stroked its nose. Charlotte was completely unafraid of the huge beast, as clumsily her little hand patted the patient horse, her bright eyes like violets in her laughing face.

Coming round a corner of the stable block, Lance saw them and paused to watch, mesmerised by the lovely picture they made. Belle and the child made a delightful scene and the impact it had on him rooted him to the spot. Their laughter was infectious and brought a smile to his lips, and he felt himself drawn towards them, to his lovely young wife and the enchanting child she was bringing, by her own efforts, to his notice.

Moving soundlessly towards them, he listened to Belle's words as she talked to the child, telling her how one day her daddy would buy her a beautiful white pony of her very own to ride, of how she would gallop over the fields as free as a bird.

It was the child that became aware of him first. Her head spun round and she looked at him, her little face aglow with such happiness that Lance's heart turned over. Aware that Charlotte's attention was directed elsewhere, Belle turned to face her husband.

'Lance! You startled me.'

Lance's gaze went to the child. Not knowing who he

was, she was shy of him and hid her face in Belle's neck, but her curiosity getting the better of her, slowly she twisted her neck round so that she could look at him. Lance saw a small dark head wearing a white frilled bonnet and two bright blue eyes looking at him. A small hand with plump and questing fingers reached out to the bright buttons on his jacket and the blue eyes smiled. They were his eyes, he saw, so blue as to be almost violet, and two tiny teeth like pearls were revealed between parted pink lips.

Belle stood and watched, not saying a word, as father and daughter looked at each other properly for the first time. Her heart was in her mouth, fearing and expecting Lance to walk away.

The small bud of feeling Lance had experienced in the nursery when he'd looked down at his daughter's sleeping face, moved somewhere inside him and began to grow. He smiled back at his child and put out his hand to her. Instantly his finger was gripped by her tiny hand. Lance felt it, and it was as though a steel band had wrapped itself round his heart and would never let go.

'She is lovely, Lance, is she not?' Belle murmured, deeply moved by this moment.

'Yes—yes,' he answered hoarsely, 'she is', and then a shutter came down on his face and he turned away sharply, disengaging his finger from Charlotte's grip. 'Excuse me. I have things to do.'

Belle watching him stride away, his shoulders stiff, his head erect, but she was satisfied. The ice was broken.

After settling Charlotte in her crib for the night, Belle went to her rooms, meeting Daisy on her way out. With a bundle of Belle's clothes in her arms to take downstairs to be ironed, she paused and pointed to a slender vase on her dressing table, which held a single pink rose.

In bewilderment, Belle moved towards it, eyeing the rose with suspicion. 'What's this, Daisy?'

'It looks very much like a rose to me.'

'But—where has it come from?'

'Your husband brought it before he went out.'

'Oh—I wonder why.'

'Looks like he's trying to make amends to me.' Daisy knew how things stood between her mistress and her husband, and was as impatient for matters to be resolved as her mistress. 'Surely you do not doubt his feelings now?'

Alone, Belle fingered delicate petals of the rose, wondering what could have prompted Lance to give it to her. And then she remembered the night she had worn her rose gown and the comment he had made, telling her the colour suited her, but reminding her that the thorns of the rose were like her and had pierced deep beneath his skin.

So what did this mean? What was he trying to tell her? She was given the answer when she removed the rose from the glass vase and saw it was without thorns. She smiled. It was his way of telling her that the barbs had been pulled from his flesh and that he accepted responsibility for Charlotte, that he no longer blamed her for Delphine's death, and that he no longer wanted to send her away. In doing so, was he also making a genuine confession of his love for her, Belle? she wondered. But, no, surely she had misread the sign, for it did not make sense. He had certainly not loved her in the beginning, so why should he love her now? No, it was not possible, for she knew the foolishness of that far-fetched idea.

Tears started to her eyes and blurred her vision, but she blinked them away, refusing to cry. It would be enough for her that he learned to love his daughter, but deep down inside her she hoped and prayed fervently that he would have a little love left over for his wife.

Suddenly a keen awareness swept over her, causing her to place the rose back in the vase. Then she turned and saw a tall, broad-shouldered form advancing towards her from the doorway. She blinked, wiping desperately at her tears. Then she saw her husband's smiling face and his arms extended toward her, and all of heaven opened up to her. In an instant she was flying across the carpet into his embrace and being lifted off her feet. She wrapped her arms tightly round his neck, laughing and crying like a crazy woman as he covered her face with kisses before his mouth snared hers in a wild, ravenous kiss.

When his lips released hers after what seemed like an eternity, Lance held her close to his chest. 'I've missed you so much,' he whispered, brushing his lips across her brow. 'You'll never know how much.'

'I do, because I've missed you also. Do you hate me for what I almost did to us?'

'Hate you?' Lance was incredulous. 'Good Lord, woman, how could I possibly hate you when I'm sure the sun rises and sets with you? Can't you understand by now how much I love you?'

Pulling herself away from his chest, but remaining within the circle of his arms, Belle searched his handsome face. 'Are you sure it's not your lusting instincts?'

His hands pulled her back to him. 'If it were, my love, I would have been able to find appeasement with any woman, but I wanted no one but you. One way or another you've held my mind ensnared from that moment I saw you at Carlton House.'

Belle traced her finger down the front of his shirt. 'Then I must tell you that I've been in love with you ever since you agreed to marry me.'

His dark eyebrows lifted in a small shrug. 'I always hoped that, but you led me to believe otherwise when you stood against me and tried to send me packing when I came to rescue you at the Schofields' ball.'

'And I thought you'd hate me for making you feel obligated to doing the gentlemanly thing.' She looked up at him, searching his face. 'I thought you had gone out.'

'I did,' he said, cupping her face with hands, 'but I came back. I wanted to be with my wife—and child.'

'Oh, Lance. And the rose? Does this mean you no longer want to send Charlotte away?'

'Yes, my darling, that is exactly what it means,' he said, taking her hand and pulling her down on to the bed beside him. Belle saw his regret, heard it in his voice when he again looked at her and said, 'I have been a fool. I should have realised my responsibilities a long time ago and honoured the pledge I made to Delphine.' His voice was harsh with self-recrimination. 'I promised her I would support her in a manner suitable to her upbringing. I gave my word and I broke it.'

'You are too hard on yourself. I don't see it like that. You made provision for her. You made sure she was taken care of by sending her to your mother, where she received the very best of care. Where she was loved.'

'But how could I have blamed Charlotte for Delphine's death? I'm not proud of myself,' he admitted. 'Fear had something to do with it—fear of recognising that her death was down to me entirely. I lived in daily dread of the day when I would have to look on Charlotte's face—when I would have to confront what I had done, because she was the living proof of it. It was the most despicable thing I could have done.'

Lance looked at Belle, waiting for her to comment, and when she didn't, he said, 'It would mean a great deal to me, and to our future together, if you could find it in your heart to forgive me.'

'I have nothing to forgive you for. That you realise it now is a good thing, Lance. Now you can honour the promise you made to Delphine and get to know Charlotte. She is a baby still. You have only a little time to make up—and I know you will make a wonderful father.'

'Nevertheless, it was wrong of me to cast her off like I did.'

'You didn't know Delphine was with child. I'm sorry to say this, but she was equally to blame. She should have told you—or contacted you in some way when she realised she was pregnant.' Belle sighed, placing her head on his shoulder. 'The fates played against you, Lance, and there is no turning back the clock to right the wrong. It is the future that counts—a future that includes Charlotte.'

Placing his arms around her, he drew her close, kissing her cheek. 'I don't deserve you, Isabelle Bingham. When I consider the way I treated you in London, when your grandmother insisted I did the honourable thing and marry you, when I finally agreed to it, you were already half-convinced my proposal was made out of pity and regret. You didn't like me very well as it was, and you didn't particularly trust me, either,' he reminded her, 'and I knew you found it extremely difficult to forgive me for hurting you, and for shaming you. I never imagined, though, the extent you would actually go to to retaliate against me by leaving my bed in defence of my daughter.'

Lance saw the pain in her eyes, and despite his belief that all this had to be said, it took an almost physical effort not to ease her hurt with his hands and his mouth.

'It wasn't retaliation, Lance, please do not think that. It's just that I knew you were a fair man and that something about Delphine's death had hurt you very badly. Your reticence to your daughter almost broke my heart. That you reacted the way you did to my trying to bring about a reconciliation between you and Charlotte was unfortunate, but I did what I thought was for the best.'

That she didn't blame him or argue made Lance realise that Belle might be very young and inexperienced, but she was also very wise.

In the flickering candlelight Lance and Belle lay together and made love with a fierceness, unable to control the tormenting demands of their bodies, as if to make up for the time they had lost from being apart. Belle's sighs were soft and seductive as she stretched out alongside this man she adored. Not only had she a husband but a lover. His irrepressible carnality enthralled her.

Blue eyes were now dark eyes, passionate eyes, burning eyes, gazing down into hers. Here they were again, doing the most wonderful things, lovely things, and a shivering ecstasy pierced her entire body, sending streaks of pleasure curling through her. One kiss led to another and soon Lance's virile body blended with that of his wife's in an erotic exchange that left them both heady with desire.

The sharp spasm was so insistently physical. Suddenly Belle felt a burst of the wildest wantonness in her body and such urgency that she did not recognise herself, so foreign was it to her, so alien, that she lost all sense of decorum as he drove her into sweet oblivion.

Lance pulled her with him on to his side, his breathing still laboured as he kissed her forehead and moved her rumpled hair off her face. 'How do you feel now?' he asked softly.

She sighed, nestling closer to him, their bodies as sleek and wet and lithe as the fish in the lake. Her long curling lashes fluttered up, her eyes still dark with passion. 'Like a wife,' she murmured. 'Like your wife.'

His expression was tender as he gently kissed her lips. 'You are, my love, without doubt.' He groaned as she writhed against him. 'Do you know how erotic you are,' he murmured, running his fingers down her spine to the swell of her buttocks with such delicate tracery, such tenderness, that Belle scarcely knew her own body as they started again, another shuddering tournament of making love.

Belle had come to the realisation that she had never been happier in her life. She was married to the most wonderful man whom she adored, and with each passing hour their love for each other deepened. They enjoyed being secluded and made much of those interludes in the privacy of their home.

Charlotte was a constant delight to them and they could frequently be found in the nursery happily watching her crawling on the rug. Lance, now a besotted father, was quite enthralled by her noisy antics and couldn't believe his reluctance to have anything to do with her. He looked at Belle, unable to believe how much he loved her, and how much he owed to her for bringing it about.

'You do not object to a ready-made family, Belle?'

Her cheeks dimpled impishly. 'On the contrary. I mean to add to it just as soon as I can,' she said softly. 'Charlotte is a darling child and I love her as if she were my own.'

Drawing his daughter into the crook of his arm, where she settled down willingly since this was where she most liked to be, Lance placed a finger under Belle's chin, turning her face towards his. He searched her eyes for a moment, then shook his head. 'You are quite remarkable, do you know that?'

Belle wasn't certain, but she thought it might be a compliment. It flustered her to have him looking at her so, as if she had accomplished some great deed rather than spoke well of his child, and his simple words flustered her more.

'Thank you,' he said, his husky voice warming her as she gazed into his eyes. After the night he had just spent with her, Lance was certain he had never experienced such fulfilment. He also knew he wouldn't have traded his freedom for his darling wife, his mate for life.

Belle felt herself being drawn into his gaze, into the vital rugged aura of him. Being so close to him was having a strange effect on her senses. She was too aware of him—of his power and his strength. She couldn't mistake the approval in the tender smile he gave her. It was reward enough, she decided, for her efforts to accept and love his daughter.

Harlequin offers a romance for every mood!
See below for a sneak peek from
our suspense romance line
Silhouette® Romantic Suspense.
Introducing HER HERO IN HIDING by
New York Times *bestselling author Rachel Lee.*

Kay Young returned to woozy consciousness to find that she was lying on a soft sofa beneath a heap of quilts near a cheerfully burning fire. When she tried to move, however, everything hurt, and she groaned.

At once she heard a sound, then a stranger with a hard, harsh face was squatting beside her. "Shh," he said softly. "You're safe here. I promise."

"I have to go," she said weakly, struggling against pain. "He'll find me. He can't find me."

"Easy, lady," he said quietly. "You're hurt. No one's going to find you here."

"He will," she said desperately, terror clutching at her insides. "He always finds me!"

"Easy," he said again. "There's a blizzard outside. No one's getting here tonight, not even the doctor. I know, because I tried."

"Doctor? I don't need a doctor! I've got to get away."

"There's nowhere to go tonight," he said levelly. "And if I thought you could stand, I'd take you to a window and show you."

But even as she tried once more to pull away the quilts, she remembered something else: this man had been gentle when he'd found her beside the road, even when she had kicked and clawed. He hadn't hurt her.

Terror receded just a bit. She looked at him and detected signs of true concern there.

The terror eased another notch and she let her head sag on the pillow. "He always finds me," she whispered.

"Not here. Not tonight. That much I can guarantee."

Will Kay's mysterious rescuer protect
her from her worst fears?
Find out in HER HERO IN HIDING by
New York Times *bestselling author Rachel Lee.*
Available June 2010, only from
Silhouette® Romantic Suspense.

Copyright © 2010 by Susan Civil-Brown